Praise for the first two Ripper novels:

Ripper

"Well written, *Ripper* will appeal to teen readers, especially fans of Cassandra Clare's Infernal Devices series. Reeves cleverly uses one of the most heinous figures from history to tell a gothic tale with a paranormal twist."

—VOYA

Renegade

"Reeves strikes a good balance between Victorian sensibilities and a strong female protagonist."

—School Library Journal

To Kristen, my fun and fearless sister.

Resurrection

AMY CAROL REEVES

flux®
Woodbury, Minnesota

First Edition
First Printing, 2014

Book design by Bob Gaul
Cover design by Kevin R. Brown
Cover illustration © Dominick Finelle/The July Group

Flux, an imprint of Llewellyn Worldwide Ltd.

Library of Congress Cataloging-in-Publication Data
Reeves, Amy Carol.
  Resurrection/Amy Carol Reeves.—First edition.
    pages cm.—(Ripper novel; #3)
  Summary: "As a series of unexplained murders again strike fear into Londoners, Abbie Sharp discovers the Ripper's plot to revive the Conclave and usurp the British throne"—Provided by publisher.
  ISBN 978-0-7387-3877-2
1. Jack, the Ripper—Juvenile fiction. [1. Jack, the Ripper—Fiction. 2. Murder—Fiction. 3. London (England)—History—19th century—Fiction. 4. Great Britain—History—19th century—Fiction.] I. Title.
  PZ7.R25578Res 2014
  [Fic]—dc23

                                        2013044669

Flux
Llewellyn Worldwide Ltd.
2143 Wooddale Drive
Woodbury, MN 55125-2989
www.fluxnow.com

Printed in the United States of America

Acknowledgments

I'm grateful for my agent, Jessica Sinsheimer, for all of her work on the Ripper trilogy and for talking me off many narrative cliffs.

I'd like to thank everyone at Flux for their support as I worked on this series. *Resurrection* would not be in its current shape without the skillful editorial support of Brian Farrey-Latz and Sandy Sullivan. I would also like to thank my publicist, Mallory Hayes.

I am greatly indebted to my sister and fearless research assistant, Kristen Smith. Thanks for following me through muddy graveyards and old chapels. You are awesome for holding my umbrella and coffee while I photographed gravestones in gloomy London rain showers and for keeping my stressed self sane.

I am also greatly indebted to the staff and parishioners at St. Pancras Old Church in London. I appreciate Father James Elston and other parishioners for discussing the history of the church and surrounding graveyard.

Prologue

By the time he stepped outdoors to escape the stifling billiard game conversation, young Lionel Millbrough the Third's head swam from the three brandies he had unwisely consumed. The cool night mist surrounding his uncle's Kensington townhouse felt wonderful, a pleasant relief after the crowds inside, the roar of voices and clinking glasses of the party. In the darkness of a small alley behind the residence, he wiped a bit of perspiration from his face with his handkerchief and lit a cigar.

In the sharp glow of the match, he saw a handsome, well-dressed young woman standing near him in the darkness. Startled, he choked on the smoke.

"Um … hello," he murmured, a little stupidly, before taking another draw from his cigar.

Long, dark, curly hair cascaded loose down her shoulders, and her dark eyes stood out against her pale skin. She wore a green gown with silk ruffles that curled about her throat. She was only about four feet from him, still as a statue, watching him as she leaned against the townhouse's brick wall.

The night air was chilly, and as Millbrough pulled his double-breasted jacket tighter about him, he wondered why this woman wore no cape, no shawl even. She seemed to be a woman of means.

Vaguely, through his slightly inebriated brain, it occurred to him that he should offer her his jacket. "Do you need something, miss?"

She said nothing, but stepped toward him. Mesmerized by her shining dark eyes, he thought of the chocolate-sauce fountain that had been flowing in his uncle's parlor all evening.

Her mouth curved into a smile, and she stepped closer.

An inexplicable chill crossed through him. But then he almost chuckled. *A beguiling young woman approaches me in the darkness, and I instinctually want to run back inside?* This reaction seemed quite silly, and he worried that his law studies at Oxford had made him dull.

So he remained in his place, trying to appear more sober than he felt.

When she was almost upon him, he noticed a smell in the air, slightly acidic or perhaps rotten, somewhat like... *a decomposing animal?*

Now she was inches from his face, and he peered at her.

Although strikingly lovely, her face was too pale; purplish half-moon circles stood out under her eyes. His urge to bolt from her resurged.

"How do you do?" she asked. She was standing far too

close to him, much closer than a well-behaved lady should. Her manner of speaking, her accent, was like that of a lady from Kensington, and yet why would she be out at night in *this* compromising situation?

His unease almost vanished when she kissed him. Her lips were cold against his, far *too* cold. Now he not only smelled that strange odor, but he tasted it on her lips, in her mouth. Yet as she pressed her body against his, he could not move from this dark little alley.

Her lips moved down his jaw. Although shocked when she began to unknot the top of his ascot tie, he didn't stop her. Her breath was cool. Then she pulled away, staring at his throat with strange greediness. Blithely, he thought of vampire tales such as *Carmilla*, those stories with the beautiful, throat-biting demons. She met his eyes once more and widened her strange smile.

Then she lunged toward him, and before he could cry out, he felt sharp pain in his neck. He tried to scream, but he couldn't make a sound. He clutched desperately at his throat, near where her jaws were locked into his flesh. Where his neck had been was now a great hole, with blood—*so much blood.*

Yet again he tried to cry out but made only small gurgling sounds.

The young woman pulled away from him, her mouth bloody, her teeth stained red. She smiled, untouched by his pain. He fell back against the wall, sliding to the cold ground. He faintly heard the laughter and conversation from inside the house. The door was so close, safety so close.

Crawling toward the door, he struggled to remain conscious.

Blood.

Warm blood everywhere.

The girl lunged at him again, biting even deeper into his throat. This time the pain felt more distant, and his world slipped further away.

"How many times have I told you not to play with your food?" a young man asked wryly. He stood immediately behind her as she crouched over the body, feeding greedily.

Soon she rose and faced him.

He placed a long, heavy, dark coat around her shoulders; the hood hid her bloodstained face. The party was dwindling, and although most guests would leave through the front doors, he needed to get her out of this alley quickly.

She looked up at him from under her hood. He was tall, with light hazelnut curls breaking out from under his turban. "You know that I have no control," she said.

"Come along," he said lightly, pulling her swiftly out of the alley. "If I'm going to expand your hunting grounds, you know that you must be smoother and swifter. There isn't time for *that*."

"What do you mean?" was her coy response.

"That ridiculous cat-and-mouse game you played back there."

She giggled. Then, together, the pair ran off, into the dark street's shadows.

When they had gone four blocks, the earsplitting scream rang out.

PART I

"It's no use going back to yesterday, because I was a different person then."

—Alice's Adventures in Wonderland

One

Damn it!" William yelled, stumbling onto one knee in the gardens and dropping his walking stick. As I picked it up and helped him to his feet, I bit my tongue, weary of his poor attitude.

Our tempers had flared despite the idyllic surroundings of the Kennilworth Estate, where a light breeze stirred the thriving greenery and bees buzzed loudly in clusters of amaryllis and larkspur. I gingerly led William to a nearby stone bench and handed him his walking stick. Then we sat beside one another in angry silence.

During the past month of his convalescence, whenever I had checked in on William, he had worn at my patience. And I was to return to Grandmother's house in Kensington tomorrow; she believed I'd spent these many weeks in Bath with Simon's sister Rosamund, rather than in Orkney dealing with the Conclave's valuables.

Simon and I had used a portion of the Conclave's treasury to purchase the Kennilworth Estate in Warwick, a town only a short train ride from London. Although the estate and its grounds were rather lavish for my taste, the mansion had an extraordinary menagerie—a room we very much needed. Simon and I had only recently finished moving the Conclave's animals here. To maintain discretion, we could only bring a few back at a time. It was an expensive and arduous task.

Consequently, I had done little else than travel, with Simon, back and forth from the Orkney Isles to Kennilworth, transporting animals, books, and papers. The Conclave had hidden these possessions with Seraphina, their shape-shifting lamia, who had served as caretaker for the animals in her underground home. During our brief stays at the estate, I had tended to William, but his aunt, Christina, had assisted him during my frequent absences.

Brushing a dragonfly off my skirts, I turned to William. He seemed oblivious to my presence. "You *heard* Simon's instructions," I reminded him.

Simon was at work, in London, at Whitechapel Hospital for Women. He had directed the hospital alone ever since William became indisposed. I sorely wished Simon could be at Kennilworth with us. His presence was always so calming.

"Simon told you that the healing process might take a very long time," I continued. "You need exercise each day, but you must pace yourself or it won't work. William, *look* at me . . ." He turned his head a bit in my direction. "It *will not work* if you are not patient and consistent in your exercise."

William leaned his chin heavily upon his walking stick and stared straight ahead into a wall of scented jasmine. "Do you know how difficult it is for me to stay here at this place like an invalid, while Simon works his miracles among the poor in the East End?"

I sighed, watching a hummingbird fly by.

Despite his attitude, William was growing stronger every day. At first, Christina and I had to push him about the grounds in a wheelchair, but in the past few weeks, he had started walking with a stick or cane. His progress was so rapid that Simon thought he might soon walk unassisted. Yet William's right thigh remained mildly inflamed from where Seraphina had bitten him. Simon had collected a sample of the lamia's saliva soon after I killed her, and he found that her venom was unique. He believed that the poison would have to work itself out of the muscle before William could walk easily again. To speed up this process, Simon recommended regular and vigorous exercise.

As I considered William now, I knew that neither he nor I would say what was unsaid between us: that his pride was wounded from the whole ordeal with Seraphina. William was aware that if he had not been drinking excessively at the time, he would not have been so easy for Max to kidnap and stash away in Seraphina's lair. The fact that Simon and I had risked our lives to save him, when he was so helpless and close to death, was unbearable to him.

"You are stronger now than you were even a week ago, William," I said quietly. "You can't let a few stumbles discourage you." In the sunlight, I could see that his appearance had also improved. Although he remained a little thin, he was no longer so emaciated and pale.

He continued to pout, saying nothing in response.

A sharp rustle sounded in the nearby bushes. Laura,

Neil MacDiarmand's granddaughter, stood close to a nearby garden wall. She stared at William and me with wide eyes.

"Is Bridget finished with luncheon?" I asked.

The little girl nodded soberly, then turned and walked back toward the house, her lavender pinafore tied as primly as it had been when I secured it this morning.

When Laura was out of earshot, William said, "You know I loathe children, but I do feel pity for that little darling."

"I pity her too."

"You still haven't heard her speak a word?"

"No."

Laura had seen Seraphina kill her older sister and her sister's fiancé. Later, the lamia had devoured her grandfather, who had raised her. On one of our final trips to Orkney, Simon and I learned that Laura's grandmother had died suddenly of a stroke, likely brought on by the shock of her husband's death. Laura had been staying temporarily with a poor relative on the other side of Orkney, but the cousin already had ten children and didn't know what to do with the mute girl. Even though we were strangers to her, the cousin happily gave Laura to Simon and me to take back to London. We gave her Simon's address, but I doubted we would hear from her.

Neither Simon, William, nor I knew what to do with Laura MacDiarmand. When we'd first met her, that night in Neil's house before our confrontation with Seraphina, Laura was catatonic. Now, two months later, she still wouldn't speak.

"I know she needs time. Still, I'm worried," I muttered.

"She saw her sister ripped to shreds in front of her," William said.

"I know. But she's so young... if she can get past this a

bit. Neil said that she was strong…" My voice trailed off. Bridget, our housemaid, would summon us again if we didn't hurry inside soon.

"Come along," I said, standing. Taking William's arm in my own, I led him back to the house.

I awoke early the next morning, not quite ready to return to Grandmother's house and my work at New Hospital.

I walked first through my favorite room, the menagerie, the early light seeping through the enormous windows along the east wall. Large, unlit gas lamps lined two of the walls at regular intervals, and a large bamboo swing hung suspended from the high ceiling along the south wall. This was my favorite place in the house, particularly in mornings and evenings. I loved the monkeys, the birds, Robert Buck's two dodos, and even Petey the tiger, ferocious and beautiful as he roamed throughout his large enclosure. Placing one hand upon a bar of the enclosure, I stared at him; he watched me sleepily through half-closed lids, his giant head upon his paws. He gave a low growl but didn't move. I thought of the photo of him in the Conclave's album, surrounded by the group soon after his capture in Asia. Notes near the photograph described him as a man-eater.

I stepped away from Petey's enclosure and stared about me one more time.

I wanted more plants in this room, but our household staff was very limited. We only had two servants, Bridget and

Miranda, who had been recommended to us by Christina (they were some of the many former prostitutes she helped build new lives). The women could barely manage caring for the animals on top of their regular duties. Unfortunately, we could not risk bringing on more staff, as we didn't want too many questions about the animals or about the library, which Simon, William, and I kept locked for our own use. In it, we stored the Conclave's albums and books, alongside some of our own.

I slipped a half-eaten biscuit to a spider monkey and returned to the main part of the house, then went back upstairs to retrieve my bags.

As I walked through Laura's small room, which adjoined mine, I saw her dark brown hair falling about her face as she slept. The book I'd read to her last night, *Alice's Adventures in Wonderland*, lay open beside her on the pillow.

I hoped that I might soon spend more time with Laura, once I finally decided how to tell Grandmother about this place. Laura enjoyed reading; it was one of the few times when a smile would play at the corner of her mouth. Simon said that she needed an education, but I didn't know how we could possibly send her to school or even hire a governess if she wouldn't speak.

After gently removing the book from her pillow and returning it to the nightstand, I kissed her forehead lightly and left.

Two

Arabella, you have been gone all these weeks, yet you only wrote to me twice. Certainly, in that extended time of leisure in Bath, you had opportunities to write. That was quite inconsiderate."

I apologized profusely.

Of course, I had expected this. I had been in her house not yet an hour, and as we took tea in the parlor I endured her verbal lashing, to the tune of the grandfather clock ticking loudly from the hallway.

Jupe furiously sniffed at my boots. I wondered if the pug could still somehow smell the lamia on me.

"And, Arabella, what is that *awful* mark on your throat?" Grandmother asked. "Were the drawing rooms in Bath *that* ferocious?"

I touched the long laceration from Seraphina's claw, which ran from the base of my throat across my left shoulder and then straight down to the lower part of my breast. The wound didn't hurt much now, but the long scar would remain.

"It's merely a cat scratch, Grandmother. Rosamund had a new kitten."

"It must have been quite feral."

"It was very feral, Grandmother. I'm lucky to have escaped alive."

"Well, it doesn't matter," she said in a clipped tone. "We've had quite an uproar here this past week."

I didn't respond. Perhaps Grandmother's friend Lady Violet had ordered the wrong drapes for her drawing room. This was a typical "uproar" in Kensington.

"The night before last, there was a murder two streets away," Grandmother continued crossly. "Lord Millbrough's nephew had just returned from finishing his degree. Lord Millbrough hosted the celebration. I was invited, but Lord Millbrough's granddaughter, who was also at the party, was rumored to have had an indiscretion—"

"So who was murdered?"

Grandmother leaned forward. "Lord Millbrough's *nephew*. Lionel. His throat was cut out savagely. Ellen said that the maid who found him told her it looked as if he'd been attacked by a wild dog."

I set my tea down a bit too hard and lightly kicked Jupe away from my boots. This seemed similar to the Highgate Cemetery murders last year, where grave robbers turned up dead with their throats torn out and their bodies eviscerated. "A *wild dog*?" I repeated.

Grandmother nodded vigorously. "Ellen swears that Lord Millbrough's maid said the throat looked rather…*gnawed*, but you know how dramatic Ellen can be. The coroner announced yesterday that it was merely a random and terrible attack by a vagabond. To my knowledge, though, there have been no arrests."

"And it wasn't a robbery? Nothing was taken off the young man's body?"

Grandmother cocked her head. "I don't believe so." Then her interest in the matter waned. "All I care about is that it doesn't happen again, and that Scotland Yard arrests the savage." She tapped her wrinkled, heavily ringed fingers against a side table impatiently. "Now where is Richard? I asked him for those raspberry scones fifteen minutes ago."

I bit my lip hard as Grandmother left the parlor to fetch Richard. I had never discussed the cemetery murders with her; in fact, I wasn't even certain if she had heard of them. Inspector Abberline had seemed anxious—as he'd been in the Ripper case—not to cause a widespread public panic; Scotland Yard had tried to keep the brutal details, such as the cannibalism, out of the papers.

I wondered if any other graveyard murders had occurred in our absence.

I couldn't jump to conclusions. Ellen indeed exaggerated, but at the same time, if Lionel Millbrough's death *was* related to the cemetery murders, then it meant that the killers were moving beyond cemeteries, into respectable London neighborhoods.

Three

Two days later, Simon and I rode in a black brougham carriage to meet with Edmund Wyatt.

Wyatt had been spying on us earlier in the spring, and then caught up with us in Orkney soon after my battle with Seraphina. He explained that he worked for the monarchy and was concerned about the Conclave. We received a brief message from him during our travels, telling us he had been detained on business abroad and would return to London this week to talk further with us.

Still, Simon and I had many questions about him.

The carriage, which he'd sent especially for us, was secured with black shutters, so we could not see where we were going. If Wyatt truly was a member of Queen Victoria's Secret Service Bureau, such secrecy was understandable, but it was also quite maddening for Simon and me.

"I still don't think I trust Edmund Wyatt," I murmured quietly.

"Neither do I," Simon replied. "But I do believe that he

works for the Queen. The emblem on his jacket did not look counterfeit. Although I suppose it could be…"

Simon kept any further qualms to himself.

The carriage stalled momentarily before lurching forward again, and I was reminded of one of our many long carriage rides from Orkney to Warwick. I had asked Simon to elaborate upon his cryptic comments regarding Richard, Grandmother's butler.

Smiling in the darkness, Simon had said, "Yes, you should know the details of Richard's interesting history. His employment at Lady Westfield's home was a returned favor after my…experience in Africa."

"He aided you?"

A faraway look then took over Simon's eyes, undoubtedly from memories of the awful sights he had seen in that village, how he killed his own uncle, how he tried to save the mutilated little boy. But nonetheless, quietly and in very few words, he told me about how, when he had returned to Port Francqui after being at his uncle's village, he'd been held there and interrogated by members of the Queen's Secret Service.

"I developed a terrible fever during my detainment. As a member of the Secret Service Bureau, one of Richard's responsibilities was to relocate the few survivors of the village and then burn the rest of it. If news of what happened there were made public, the village, as well as my uncle's madness, would be a blight upon Her Majesty's empire. I believe that the Bureau, except of course for Richard, half wished that I would simply perish—I feared they might decide to put a bullet through my head. Who would know? My mother and sisters would simply receive a letter saying that my uncle and I had died from illness. However, Richard was kind to me, very kind. He gave me food and water and ordered a nurse to attend to me. When Richard retired from the Queen's service, I knew that he wanted employment. His pension is deplorable, and he often gives money to his niece. I found him the position in your grandmother's house."

"I had no idea."

"That is why I had full confidence in him, this past autumn, to protect Lady Westfield on the night we confronted the Conclave. I told Richard we had become embroiled in a 'dangerous matter.' That was all I told him, but I knew he would watch over her." Glancing at me, Simon had smirked slightly. "He handles a pistol remarkably well. And a saber, for that matter."

Now, as we made our way to our meeting with Wyatt, I thought of how so much finally made sense—Richard's tattoo, the way Simon had offered him money when we left Grandmother under his protection that horrible night.

Breaking the silence, I asked, "Is it because of your experience in Africa that you think we should not trust Wyatt, or the monarchy as a whole for that matter?"

"I have no faith in the ways of the empire overseas," Simon said with a sigh. "My uncle's actions reflect how our nation treats those we're supposed to rule. England is worse than a bully, and the monarchy's initial decision to sanction the Conclave was far from ethical." His voice drained away bitterly. "If Wyatt indeed works for the monarchy, I think it would be unwise to trust him *or* them."

My mind flashed to the Conclave's yearly ritual, at which they took the elixir of life to maintain their immortality. By replenishing their systems with the elixir, which they had created from the philosopher's stone, they kept themselves from aging or dying of natural causes. Until that night—the night I murdered them—they'd lived this way for centuries, pursuing scientific and scholarly projects "for the greater good" without a trace of conscience or concern for individual human life.

If the current monarchy allowed things to continue in this vein, even knowing about the Ripper murders and the lamia, it would be too terrible.

"I'm inclined to agree with you," I told Simon. "I'm not naïve enough to think that the monarchy would care about you or me or our safety. They are most certainly using us, but Wyatt said that Max must be stopped or the entire monarchy would be threatened. Might they at least share the same goal as us—to stop Max?"

Even as I spoke, the words about sharing any goals with the monarchy felt distasteful.

The carriage came to a sudden halt, and Simon lowered his voice and spoke quickly.

"The monarchy's goal is to protect themselves, whereas our goal is to protect ourselves and those we love. Even if we work with them to kill the Conclave's last remaining member, they are the very establishment that created the Conclave three hundred years ago. I don't know who exactly Wyatt is, or why he wants to meet with us, but we have breached the monarchy's deepest secrets. Make no mistake—if we cooperate with them, we will be involved in a dangerous game, and we and all whom we hold dear might be crushed in the end."

Voices approached the carriage.

"But won't we be in over our heads if we continue this fight against Max alone?" I whispered.

Simon smiled serenely before saying, "We've been in 'over our heads' for a long while now, and I believe we will be a great deal better off continuing as we have been."

"Quite true," I said quickly, returning his smile.

His tone turned serious again. "Our path might cross the monarchy's path, but we cannot trust them. It's far too dangerous."

As the driver swung the door open, I met Simon's eyes and nodded slightly to let him know I agreed.

In the late afternoon light, I saw that we were in a narrow alleyway. A light rain had begun. I looked about me but did not recognize any streets or landscapes. We had been riding for only about half an hour, so I assumed that we must still be within the vicinity of London.

Then I saw Edmund Wyatt waiting for us. He still sported ash-blond hair and seemingly sunburned skin, which had always struck me as out of place in London. But something else about his appearance was odd. He seemed gaunt, and his already flushed face appeared bloated. His hand trembled a little as he shook our hands. I wondered if perhaps he'd become ill during his trip abroad.

After briefly greeting us, Wyatt led us through the late afternoon drizzle to a door, then up a narrow set of stairs into a small, modest flat.

The flat was dark, even a bit dingy for a man who presumably worked for Queen Victoria. Still, I was impressed by the weapons and instruments in the rooms. The walls were covered with swords, sabers, and mahogany bookcases. A telescope rested near a heavily draped window, and a strange, enormous picture of all of the constellations hung over a desk.

Wyatt led us through the long flat until we reached a small back room with an extremely large oak table. It reminded me of the table the Conclave once had, at their house on Montgomery Street.

"I am certain that you both have many unanswered questions about this Conclave business," Wyatt said after we'd seated ourselves. He sat directly across the table from us, a good five feet away.

"To begin with, why did the monarchy not stop the Conclave when they began murdering women in Whitechapel last year?" I asked sharply.

Wyatt looked down at his folded fingers and then back at us. He gazed hard at me for a few seconds before turning his attention to Simon.

"Your hospital flourished, did it not, Dr. St. John, after the deaths of those women?"

Simon hesitated, watching Wyatt coolly. "Whitechapel Hospital received significant charitable donations last autumn."

After a few awkward seconds of silence, Wyatt continued, his voice slightly raspy. I wondered if he was nervous. "The journalistic attention to the area caused public awareness of the East End to surge significantly. And last I heard, Miss Sharp, you and Dr. William Siddal are planning to establish a school for the children in one wing of the hospital. Now you have almost all the funding you need to do this."

"*At the cost of—*"

Simon silenced me with a sharp tap on my knee and I struggled to subdue my anger.

"At the cost of five alcoholic prostitutes, Miss Sharp," Wyatt continued. "Her Majesty does not endorse the *deeds* of the Conclave—that's why they were instructed by Queen Elizabeth to remain independent of the monarchy, to make their own decisions about what was right and wrong as long as their works benefitted the public good. As long as their actions do not hurt her empire—as long as they use their knowledge to *benefit* her city, nation, and empire—then she doesn't bother herself about the means by which they go about it."

"Did you know about the lamia?" I demanded.

Wyatt sighed. "I only learned of her recently. The Conclave did well at keeping her existence a secret. We have never had much information as to the details of their work. Historically, there's been *one* member and one member only in the Bureau who even knows of the existence of the Conclave, or Case X as we call it. Francis Walsingham, who was Queen Elizabeth's advisor, established this system years ago in case the Conclave became too roguish in their independence. There was always a concern that they might turn against the empire or publicly reveal the elixir."

"Murdering women wasn't considered *roguish*?"

Wyatt narrowed his eyes. "Your mouth, Miss Sharp, is unbecoming and will gain you no favors as a gentlewoman."

"I'm not looking for favors from you, and whoever said that I was a gentle—"

Simon cut me off. "Miss Sharp and I have grave concerns regarding the Conclave's unethical practices."

Wyatt sat back in his chair and straightened his posture. "I'm not here to quibble with either of you about how the Conclave has behaved in the past. The truth of the matter is that they have mostly been left alone by the monarchy—although they have always been paid generously upon an annual basis, and occasionally met with the king or queen. Often, the advisor for Case X never even meets a single member of the Conclave. I only took this job last year, when there was that mysterious fire at their London property and the members of the group perished."

He folded his hands carefully in front of him, and I sensed that Wyatt was getting to the heart of the matter.

"We knew that the Conclave had taken in another member several years ago," he said. "An assassin from France, who apparently survived the fire. On this front, a problem has arisen. This assassin has ensnared you two—and the young physician, William Siddal—into the Conclave's business."

Simon and I remained silent.

Upon receiving no response, Wyatt leveled his gaze at Simon. "I'm learning many interesting details about the Conclave. They have become bolder in recent years." He turned to me. "Miss Sharp, did they not try to make your mother a part of the group?"

A lump rose in my throat. "Yes."

Wyatt paused. "Do you know anything about her relationship with the assassin, Max Bartlett?"

Thoughts that I couldn't quite piece together formed in my head. I felt Simon's gaze upon me.

"Did she tell you anything about him, Miss Sharp?" Wyatt pressed.

"No." My answer was firm. She hadn't. But Max had been there, that day in Ireland when I'd almost drowned. He had rescued me, and as I regained consciousness I heard him arguing with Mother. How many times had she spoken to him or seen him in the years after she fled from London?

Wyatt eyed me carefully for a few seconds, skeptical. "I have tried to follow him, but he is a strange, shadowy character. Over the past few weeks I have been in France, trying to learn more of his history. His past is virtually untraceable. I *do* know that not only is he a skilled assassin and a psychic, but the elixir gives him powers it did not give the other members. He became an aberration."

I recalled all the times I had seen Max climbing walls, how he could sometimes possess the bodies of others. I thought of his strength. His speed.

"Although apparently French, he speaks English well, with no French accent. In fact, he speaks several languages and can adapt his speech to any accent or dialect."

I remembered Max's Austrian accent that time he'd arrived in Grandmother's parlor. I remembered hearing him speak in German to Dr. Buck once at the hospital. Yes, all that Wyatt said seemed accurate.

"As you know, in taking on the name Bartlett, he is pretending to be Dr. Julian Bartlett's nephew. We're almost certain it's not his actual name. He is elusive. Dangerous. And now, he's gone underground. We keep trying to track him, but we cannot even determine where he lives. He was spotted in London this month by one of my men, near the Thames, but chasing him thus far has been futile. He cut the throats of two of my men recently."

As he spoke, Wyatt seemed increasingly agitated. I noticed his fourth finger trembling.

"So, what do you want from us? If the Secret Service

Bureau can't locate him, why would you think that we could?" I asked.

Wyatt, brimming with impatience, leaned across the table. "Because, Miss Sharp, he always seems to come back to *you*. What is it about you? Why won't he leave you alone?"

A ticking clock sounded loudly from across the room.

"What does he want from you, Miss Sharp?"

But I didn't speak a word. I wasn't about to tell Wyatt my entire history with Max.

As if reading my thoughts, Simon spoke quickly. "We have nothing more to discuss here." He stood up and I followed his lead, wanting only to leave this place.

"There have been more murders during your cavorts in Orkney," Wyatt said abruptly, pulling a file from a bag at his feet that I hadn't noticed before. "In fact, there have been many more than we've made public. At least twenty cannibalistic murders have occurred since your first journey to the Orkney Isles."

Standing up, he placed a photograph on the table for us to see. "Highgate Cemetery."

I saw a young male victim whose throat and stomach had been eviscerated, exactly like the body I'd seen earlier this spring.

"Brompton Cemetery." Wyatt laid out another photograph. This one depicted a young female gravedigger, a great gaping hole in her chest.

"Abney Park. Kensal Green." He laid out two equally grotesque photographs of bodies. All looked as if they had been attacked by wild dogs.

"The dead have all been resurrection men, common gravediggers. No one would inquire after them, so we've disposed of the last seven bodies quietly. However, two weeks ago, a priest near Covent Gardens was murdered in his own parsonage, cannibalized just like the gravediggers. Then, as you likely know, Miss Sharp, a young law student in Kensington was murdered. The murderer, or murderers, are becoming more brazen, expanding their 'hunting' territories beyond the cemeteries."

It was as I had feared.

Wyatt drew a deep breath. "And there have been rumors, by some who live or work near the cemeteries, of odd-looking figures roaming near the walls. One individual reported seeing a pale woman, blood smeared upon her face. We have reason to believe—particularly since we found the Conclave's symbol near the murdered men in Highgate this spring—that Max Bartlett is involved, and that he has these strange others working for him. He is taunting the authorities, just as he did in the Ripper case."

"I find it difficult to believe," Simon said quietly, "that you and your men cannot patrol these areas better. That *your* men have not seen these figures."

Beads of perspiration popped out across Wyatt's red forehead. "I actually have few men at my disposal—less than ten. And now, because of Bartlett, I am down to eight. Because of the highly sensitive nature of the Conclave, only Her Majesty and I know of the matters surrounding Case X; my men only know that we are pursuing Max Bartlett, thought to be a Ripper suspect, and a group of cannibalistic lunatics." He wiped his face. "I met with Her Majesty yesterday. We need to find Bartlett, and whoever else is involved, before the situation becomes any more difficult."

"Why do you suddenly care so much that a Conclave

member is murdering people?" I snapped. "It almost sounds like it's because the victims now include a wealthy Kensington youth from a prominent family."

Rather than answering me, Wyatt merely glared. His hands trembled as he began collecting the photographs. Although I didn't really care, I wondered vaguely if the trembling was from anger or from illness.

Of course, Wyatt couldn't respond to my question because it hit too hard against too many truths. It was perfectly acceptable for the Conclave to murder so long as they were discreet, so long as they didn't murder anyone "important." But now Max had splintered away from the established pattern; he was an immortal who paid no heed to the monarchy's will. He mocked them with his painted chalices on tombstones; he engaged them in his reckless, high-stakes games. I fought an urge to chuckle. Like Victor Frankenstein, the monarchy had created a monster beyond its control.

Shoving the photographs back into his bag, Wyatt stepped away from the table. "I'll be talking with you both at a later time."

"We have nothing more to discuss," Simon said again, as we were ushered out of the flat and back downstairs to the carriage.

Max stood at a distance, a wide-brimmed hat guarding his face from the drizzling rain.

His two male companions stood with him atop a nearby

building, their eyes upon Abbie Sharp and Simon St. John stepping into the dark carriage.

"Things are about to get interesting," the man closest to Max remarked. His intense blue eyes gleamed under his short hazelnut curls, like he was a child impatient for Christmas.

"Yes," the other young man said. This man was tall and strikingly beautiful, with dark curly hair and dark eyes. "Impressive, that work in Orkney. It would be a shame to kill her. A terrible shame. She's too pretty."

"*Far* too pretty," Max said. He kept his eyes upon her. "And too much like her mother."

The three men stood silent and still as statues for a few minutes, not bothered by the building rain as they watched the carriage pull away.

"Come along," Max said abruptly. "This will do no good. We've got too much to do, and it's almost time to introduce Miss Sharp to our friends."

His blue-eyed companion smirked, his cape swirling in a stream of weak wind as he turned leave. "I hope she survives."

"Yes," Max said, almost to himself.

He lingered in his place as the others walked away, watching until the carriage was out of sight.

Four

The leaves of the great cedar tree rattled high above us as we eased, with the crowd, through the Circle of Lebanon in Highgate Cemetery. The corridor felt tight with the crush of warm bodies, and I tried to stay close to Simon. While Mariah's funeral had been sparsely attended, Lionel Millbrough the Third's funeral attracted half of Kensington.

Grandmother walked ahead of us with her friends, Lady Violet and Lady Catherine. All three women were clad in noisy black crinoline, but they spoke in hushed whispers and dabbed daintily at their eyes with embroidered handkerchiefs. Grandmother hadn't known the young man very well, but as one was expected to cry at a funeral, she cried. As for me, I couldn't even pretend to cry. My mind was still reeling from our meeting with Wyatt yesterday.

Simon and I had not had much time to talk about the meeting. Although I was once again working at New Hospital, I still often helped out at Whitechapel, and that evening Simon and I had delivered three babies. Today, my feet ached from spending my morning assisting in the operating theater at New Hospital. In addition, my books and notes for the medical school examinations awaited me upon my desk at home. I planned to start at the London Medical School for Women in the autumn, and often I studied to the point of exhaustion.

The crowd was entering a dark mausoleum. I held back. The place was far too cold and, in spite of the cement-encased coffins, smelled of decomposition.

Simon must have had the same thoughts because he remained where he was, leaning against the wall. He nodded his head at me, and as Grandmother and the others walked past, we hung back together, easing ourselves slowly out of the Circle of Lebanon and through Egyptian Avenue.

When we reached Egyptian Avenue's impressive entrance, we paused. Simon laid his long, pale fingers lightly on one of the column's carved lotus petals.

In spite of its tombstones and the gnarled overgrowth, I'd always found Highgate Cemetery comforting. I liked meandering around the tombs, the thick tree trunks spiraling out like fingers. The cemetery teemed with wildlife—hares, foxes, red-bosomed sparrows. As there were no crying children or barking dogs, I preferred this place to any London park. As did William; I remembered the time I ran into him near his family's gravesite.

"Have you been here since Mariah's death?" I asked Simon.

"A few times. During daylight hours, of course." He glanced away for a second, shielding his ice-blue eyes from the sunlight with one hand and lowering his voice. "I don't think that we should bother anymore with Wyatt."

"I agree. He knew that the Conclave was behind the Ripper murders and yet he did nothing. He doesn't strike me as being morally tortured. I'd be fine if I never heard from him again."

"And yet..." Simon still squinted out over the tangled sea of graves beyond us. "I fear we will."

I wasn't finished venting my spleen. "Did you notice how awful he appeared yesterday? How his hands and fingers trembled? How gaunt his appearance was? If he does indeed work for Queen Victoria, perhaps his work has made him ill...which would be a proper sort of justice."

Simon looked down at me, smirking a little. "In terms of our initial qualms about his credentials, I'm convinced that he works for the Queen, given all that he knows about the Conclave's history. It would be an extraordinary charade if he did not. And yes, Abbie, I also noticed his appearance. His entire demeanor seems different than it did in Orkney, and it troubles me."

"Why?"

Simon hesitated. "I'm concerned that he is perhaps... untrustworthy."

"What would his health or appearance have to do with being untrustworthy?"

Simon started to speak, then stopped and shrugged. "I'm not certain exactly. I just have some...premonitions."

"Might you clarify?"

Simon seemed to be trying to come up with the right

words. "Let's just say that Edmund Wyatt might be a ... complicated individual."

He turned his attention back to the surrounding graveyard. I followed his gaze, watching a large raven burst away from a tree, cawing loudly; a cloud of dried leaves rained down behind it. "I would love to know what happens here at night," Simon murmured.

Then he nodded in the direction of the Millbrough mausoleum. "And evidently, it's happening *outside* of here. Be careful, Abbie."

"I think Kensington has had enough gruesome happenings for one week," I said, following his gaze to a young fox running nearby.

The sun glinted on Simon's light lashes, illuminating his angel-like features. He made no reply.

Three nights later I awoke, startled by a distant, off-key shriek.

Confused, I surveyed my dark bedroom.

I had fallen asleep slouched in my desk chair, my anatomy book still open in my lap. The candle upon my desk had long since burned down. I squinted, my eyes adjusting to the darkness, at the clock above my bedroom fireplace. It was two o'clock in the morning.

The house was silent now. I wondered if perhaps I'd been dreaming.

Rubbing my eyes, I returned the book to the desk and walked heavily to my bed.

Just as I slipped under my bedcovers a loud thump sounded, as if someone had thrown a large sack of flour against my bedroom door. I sat up, jolted.

Leaping quietly from the bed, I laid my hand on the doorknob.

Silence.

I held my breath and swung the door open.

I screamed.

Ellen, our maid, tumbled into my room, her throat ripped out. The back of her head hit my bedroom floor, and her life-less eyes stared up at me.

Covering my mouth to keep from crying out again, I crouched down and felt her wrist for a pulse. Her body was still warm, but she was dead. There was no breath, no heart-beat. Her strawlike, graying red hair spiraled loose about her shoulders, and her nightgown was ripped open near the gap-ing wound at her neck. Blood seeped rapidly out, spreading across and staining the carpet at my feet.

Jupe began to bark from Grandmother's downstairs bed-room, immediately below my own.

Grandmother.

I ran to my closet, my fingers shaking violently as I grabbed my bowie knife from my trunk and bolted back across the room.

But then *she*—my beloved dead friend Mariah—stepped into the doorway, blocking me. She stood above Ellen's body. Even though it was night, she wore no coat or shawl over her green gown. Blood was smeared upon her mouth; she was like a predator guarding its prey.

I blinked, unbelieving.

"Mariah..." I whispered.

Even now, with the blood upon her face, she was beautiful. Her hair hung dark and curly around her face. Mariah had always had a china-doll complexion, but now her face was alarmingly pale. Her eyes shone wide and dark, with curious purple crescents under them. Something about Mariah seemed like a blurred painting that had been wiped by a hand before it dried.

She smiled, wiped some blood from her mouth, stepped into my bedroom, and walked straight toward me.

Horror and longing washed over me.

She had been my friend.

She was dead.

I'd seen her die, that night in Lady Violet's attic.

I thought of the ways Max had used her, both while she was alive and then shortly before her death. I stuttered as I stepped backward, still clutching the knife; my thoughts grew scrambled and increasingly incoherent. As I backed away from her, breathless, my back hit hard against my bedpost.

It was unbelievable, but I wanted to embrace her.

And yet... there was something feral, something strange in her eyes that I'd never seen when she was alive. I stared from her bloodstained mouth back to Ellen's body. I thought of the strange people who'd pursued me when I'd ventured alone into Highgate Cemetery this spring.

"Mariah..." I stuttered. "You're dead."

She continued advancing upon me.

Vaguely, I remembered to keep my grip upon the knife.

"I *am* dead."

In my shock, I hadn't noticed how quickly she was moving.

Now she stood immediately before me. In a single movement she ripped open the buttons on her gown, baring her chest to me. She wore no corset, no undergarments even. A great purple wound, which looked as if it had been crudely sewn together, spanned her breastbone.

She grabbed my free hand and pulled it toward the wound. "Touch me, Abbie."

A tear fell down my cheek, and I couldn't pull my hand away.

"Yes, it was a violent death, wasn't it, Abbie love? Don't you remember? I fell three stories onto that pile of splintered wood."

"You're cold." I whispered. Under my fingertips, her scarred breasts felt cold as marble.

"I was dead. But now I'm alive. Resurrected." She giggled. "Isn't it wonderful?" Her laugh was almost musical.

My mouth parched and I couldn't speak. I took a deep breath. "*How?* How did this happen, Mariah?"

She smiled mysteriously.

She was so beautiful, even in this deathly pale and frightening form. She leaned toward me, her bloodstained mouth nearing my own; my hand still rested upon the stitched wound. I froze. Her breath was a winter breeze, soothing yet tinged with some vaguely rotten odor. Again, I couldn't move. I searched her face, sought traces of my friend. But this Mariah seemed so cruel, not the witty, kind companion I had known.

I tried to pull myself away from her spell, surface from my shock. Jupe's bark continued downstairs, and I heard Grandmother fussing at him. Grandmother couldn't see this—Ellen's body, Mariah.

Against my instinct to run, I remained frozen.

Mariah smiled.

My breath came out ragged as I stared into her eyes. I felt the stitches under my fingertips, rough blights over her cold skin.

Suddenly Mariah kissed me, her lips pressing hard against mine. I retuned the kiss, still under her spell. Her mouth was cold, my tears warm.

Then I tasted the blood on her lips.

I pulled away, regaining all of my senses and remembering that I needed to get to Grandmother. I pushed Mariah away hard, and she landed on the floor.

"Get away!" I yelled, holding the knife in front of me. I reminded myself that this fiend was not the Mariah Crawley I had known.

She bared her teeth at me, crouching between me and Ellen's body in the doorway, her hair loose and wild about her shoulders. She seemed oblivious to her exposed breasts. Her fingers, long and pale, curled in front of her against the carpeted floor like an animal's claws.

"What did you do to Ellen?" I demanded, hoping that she could not hear the fear in my voice.

Mariah curled her lips back from her teeth like a snarling dog; she crouched lower, as if she would pounce at any moment. "My appetite has changed a bit since I returned. I could tear your throat…"

Grandmother's door opened downstairs. "Arabella?"

Then I heard a crash from somewhere in the back of the house.

Were there more of them?

Richard! Where was Richard? Had he heard this from his attic bedroom? Panicked, I wondered if he was lying dead like Ellen.

Mariah smiled and glanced toward the door, then looked up at me viciously through her thick, dark lashes. "Actually, I'm supposed to leave *you* alive. But Lady Westfield ... " She licked her lips. "Do you think she'll be happy to see me again?" She sprang over Ellen's body and ran toward the staircase.

"*No!*" I screamed, running after her, gripping my knife. As I lunged out of the room, I felt Ellen's blood on the soles of my bare feet. Taking the steps three at a time, I saw, in the dimness, Mariah running ahead of me, surprisingly lithe in her green gown. Through the bannister spindles, I saw light spreading from Grandmother's doorway.

"Grandmother!" I shouted, almost falling headfirst down the last five steps. "Get back into your room and lock the door! *Now!*"

Another great crash came from the back of the house, in the direction of the kitchen.

Whining, Jupe bolted away from Grandmother's bedroom.

Turning the corner, I stopped, frozen in my tracks.

Grandmother was standing in her bedroom doorway, staring with horror at Mariah. She wore a robe; her hair was still in paper curlers. At the end of the hall, past Grandmother and directly across from me, were three men, all frighteningly pale like Mariah.

One was very young, no more than fifteen. Another wore an old constable's uniform—I recognized him immediately as the man who had pursued me in Highgate

Cemetery. The third man was older, perhaps in his fifties. They stood silently in the hallway, all with that same feral, hungry look on their faces.

Trying to decide how best to protect Grandmother, I watched all of their positions at once: Mariah in front of Grandmother, the others paused at the end of the hallway. I thought of the illustrations I had seen in zoology books of lionesses surrounding their prey.

Grandmother didn't seem to see the others; her eyes remained locked upon Mariah.

"Mariah..." she muttered, her voice no more than a croak. She swayed on her feet a bit and clutched the door frame in support.

Mariah threw her head back in a hysterical laugh. "It's a miracle, Lady Westfield! I'm back from the dead!"

"No!" I yelled, leaping between them. I shoved Grandmother back into her room. But before I could shut the door, a searing pain, like fire, shot through my shoulder as Mariah bit me. I heard the sound of tearing fabric.

Suddenly, the three others charged down the hallway toward us.

Ignoring the wetness spreading down my arm, I shoved Mariah hard, throwing her against the wall and swiping at her with the bowie knife. Outnumbered, I spun around to fight the others.

Then the older intruder fell forward, dead, a knife in his back.

Richard!

I saw Richard pummeling the constable to the ground. Mariah, frenzied now, lunged at me, aiming for my throat.

I pushed her so hard against the wall that a mirror fell, missing her head but shattering to pieces about her.

While Richard struggled with the constable, the boy sprang at me, and I kneed him hard in the ribs. He howled in pain and lunged again, his teeth bared like an animal.

Who were these beings?

"Get back, Grandmother!" I yelled. "Lock the door!"

But she didn't move.

"Bitch!" Mariah yelled as she stood up, mirror fragments caught in the ruffles of her gown. The glass had cut the exposed parts of her breasts; the blood seeping out was rust brown, not bright red like my own.

I stabbed at the boy but missed his chest; my knife blade grazed his arm. We struggled and he wrested the knife from my grip, swinging it clumsily at me.

As I fought both the boy and Mariah, I saw that Richard and the constable were still locked in struggle. They both fell into the grandfather clock, which teetered briefly and then crashed to the floor loudly. Wood and glass splinters flew everywhere.

"This can't *be*!" Grandmother screamed from behind me as I continued fighting, blocking the boy and Mariah from Grandmother. I tried to remember everything that my old friend Roddy told me about fighting, but my strength was waning. My shoulder ached, and the boy still had my knife.

"It *is*, Grandmother! It's *Mariah*! Now get me a weapon!"

Grandmother must have regained some of her composure, for in a split second I had a poker in my hand.

I smacked Mariah hard in the chest and then struck the boy across the face. Both stumbled backward.

Richard now held the constable up against the wall, his hand squeezing the man's neck.

Suddenly, the front door burst open. Everyone, including our attackers, froze.

Max strode into the foyer.

There must have been a slight rain outside, for water glistened in the wild dark curls around his head. His leopard-green eyes gleamed. Two other male figures stood behind him, framed by the front doorway, their faces shadowy in the misty night. I strained my eyes past Max's large form while keeping a tight hold of the poker. One of the men wore some sort of cape and turban; the other one had dark curly hair. I could not see their faces.

Quickly I turned my attention back to Max.

"Oh, thank heavens!" Grandmother exclaimed from behind me. "It's Mr. Bartlett..."

She tried to push past me.

"Grandmother, *no!*" I blocked her with my arm, keeping her behind me in the bedroom. Mariah glared daggers at me but remained still. The other attackers and Richard also froze.

Max walked slowly toward us, surveying the scene: the subdued attackers, the broken mirror, the stained carpets and shattered grandfather clock. His eyes rested upon the dead attacker on the floor. As he neared me, I saw that he was holding Jupe in his arms.

Grandmother said nothing else, but I heard her catch her breath. She was no fool; she realized something was amiss.

I was still breathless from the fight; my heart pounded and my chest heaved. Goose bumps prickled upon my neck—Max had almost reached Grandmother's doorway, where I stood.

My thoughts spun frantically as I tried to make sense of it all.

"Your dog, Lady Westfield," Max said without even glancing at her. He threw Jupe into the bedroom. The dog yelped as it hit the far wall.

Everyone remained silent. Richard cast me a glance. A small gash ran across his cheek, and a lock of his thin white hair fell across his forehead. Still, his hand remained clutched tightly around the constable's throat.

"It's time to go," Max said sternly to our attackers.

I glared at him. I could not fight him here. Richard, Grandmother, and I were outnumbered, and Grandmother and Richard meant nothing to Max. He would kill them in a minute.

"What are you doing here?" I demanded. "Who are these people?"

Max stared down at me, his eyes glinting.

Grandmother clutched my arm tightly, protectively, trying to pull me back toward her. This version of Max was far removed from the well-behaved gentleman who had paid her a visit this spring.

Max smiled widely and leaned toward me. The scent of Oriental cigars lingered upon his jacket. "Did you like the little show tonight?"

"Get out of this house," I said through gritted teeth. Grandmother's grip tightened on my arm.

He was too close to me, and to her. I swung the poker at him, but he caught my wrist in a painful vise-grip. He was always one step ahead of me, always flawlessly interpreting my next move. I needed to regroup, come up with a better plan, if I was going to rid myself of him for good.

One of the men in the doorway chuckled softly, and I turned sharply to them. Maddeningly, I could still only see the outlines of their figures.

"We're finished for tonight," Max said.

The constable pushed Richard away from him.

Mariah gnashed her teeth at me and Grandmother. She obviously still wanted to tear my throat out, but she was cowering in Max's presence.

What had happened to her?

The Mariah I had known would never have cowered to anyone, particularly a man.

Max stooped, picked up the man Richard had stabbed, and flung him over his shoulder like a sack of potatoes. He glanced toward the men still lingering in the open front door. "I'll take them out back."

The turbaned man nodded, bowed a bit, and quietly closed the front door, shutting himself and the other man outside, while Max, still holding the dead man, glanced back at me, locking his gaze into mine. A smile played at the corners of his mouth. Richard stepped quietly aside, his hand clutching a long shard of glass as a weapon. Mariah, the constable, and the boy followed Max out quietly.

The moment the door closed, I turned to Grandmother.

She clutched me tightly to her. My blood was still rushing, my head spinning. I heard Richard firmly bolting the back door in the kitchen.

Suddenly Grandmother pulled away, gripping her chest.

"Grandmother!"

Her face was so pale. Alarmed, I led her to bed. She had never had heart trouble before, but I feared for her now because of her age and the shock of what had just happened.

"Lie down. I'll bring you some hot tea."

Jupe, cringing but unharmed, leaped onto the bed beside her.

"They're gone, Grandmother." I kissed her cheek and left, shutting her bedroom door behind me. She could not see Ellen's body.

I retrieved my bowie knife from the floor where the boy had dropped it and found Richard upstairs, kneeling over Ellen. He had closed her eyelids. Soberly, he looked up at me. The long deep scratch on his cheek glistened with blood in the darkness.

"Do you have something to tell me, Miss Sharp?"

"I can't…"

But he continued. "This is merely an intuition, but that attack…I feel as if you and your friend, Dr. St. John, might not be altogether *surprised* by tonight's events." He narrowed his eyes. "What muddles have you involved yourself in?"

I had to look away from Ellen's body, a lump in my throat. She was yet another casualty of my ties to the Conclave. It would be impossible now to keep Richard and Grandmother out of this.

"How much did Simon tell you during the Ripper murders?" I wiped a tear away from my face.

"A bit. He said that you were involved in some sort of very serious business. That there was a killer after you."

I slumped onto the top of the staircase. The pain in my

shoulder wound throbbed hard. The coagulating blood glued the thin fabric of my nightgown to my skin.

"Please," I muttered wearily, "please summon Simon and Scotland Yard."

"And tell them *what*, precisely?" Richard asked pointedly.

"Tell the police that we found Ellen this way. That she was murdered like the Millbrough youth the other night. Tell them the killer was here, but that we saw nothing."

Richard hesitated, then nodded. "I will. But I must know *everything* regarding this matter. That's only fair for Lady Westfield and her safety. We will leave Ellen's body here, but I do not want Lady Westfield to see this sight."

"I won't let her out of her bedroom."

I tried not to look at Ellen's body. I winced, fought back tears. The pain from my shoulder wound began to spread down my arm.

Richard's eyes lingered on the bite. "You're wounded."

"Simon will examine it when he arrives."

Richard started down the stairs, pausing after a few steps.

"Is there something else, Richard?"

He started to speak, then shook his head. "I hardly know what to say. Please attend to Lady Westfield."

Five

You and your grandmother cannot stay in this house," Simon said quietly. Although Scotland Yard wouldn't arrive for another few hours, Simon had come within minutes of Richard summoning him.

I winced, biting my lip as he cleaned my shoulder wound with carbolic acid. We were in the kitchen, and although I was now dressed and wearing a corset, I had folded the top of my gown to my waist so that Simon could attend to the wound. It was improper, but it couldn't be helped. I wrapped a shawl around my other arm and my corset for the sake of modesty.

"I know," I murmured quietly, looking away as Simon fumbled lightly through the instruments in his medical bag. This was going to hurt, and I would rather not see the scalpel, the needle.

Simon gave me a very small dose of laudanum to dull the pain.

"I can't leave my work now, Simon. I told Dr. Anderson I would shadow her in the pediatric ward tomorrow."

I turned my head a bit to gauge Simon's expression, but he seemed wholly focused upon threading a long needle. "Fine," he said. "Complete your immediate responsibilities at New Hospital. You and Lady Westfield can stay at my house for a few nights. Then we'll take her to Warwick, and you shall stay at the estate with her. It's too unsafe for you to be in London."

"But my work," I repeated. "My examinations are soon. And how could I explain another long absence to Dr. Anderson? I already was gone too long with the Orkney trips."

"I'll speak to Dr. Anderson, vouch for your dedication to the hospital and your seriousness about entering her medical school. Your safety is more pressing."

Images of Ellen's lifeless eyes … Mariah … and Max kept invading my thoughts.

"There were two other men, Simon." I quickly described the men in the doorway. "But they didn't seem to be undead, like our attackers were. Of course, I couldn't see them very well. Max spoke to them as if they were his equals."

A pause. "We cannot assume too much at this point, Abbie."

I'd known Simon long enough to hear the weight in his voice. "What do you know, Simon?" I asked.

"I *know* only that it is a miracle no one other than Ellen died last night, and that you and Lady Westfield will be on the train to Warwick by the end of this week."

I decided to postpone mentioning that I wouldn't be *staying* in Warwick. I was too exhausted to press the matter now, but I certainly couldn't imagine living at Kennilworth and leaving Simon to sort out the Conclave matters alone.

As the sun rose, the mottled shadows in the kitchen deepened. Simon needed to finish stitching my wound before Scotland Yard arrived.

He looked at me pityingly. "You already know that this is going to hurt."

"Yes, do it."

He handed me a clean cloth, which I promptly balled up into my mouth to keep from crying out. Grandmother was sleeping soundly, as Simon had given her a heavy dose of laudanum. Still, I didn't want to risk waking her.

I looked away.

Simon paused.

"Go on," I said awkwardly, through the rag.

Tears ran down my face as he stitched up the wound.

It helped to have Simon near as the police photographed Ellen's body and questioned me. I asked that Grandmother be left alone, as her nerves were unwell. Detective Inspector Abberline arrived around five o'clock and I did my best to avoid him, disappearing into Grandmother's room or staying near Simon.

Unfortunately, when the morgue carriage arrived and Simon and Richard were occupied with the removal of Ellen's body, Abberline cornered me in the downstairs hallway just as I left Grandmother's room.

"Miss Sharp, I need to ask you a few questions in the parlor."

It was a command, not a request. I cut my gaze from his four-fingered right hand to meet his eyes. He hadn't shown me the least bit of gratitude, even though it was because of me that he'd merely lost a finger that night in the alley with Max.

I walked wearily behind him, into the parlor, still in pain. Although Simon had been quick, my stitches still ached under the salve and bandages.

"Miss Sharp," Abberline said once he'd shut the parlor door. "I have a strong suspicion that you know who is behind all this."

I said nothing.

"That man who attacked me, that evening several months ago—who *was* he?"

I'd forgotten how much I disliked Abberline's smell, which was overpowering me in the closed parlor. It was like stale tea. I tried to determine whom I disliked more, Abberline or Wyatt, and decided quickly upon Wyatt. An image of his trembling finger came to my mind; he seemed unpredictable and very close to unraveling. Abberline, on the other hand, was generally predictable, like a loud but reliable clock.

"You would be wise to tell me what you know, Miss Sharp. You need our protection."

I chuckled. Abberline cared nothing about my safety, and it seemed absurd that this middle-aged man, who didn't even know half the truth behind these murders, would suggest that he could protect me.

Abberline's gaze darkened. He was about to attempt to frighten me as he had during the Ripper investigation—I still remembered how he had taken me to that suffocating back room at Scotland Yard, shown me that kidney floating in the jar.

He lowered his voice and leaned forward. "This is no laughing matter. All of the bodies have been *consumed*, Miss Sharp. The bite upon your housemaid was done by human teeth—I *must* know what you saw or heard."

Abberline wanted information from me. Wyatt wanted information from me. It did seem ridiculous—as if *I* had all the answers about this grotesque web Max was spinning around us. I had enough before me without Abberline bungling matters with his bullying tactics. He could never solve this case, and if he continued trying, he would end up dead.

"We have been doing our *damnedest*, Miss Sharp, to keep these murders out of the newspapers. We don't want another situation like the Ripper case."

Of course, I had heard all of this before. Scotland Yard, the Secret Service Bureau...

"Do you have anything else to say, Miss Sharp?" he demanded. I was reminded of my first impression of him, how he resembled a bloodhound with his tenacity. He pursued his cases at all costs. I remembered those stacks of empty teacups, the papers on his desk at Scotland Yard. Oddly, I thought of that little photograph of the woman, likely his wife, on his desk. I remembered when he grabbed my arm outside of Highgate Cemetery last year. I'd had enough experience with Abberline to wager that he wasn't vengeful; still, with an open case before him, everything else fell to the wayside.

He waited for my response in irritable silence.

"How is your wife, Abberline?"

He stood silent in front of me, his anger melting to bewilderment.

When he started to speak, I cut him off. "I mean, we talk about these murders all the time, but we never talk about *you*," I said. "I'm just wondering if you are flesh and blood or merely a well-oiled clock that won't cease until it reaches the next hour and solves the next case."

Abberline's expression was mingled with anger and confusion, yet somehow disarmed.

Simon suddenly swung open the parlor doors and stepped into the room, Richard just behind him. The police were ready to leave.

A small scowl on his face, Abberline tipped his bowler hat at us and left the room. His back was hunched; he'd lost his usual confidence.

"If he weren't such a bully, I would almost feel sorry for him," I said to Simon as he stood beside me, watching the Inspector leave.

When Grandmother awoke, I helped her dress. She kept asking for Ellen, as I still hadn't told her about the maid's death. I put off her questions, gently slipping her chemise over her head and securing the buttons at the back of her dress. As I brushed her hair while she sat at her vanity, I knew that I had to tell her almost everything. Still, I feared how it might affect her.

I sat next to her on the small vanity bench.

"Grandmother, Ellen is dead." A lump formed in my

throat. My fingers still felt raw from the hours that Simon, Richard, and I had spent scrubbing the bloodstained walls. The more heavily stained portions of carpet would have to be replaced.

Grandmother's hand trembled violently as she fastened her earbobs. "Will you please leave me alone for five minutes, Arabella?"

I nodded and left, then stood outside her room. My head throbbed and I leaned heavily against the door. Vaguely, I heard Simon in the parlor stirring his tea.

When I stepped back into her room, Grandmother was sitting in a chair at the bottom of the bed with Jupe and her long-dead husband's flintlock pistol in her lap. The frizzen opened; it didn't appear to be loaded. The pistol's velvet-lined case lay open on her bed.

"Is that loaded?" I asked, to be sure.

"No, it hasn't been fired in over forty years. I'll need Richard to purchase some gunpowder later and show me how to load it."

Although Grandmother seemed better at hosting tea parties than handling a loaded flintlock pistol, I remembered last night when she'd thrust the poker into my hands as I fought Mariah. I smiled at her peculiar steeliness.

"Arabella, I *must* know what happened last night."

"Yes, you must. Please come to the parlor." Simon and I had talked this through with Richard while cleaning things up.

She followed me, the pistol still in her hands, Jupe at her feet. Richard stood near the parlor doorway.

"Come along, Richard," I said. "Please sit with us."

Awkwardly, Richard sat down on a small wooden chair

near the sofa. Simon glanced at the pistol and cast me an amused expression as I seated myself near him. I shrugged.

Grandmother placed the pistol in her lap and poured herself tea from a nearby tray. "I demand to know what happened last night. What you know about all of this. Why Mariah was here, behaving so ... *wickedly*. She is *dead*. I attended her funeral." She took a sip of tea. "Did *she* kill Ellen?"

"Yes," I said quickly, wondering how I would explain.

"Lady Westfield, what happened last night is a result of something that has been happening since Caroline left you many years ago," Simon said quietly.

In what seemed like one breath, I told Grandmother about the Conclave—about how they had pursued Mother as a member and then pursued me. I told her a much-abridged and slightly altered version of that night at the Conclave's house, when Simon and William had helped me kill them after they gave me the choice to join them or die. I left out everything about the visions that had afflicted Mother and then me. I then told her the truth about my long absence this spring. Her eyes widened as if she didn't believe me. I unbuttoned my collar a bit so she could see again the top of the "cat scratch" I'd received from Seraphina.

She stared quietly at me before turning to Simon.

"It's all true, Lady Westfield," he said evenly.

"That portrait of the lamia, Grandmother. The one that Mother posed for ... "

Grandmother's expression darkened.

"I think it was a warning. Somehow, I believe Mother knew of the lamia the Conclave was keeping. She wanted Dante Gabriel Rossetti to paint it as a warning."

"Caroline..." Grandmother muttered. Lifting a hand from the pistol to her heart, she paled. "Caroline. Why couldn't she have talked to me about all of this?"

"It would have been too dangerous for you to know," I said limply, leaving out the other obvious reason—that they had been estranged.

Simon went on to tell Grandmother the truth about Richard. "Although Richard was ignorant, until now, of the existence of the Conclave, he knows that the monarchy has historical and very sensitive political *secrets*. Richard assisted me once during a very... terrible illness that I contracted in Africa. I wanted to help him upon his retirement from the Secret Service, so that is why I provided such excellent references for him when you needed a butler."

Grandmother stared wide-eyed at Richard, fidgeting with one of her earbobs. "That explains why you didn't know how to prepare a proper omelet when you first arrived."

A smile played at the corner of Richard's mouth.

Simon continued. "The point, Lady Westfield, is that Max Bartlett is now the only remaining member of the Conclave, but he might not be acting alone. Earlier this year, he threatened Abbie and referenced an ongoing 'project,' but we're not sure what that is. I do believe that it somehow involves those... people... who attacked you last night. He has done something dreadful to bring Mariah back to life. I must emphasize that no place is completely safe until we solve these matters. You *cannot* remain here."

Grandmother sighed.

Then, after an uncomfortable silence, she said, "Do you

have anything else shocking to tell me, Abbie? Perhaps your mother was part lamia?"

I met Simon's eyes. He smiled and shook his head.

But I couldn't resist. "My real father was not Jacque Sharp. It was William's adoptive father, Dante Gabriel Rossetti."

Grandmother fainted, falling hard on the floor.

Six

As rain poured unceasing throughout the day, William took his exercise in the menagerie.

Simon and Abbie would be arriving in a few days, and William thought bitterly of how he might enjoy even Simon's company to ease his loneliness. The beautiful estate was insufferably dull and quiet. He played dominoes, chess, and card games with Laura and read books to her, but of course there was no conversation. Bridget and Miranda performed their duties like automatons; they cooked, fed the animals, dusted, and closed the drapes silently and efficiently at the same time every day.

In spite of his boredom, William remained determined to heal. It galled him to no end that Simon was living an active life now, working day and night at Whitechapel while he persisted as an invalid here. Since he'd last seen Abbie, over a week ago, William had increased his exercise routines to three times daily. Certainly the increased circulation from exercise would flush out the lamia's venom more quickly.

William limped, alone, through Kennilworth's corridors, leaning upon his walking stick. Although his Great Dane, Hugo, normally accompanied him, tonight the dog preferred to sleep at Laura's feet as she read in the parlor. As he walked heavily down the long carpeted hallway to the menagerie, William felt the fading but still sharp pain of the remaining venom in his leg.

He hated the intemperance and selfishness he had exhibited this spring; guilt weighed heavily upon him.

The tiger roared in the distance as William approached the menagerie. He heaved himself through the large doors, a difficult endeavor with the cane.

Entering the room, he paused.

The menagerie seemed darker than he'd expected, even for a stormy evening.

Why had Bridget only lit three of the gas lamps lining the room? He had told her he would be coming in here.

Grumbling and cursing under his breath, William stepped deeper into the enormous room; Petey roared ferociously and the monkeys clamored within their cages, nervous about the impending storm.

Petey's rage escalated; his enclosure rattled as his growls and snarls echoed throughout the room. William heard his claws raking hard upon the steel bars. The hair on the back of William's neck prickled as he squinted into the darkness; he thought he saw movement at the far end of the menagerie, just outside of the tiger's cage.

But it was too difficult to see clearly. Bridget had closed the heavy drapes over the large windows.

He blinked; saw the movement again.

"Hello!" he called in the darkness.

Nothing.

That prickle upon his neck began again when William saw a form. His initial thought was that a monkey had escaped, but the form was too tall, the movement too intentional.

It was definitely human.

William tried to walk fast toward that part of the menagerie. But his leg cramped tremendously at the effort, and the walking stick was cumbersome.

He stopped, breathing heavily and leaning hard upon the walking stick. He was now in the middle of the dark menagerie, and his eyes adjusted to the darkness a bit more.

He heard something again, the slough of a footstep.

A bolt of lightning streaked across the sky outside, the light breaking through the folds of the drapes.

In the flash, he saw, near Petey's cage, a man staring straight at him.

No.

Horrified, William stumbled forward a bit, dropped his stick, and landed on his knees.

It couldn't be.

He had been easing himself off of the laudanum as Simon had advised, but this man *must* be a drug-induced hallucination. No other explanation was possible.

William reached for his cane, stood up on trembling legs, and rubbed his eyes. When he peered again, the figure was gone.

It hadn't been Max.

It hadn't been a monster.

It had been *him*—William—staring directly at himself

across the room. But the other William stood tall and did not limp on a walking stick. He had been impeccably dressed in a jacket and a cravat. And there had been something else, an unnerving glint in the other William's eyes.

William walked toward the tiger's cage, but his legs shook violently from shock. He heard another footstep behind him and spun around, prepared to attack even this hallucination with his walking stick.

But then he stopped, feeling a mighty relief. Laura stood before him, staring at him with wide eyes.

"Could you please help me?" he asked, leaning unsteadily upon the stick. "I'd like to see the tiger."

In spite of the girl's muteness, William knew that she wasn't daft. She was quick-witted, and, particularly lately, he had seen increasing glints of expression behind her eyes. At this moment, her gaze held a spark of amusement. Indeed, he must look silly standing upon wobbling legs in the darkness, scared out of his wits.

Taking his arm, she walked beside him as he limped further toward the door near Petey's cage. He had to know if he was losing his mind, or if someone else had indeed been there.

As he approached, Petey's attention turned toward them. The tiger snarled, his great white incisors gleaming in the darkness.

William stepped behind the cage. Mindful of Petey's claws in the darkness, he muttered, "Laura, stay back."

Then, in the next flash of lightning, he saw two small puddles of rainwater—muddy boot prints, too large to be from one of the maids. Indeed, the prints seemed to be made by feet about the same size as his.

He thought of the lamia. Since discovering the Conclave, he had seen the strange and bizarre, but he shook his head in disbelief.

Laura watched him. Not wanting to frighten her, he turned and spoke gently. "Would you like to share some hot cocoa with me?"

Silence.

"Of course you would." He rested his hand upon her shoulder as they walked away from Petey's cage and slowly out of the menagerie. They sat in the library for the rest of the evening, until Bridget came to put Laura to bed.

William was unable to shake his unease. He told Bridget that he would be sleeping in Abbie's room, near Laura. Before retiring, he unlocked the revolver case he kept stored in the library.

Tomorrow he would begin exercising *four* times daily.

Seven

The next morning, Richard went back to Grandmother's house to pack her bags for Warwick, and I spent my time wrapping up business in London. I planned to stay with Grandmother for a few days at Kennilworth, and I needed to make certain that she was well settled at the estate before leaving her to rejoin Simon in London—regardless of whatever Simon might have to say about that. More specifically, I wanted assurance that Grandmother wouldn't shoot William with my grandfather's pistol. She had kept the weapon within arm's reach since the attack.

Simon accompanied me to New Hospital, where we spoke to Dr. Anderson. As the founder of New Hospital and the London Medical School for Women, she had become my mentor. Simon told her that I would be out of town for a while. Although Dr. Anderson already seemed empathetic, Simon told her about the many hours I spent assisting him in Whitechapel in my free time. She assured us that I would still be welcome at New Hospital when I returned from my absence and reminded me, yet again, to study for my entrance examinations. By the time Simon and I left her office, she had loaned me three more books to study.

When we reached Whitechapel Hospital, Simon went immediately to the laboratory, and I took my heavy load of books down the hall to William's office, which was currently my study. The room was quiet, but a dark and cramped place to work. Through the window, I watched dingy Commercial Street far below—the crowded carriages and carts, the dock and railway workers going to their shifts.

All these people lived out their lives ignorant of the small band of immortals who, for centuries, had effected the murders of so many among them. I remembered them so clearly: Dr. Julian Bartlett, the physician who had directed Whitechapel Hospital. Robert Buck, Marcus Brown, and chilly Reverend John Perkins. I stared at the medical books on the desk with mixed feelings of fury and frustration. Simon and I should be devoting all our time to our work, and I should be focused on my impending medical school examinations, but instead we had, once again, the Conclave before us.

The rain began. Water slid down the glass, blurring my view. I turned from the window and bumped into the strange skull Dr. Bartlett had kept upon a small pedestal. Carefully, I picked it up, examining the pen marks with notes about the brain's phrenology and the lobes associated with each of the four humors. I wondered, as I had a million times since learning of their existence, how much the Conclave really knew about the workings of the human body. They had turned a young woman, Seraphina, into a lamia through manipulating her cell structures. Now Max and perhaps others were bringing the dead back to life.

Gingerly, I set the skull back upon the pedestal and left the room.

I found Simon down the hall in the laboratory, dissecting a naked female corpse. Her head had been shaved and her mouth hung open, revealing few teeth.

The entire cavity of the corpse was open. Simon bent over her, his wavy blond hair falling over his forehead. His sleeves were rolled far up, and blood smeared his arms to his elbows. I saw then that he had not only cut open the chest but also removed the top of the corpse's skull. The gray and bloody brain sat nearby on the dissection table.

After greeting me, Simon turned his attention to slicing up the brain tissue.

"What is your purpose here?" I asked as I stood over the body. During a dissection, we always had a focus. If the individual had been an alcoholic, the liver might be of interest. One time, William and I drained the spinal fluid of a patient deceased from syphilis.

"Nothing in particular. I'm mostly interested in understanding the state of organs upon death." Simon's white, marble-smooth forehead wrinkled slightly in concentration.

I tied an apron about my waist and rolled up my sleeves.

After Grandmother had gone to bed last night, in the room we shared at the St. John house, Simon and I had stayed up late in his study talking about the attack—what I had seen—without coming to any conclusions. We could only speculate on how Max was able to bring corpses back from the dead, and upon the identity of the two men in league with him. Max's motives and intentions remained a mystery.

Simon sat on a nearby stool, put a small slice of the brain on a slide, and placed it under the microscope. He peered into the lens before asking quietly, "Abbie, when does death occur?"

I chuckled. "That's obvious."

Simon's face remained frozen and focused as he peered through the lens. "Not always. Please answer the question."

I sighed. It seemed a waste of time, but perhaps this would prepare me for my exams.

"Usually death occurs when the heartbeat and breathing cease. This is followed by an immediate flaccid state before the onset of rigor mortis, a condition that sets in some six to twelve hours after death depending on the individual's physiology."

Still peering down the microscope, Simon asked, "Abbie, have you heard of Luigi Galvani?"

"Of course. Mary Shelley studied his works before writing *Frankenstein*. He was an eighteenth-century physician who conducted tests upon dead frogs—he would try to reanimate their bodies by passing electrical currents through them."

Simon took another slide and placed it under the lens.

"I read about his studies in one of my medical textbooks," I continued. "However, Dr. Anderson told me that there was no real science behind his work at all. He is of interest only as a historical figure."

"For the most part, that is my assessment also," Simon said, pushing his seat a bit away from the microscope. He looked hard at me in the darkening shadows of the laboratory.

"But the actual moment of death, I believe, can be murky. While waiting for the coroner to arrive, I have seen bodies of our recently deceased sit up, jerk, or groan several minutes after the heart stops beating." He paused, watching me carefully before he continued. "Abbie, are you certain that the girl who murdered Ellen, who attacked you and Lady Westfield, was indeed Mariah?"

"Absolutely certain."

Apart from the fact that Mariah had told us who she was and that she was "resurrected"—whatever that meant—I had clearly seen her dark eyes, her smile; I had heard her familiar tinkling voice as she spoke to Grandmother and me.

"It was Mariah, Simon. But she wasn't as she'd been when alive. She was so *cruel*."

Blinking back tears, I walked over again to the corpse, considered the dead face. "I saw Mariah die..."

That night in Lady Violet's attic, I had locked eyes with Mariah as she fell from me, down onto that splintered pile of wood. I had seen a piece of wood burst through her chest, blood spurting out all over her nightgown. Even from my position high above her, I saw the life drain from her eyes. The next morning, her body had been taken away to the mortuary.

"There is *no* possibility that Mariah could have survived," I added. "When I felt her breastbone the other night..." I stopped.

"Did you feel a heartbeat?" Simon asked eagerly, leaning closer to me.

I kept my eyes on the corpse. *Why the bloody hell hadn't someone closed the corpse's eyelids?*

"I felt a heartbeat, Simon. But her chest had been crudely

stitched up. Her breath, her skin, were cold. She smelled like a decomposing animal..."

Simon handed me a handkerchief to wipe my eyes.

"If I hadn't been there, I believe that she would have killed Grandmother just as she killed Ellen. She would have eaten Ellen if she'd had more time—she crouched like a lioness over Ellen's body. But later, she *cowered* around Max. She would never have submitted to anyone when alive. *Never.*"

I chuckled even amid my tears. Mariah Crawley had been so independent.

"Come here, Abbie," Simon said gently. "I want you to look at this."

He stepped away as I sat on the stool, blinking away tears as I peered into the microscope. Slide samples, whether of an insect or a piece of body tissue, always fascinated me. Under the microscope, the view was so wildly different. Even a piece of brain matter or saliva became all swirling patterns and colors.

"But I've seen this before, Simon." The usual small, spindly cell structures.

"Yes, but we need to be quite aware of what the brain of a standard deceased corpse looks like. *This* is normal. We need to understand the normal before we can understand the abnormal. In the same way that Seraphina's venom exhibited strange structures, different from other venom I have seen, I feel, with absolute certainty, that the brain matters of your attackers the other night would appear quite different from what we see in this woman's brain."

"I see." I tried to detach myself from my emotions, focusing instead on the science. "I would like to know why they consume human flesh, and how they can recall their friends.

Mariah *knew* me and Grandmother. She remembered us. Yet why do they seem so feral in many respects, willing to kill and eat those whom they used to care about? I also want to know why they obey Max as if they are his servants."

"I have all the same questions," Simon said flatly, his gaze detached. But he said nothing more as he removed the slides from the microscope tray.

I shook my head. "How can this happen? The body and organs *decompose* after death, and nothing, *nothing*, revitalizes them."

"Abbie, the best scientist is the open-minded one." Simon began placing the brain samples into formaldehyde jars for later study. "Apart from Galvani's ridiculous electrophysiology studies, there might be other ways to bring back the recent dead. In my research, I have heard stories from the Caribbean of spells reviving the dead so that they obey the orders of the living. Although attributed to voodoo, it's most likely a concoction of herbs that revitalizes the body in those cases."

I thought of the many photographs in the albums that documented the Conclave's experiments. "The Conclave traveled extensively."

"Yes. They had many lifetimes to delve into the mysteries of such matters. And now, if Max has gained access to their scientific methods...Abbie, we thought that the notes at the Montgomery Street house perished in the fire, but perhaps Max has gotten them somehow."

Simon placed the formaldehyde jars on a shelf, next to one of Robert Buck's preserved jellyfish. "I'm not certain what Max is doing, or why he would include others in his business. Unlike the original Conclave, Max seems to be strategically *drawing attention* to his projects—leaving the Conclave's symbol on cemetery gravestones, unleashing these attackers, these revenants."

We stood in silence for a moment, until Nurse Josephine ran into the laboratory to inform Simon about a second floor patient with infected surgical stitches.

As Simon followed Josephine downstairs, I began collecting instruments to be washed.

After cleaning up in the laboratory, washing the instruments, and covering the corpse to be taken away, I walked back down the dark hall to William's office. It was early nightfall now, and moonlight streamed through the office doorway. As I entered the small place and collected my books, I wished that after all that we had been through, I could feel braver and calmer about what lay ahead.

Eight

When Simon and I returned to his house, I found Grandmother in our shared bedroom, seated in front of her vanity, vigorously rubbing lotion into her wrinkled hands. Jupe lay on the bed near her pillow, asleep. He snored loudly, his little legs up in the air.

Grandmother made her way over to the bed and pulled the covers around her. "I cannot stop thinking about the attack," she muttered, playing with her rings a bit. Her voice cracked. "Ellen, she was such a fool . . ."

"Grandmother—"

"I tried to convince Richard to come here with us, but he insists upon remaining at the house. I left him the pistol. I don't know if I can *ever* stay in that house again."

I sat on the bed with her. "You won't have to. We can sell it, buy another house even in the same neighborhood." Although I didn't like the idea of him staying there alone, I wanted to reassure her. "And Richard can take care of himself."

"But those *people* . . ."

"Grandmother, the Conclave had so many secrets. This is but another one…"

The clock approached nine. Simon and I were going to meet in his study for a bit before going to bed.

I kissed her forehead. "I'll come to bed in a little while."

But then she grabbed my wrist, hard. "Arabella, come stay with me at Kennilworth. I have a terrible feeling that you'll return to London, to work and to pursue these matters."

I said nothing, cringing a little. I had not yet told Simon of my plan. I certainly didn't want to tell Grandmother now, given her fearful state.

"Please…" she implored. "Forget about this. Take a year off and then, if you are still determined, you may apply to medical school."

"That's impossible at this point." I held her hand a moment longer, touched by her worry for me. I searched her eyes, suppressing a smile as I wondered if she even remembered my revelation yesterday morning about who my biological father was. Whether she remembered it or not, I suspected that we would never speak of it again.

As Grandmother stuttered, attempting to argue further, I kissed her wrinkled cheek and left the room. She was so frightened; her neatly ordered world was upturned by all of this.

I was furious that Max had brought her into the Conclave's world. I had preferred she remain innocent of it.

I found Simon behind his large oak desk in his study, with papers and scribbled notes spread out in front of him. He was holding a volume of *Frankenstein.*

"And how is Lady Westfield?"

"She is still very shocked and worried for me."

"And she still has her pistol?" Simon arched one of his brows.

I chuckled as he poured us each a brandy. "No, thank God. She gave it to Richard."

Simon shook his head. "I tried to talk him into coming to Warwick with us, but for now he prefers to stay in London." He smirked. "He's almost as stubborn as she is."

"Speaking of stubbornness," I said firmly, "after we settle Grandmother at Kennilworth, I'm returning to London with you. You can't convince me otherwise. I'm not going to leave you alone to figure out this mess yourself."

Simon paused, glancing down at his half-opened novel. "I had hoped, rather than believed, that you would stay out of harm's way."

I chuckled. "I expected to have more of an argument about this."

"Pointless, Abbie. It would be pointless to argue with you when you're so determined."

His tone was affectionate and warm. I blushed and looked away, wondering for the hundredth time why I loved William instead of Simon.

In an effort to change the subject, I nodded to his desk. "*Frankenstein*? I thought you rarely had time for fiction anymore."

He shrugged. "I've had some interest in this novel lately."

"In what, specifically? Bringing people back from the dead, I suppose."

"Yes, and doppelgangers."

"Doppelgangers?"

"For some reason, I cannot get them out of my mind." Simon closed the book and set it down. "Tell me more about those men with Max the other night," he added.

"It was difficult to see them, but they did not seem to be revenants—their stances were too strong. One wore a turban. The other seemed to have dark curly hair."

Simon leaned back in his chair, his long fingers wrapped gracefully around his brandy glass.

I sipped the burning amber liquid. "It seems absurd. I mean, who wears turbans in London?"

Simon's ice-blue eyes stared ahead, thoughtful. "Indeed."

Nine

As the carriage turned onto the long driveway to the Kenilworth Estate, I bit my lip, hoping that Grandmother could adjust to being outside of London. Simon and I had agreed not to tell her about Miranda and Bridget's previous profession as prostitutes. If she knew, she would never allow herself to be waited upon by them.

The persistent rain of this week stopped as the wide, wet lawn came into view. I saw Hugo running after a ball. The mansion stretched out, wide and expansive, with many large second and third story windows spanning its front like wide-open eyes. As it was a little over one hundred years old, the exterior of the house was rather simple. I preferred this Neoclassical style to the current trends in architecture, which were abundant in gables and turrets.

"You need a gardener, Arabella," Grandmother said, staring out the carriage window at the garden, which was so overgrown that foliage nearly covered the front entrance. "The grounds are indecent."

"I like them as they are," I said, peering out the window, sunlight warming my face. I had no desire to prune the foliage.

I saw Christina stepping outside to meet us. Tiny, in a dark dress, she might have been a miniature figurine for a dollhouse. William followed her closely, walking unassisted. His steps came slowly, and Christina supported him when he wobbled.

I smiled, not believing his remarkable improvement.

Luncheon was a strained, awkward event with Grandmother, Christina, William, Simon, and Laura—all of us sitting around the large table. Grandmother seemed terribly uncomfortable taking a meal with a Pre-Raphaelite like Christina. I tried to ignore Simon's weighty silence, which always developed when William and I were together. This silence, though, came less from jealousy than from reproach. I knew that Simon thought that William was beneath me in character and intelligence.

As Miranda refilled our water glasses, Christina caught my eye from across the large bowl of floating roses between us. It would be up to us to keep momentum within the conversation.

"William," she began, "has quickened the pace of his exercises these past few days. Yesterday, he walked from one side of the gardens to the other and only stumbled once."

Grandmother remained unimpressed, saying nothing.

"He seemed inspired…" Christina continued, catching my eye.

Simon gazed darkly into his water glass.

William remained silent, his face sober. Since my arrival, he had seemed distant, troubled. I'd thought he would be happier to see me.

Laura watched us all with wide dark eyes as she tasted a small spoonful of soup. I had told Grandmother about the Scottish orphan's history, and she watched Laura with uneasy curiosity.

I smiled as I lifted my soup spoon to my lips. Unfortunately, I knew that look of Grandmother's well. It was the exact expression she'd worn when she arrived last year at Mother's funeral to take me back with her to London. It was like the overwhelmed gaze one casts a wolf pup that must be tamed.

"Have you decreased your laudanum as I advised?"

Simon asked the question icily as he leaned upon the side of a bookshelf in the library. He didn't even look up as he silently turned the pages of one of Robert Buck's books about herbal remedies from the Amazon.

"Damn it, Simon. I've weaned myself off of it over the past couple of days." William, seated next to me on the sofa, cast a glance toward me. "And I'm not drinking anything stronger than water at the moment."

"That's a step." Simon closed the book, returned it to the shelf, and seated himself on a nearby ottoman. "If you could just stay out of trouble while—"

"If you hadn't saved my life, I would—"

"But I *did*, in fact, save your life. And you are presently too weak to attack me, as your leg is still injured from the venom."

William scowled.

The three of us hadn't been able to talk alone until now, in this hour after dinner in the library. Tensions between William and Simon, which had been strained since we'd brought William home from Orkney, were more so now that we'd told him about the attack by Mariah and the revenants. William told us, in turn, about seeing a man in the menagerie who had appeared to be a perfect replica of himself.

Because of Simon's interest in doppelgangers, I glanced at him after William told the story, but Simon's expression remained unreadable.

"I'm leaving," William said, reaching for his cane.

"No, William." I pulled him back down beside me. I could do without his short temper.

Something twitched in Simon's expression. "Perhaps we should all go to bed now. I think it is futile to discuss these issues any further tonight. Tomorrow morning, immediately after breakfast, we'll resume this conversation.

He stood up and started walking out of the library, but just as he reached the closed door, he turned to William. "I must get this out of my system if we are to speak again..."

"By all means, go ahead," William muttered sullenly.

"If you ever, by your own stupidity, endanger Abbie's life again, and if she dies as a result, I will kill you."

William tossed his head back, laughing. "What, will you drown me in holy water?"

"Nine o'clock tomorrow morning," Simon said as he left. "Good night, Abbie."

"Good night."

William chuckled.

"Careful, William. He's murdered before."

William stopped laughing and turned to me, intrigued. "When?"

"It's Simon's story to tell."

Refusing to use his cane, William walked by my side all the way from the second floor library to the menagerie. He winced often, but he seemed very determined. Much more determined than he had been the last time I was here.

The heavy doors swung shut behind us, and the room seemed even lovelier than I had remembered it. Although it was night, Bridget had still not closed the drapes, and the room seemed aglow with stars and lamplight.

Slowly and unsteadily, William led me to the nook of the menagerie with the bamboo swing. We sat upon the cushioned seat; one of the room's many enormous windows rose behind us, the sky beyond it a burst of movement. Although the moon and stars were out, storm clouds rolled eastward. The gaslight reflected in the glass and starlight stretched beyond, spanned out like spun gold over the gardens and the Warwick countryside.

A spider monkey squealed from its cage nearby, exciting the others into a small cacophony of cries.

William remained quiet, his eyes dark pools. "You and Simon. It seems as if it's always the two of you figuring out these mysteries, cleaning up after me."

"That pretty much describes what happened in Orkney." I caught myself before I said more. I understood why Simon had lashed out in the library just now. Now that William was feeling better, I couldn't hold my tongue against my rising bitterness.

"I'm paying my penance," William murmured sullenly.

I twisted my arm around the swing's taut suspension and looked away. "When I left you this spring, you lost all self-control. Your drinking made you unable to work. It was easy for Max to capture you. Simon and I almost died saving you. I would do it all again for you, but I cannot be the source of your stability for the rest of our lives."

William remained quiet for several minutes.

"I have no defense, Abbie. The way I behaved was rotten and inexcusable. You have every right to turn on your heel and walk away from me. But as I've told you, I love you. My feelings are sincere and will not change."

I turned to him. The animals quieted a bit; William's face in the darkness nearly undid me. Dark stubble framed his chin. His hair needed to be trimmed, but this only added to his beauty. I looked up at the enormous chandelier, dusty and cobwebbed, hanging long and heavy from the ceiling. It didn't work anymore and was far too high for Bridget and Miranda to bother with. I tried to imagine this room as a ballroom, as it had been before the previous owner converted it into a menagerie. Thinking of the house's history, its unique architecture, helped me ignore my rapid heartbeat.

"But what happens if I leave you again?" I asked. "Or if I die?" I stared at the raised plaster roses upon the ceiling. "Will you crumble again? Will you drink too much? Become like your father?"

I felt a warm palm on my cheek as he turned my face to his. "No. All I can offer is my promise. Is that enough?"

Before I could answer, William leaned over and gently kissed my jaw, his stubble scratching lightly against my skin. His mouth, feather-light, traveled up my jawline to my ear as he whispered, "Please, let it be enough."

Think, Abbie.

Think.

Although I told myself not to get carried away, not only did I let him kiss me but I returned the kiss, pulling my hand away from the rope swing and pressing my body against his. I ran my fingers through his hair, not having touched him much these last few months other than as his caretaker.

A light rain began melting the window reflection of stars and gaslight behind us. Petey emitted a sleepy roar, and the monkeys settled in their cages. One of the dodos fluttered its clumsy wings, sending out small clouds of dirt. But this all became peripheral as I leaned further into William. The bamboo swing twisted from our shifting weights, and both of my boots lifted off the floor. I toppled against William, knocking him back and falling on top of him. Our position was awkward—his feet still on the ground, his torso under my own, my hands still against his chest—and we chuckled. I knew it would be wise to shift myself; better yet, to sit up like a lady. But I couldn't. I liked being close to him like this, feeling his chest under my own. I could feel his heartbeat under my hand.

"Don't move," he whispered. Leaning up, he placed both of his hands on my cheeks and kissed me. I groaned, deepened the kiss.

"Abbie..." he muttered through half-closed lids. Suddenly he pulled away from me, his eyes wide.

"What?" I gasped. I turned and saw Laura standing about ten feet away, a small glint in her eyes.

"Dear God!" I exclaimed, moving too quickly and collapsing heavily onto the floor in a crushing heap of petticoats and crinoline.

William stood up immediately, taking my elbow as I pulled myself off the floor. My thigh throbbed in pain.

"Dear Laura, I completely forgot," William said, quickly running his hands through his hair and smoothing his rumpled shirt. Then to me, under his breath, "Laura likes to come in here after dinner to feed the dodos."

"Yes, of course," I muttered, pushing an escaped lock away from my face. I left the room as William began helping Laura pull a bag of dried pumpkin seeds from a supply box.

Ten

Arabella!" Grandmother met me in the first floor corridor immediately after I left the menagerie. "Where have you been?"

"I was just in the menagerie," I said, my skirts still rumpled, my thigh aching. I would have a large bruise by tomorrow.

"With whom?"

"Laura is in there with William now, feeding the dodos."

"The child has been with me for the past hour. Simon retired to bed, so you must have been in there alone with William." She leveled her gaze. "Arabella, I have some conduct books I shall give you. There are proper ways of etiquette here. You are not in Dublin anymore."

My face burned in embarrassment. "I'll take more care in the future."

"Please see that you do," Grandmother said, then changed the subject. "I wanted to speak to you about Laura. She will never improve if she cannot speak."

I groaned inwardly. "Grandmother, I have *tried*—"

"If she cannot talk, we will never get her a governess," Grandmother said, cutting me off. She paused and pursed her thin lips. "Of course, once she starts speaking, everyone will know she is Scottish, and you know how they are—almost as bad as the Irish, so *tribal*. But perhaps we can work the accent out."

I stifled a moan. "So how do you plan to get her to talk?"

Grandmother turned and beckoned for me to follow her to the parlor. "Laura draws remarkably well. You must see."

Once we were in the little parlor, I saw that Grandmother had several sheets of paper lying out on a writing desk, charcoal pieces nearby.

"She followed me in here after dinner—I hardly know why. But I could not very well read while she stared at me from across the room. The situation was quite awkward. I suddenly thought that if she would not speak, she might at least draw. So I had Miranda bring me some materials, and Laura began, completing this in the span of half an hour."

Grandmother pointed to a surprisingly sophisticated sketch of William hobbling across the gardens. Christina stood small beside him, not assisting him, and he walked without a walking stick. Laura had captured all the small details, deepening the character of the picture: William's furrowed brows, Christina's slightly bulging eyes, and even the small wrinkles near her eyes, which were like hairline cracks in porcelain.

"This drawing, Arabella, depicts a talented little girl. Perhaps if we urge her along in this, we will be one step closer to getting her to speak."

I chided myself for not thinking of this sooner. "That is a

wonderful idea, Grandmother. But," I added with a smile, "I thought you disapproved of artists?"

She tightened her lips, leaning over my shoulder as she peered at the drawing again. "I do. But she is only eight years old, and we might guide her toward proper subjects. Flowers and landscape stills, perhaps."

Max lit his cigar as he lay upon his bed. Through the warm cloud of smoke, he gazed at the red tapestry hanging directly above him. He had salvaged it on his last trip to the Conclave's villa in Italy. All of their beautiful homes abandoned across Europe, and one in the American West. They were his now.

He took a long draw from the cigar and became lost in his thoughts; he needed this time away from the others. He preferred solitude, but he needed them. Their work had turned out to be quite valuable to him, particularly after the loss of the Conclave's residence on Montgomery Street.

The letters rested about him, old and fragile as butterfly wings. He had read them often throughout the years.

She had loved many, unashamedly; she had seen them as varied prism lights, textured, multifaceted. The extravagance of her love fascinated him. She had been like a Cabinet of Wonders—the flip side of his own greedy love.

He continued staring at the twisting vines and nightingales on the tapestry.

The daughter … he had wanted to kill her so often. He *should* have killed her.

He recalled walking through Seraphina's empty lair during the weeks that Abbie was emptying it. He remembered his final visit, after she'd left for the last time. Everything at that point had been removed except for Seraphina's bed and her many unfinished paintings. His footsteps echoed in the empty halls as he watched the place begin to ruin. Birds nested near the beautiful ceiling mosaic, their droppings splattering the walls, staining Effie's half-completed portraits of the Conclave members. The lair's menagerie stood bare and gloomy. He recalled chuckling as he stepped into the emptied treasury, oddly impressed that Abbie could wipe out so much. Her success in killing Seraphina hadn't been a defeat for him; he had wanted it all along. Even the stolen money had not been much of a problem, as the Conclave had investments throughout the Continent. But every step in his strange dance with that girl made him want her all the more, and sharpened his memories of Caroline.

Screams from outside his room interrupted his reverie. Max sighed, threw the cigar butt into a nearby ashtray, and locked away the letters.

Picking up his revolver, he made certain that the chambers were loaded and left. He preferred knives, but this was so much quicker, less messy.

There would be another culling tonight.

The next few days at Kennilworth were intolerable. I was restless, bothered, and on edge every night, worried that an attack might happen here.

Simon traveled by train to Whitechapel Hospital every day, returning to us in the evenings. He assured me that he'd made arrangements for his servants to leave his house before we returned to London, as we didn't want to put them in danger. I spent the days helping William exercise or reading to Laura. She continued to draw, sketching everything around the house.

But this night, two nights after my arrival, I wandered into the library after William went to bed. Most of the books there were general history and science books. I opened a large one that classified various species of moths and butterflies, written by the lepidopterologist Pierre André Latreille. I recognized Robert Buck's neat, spidery notes in the margins. Numerous lines had been underlined. Some pages were torn out.

The Conclave had studied so much. I envied all that they knew, but could not forget their almost detached expressions the night I faced them across the table at the Montgomery Street house. All that knowledge, and yet they had forgotten—or lost—their essential humanity.

I pulled many different books off the shelves. Tattered Greek Bibles marked by John Perkins's handwriting. One of Marcus Brown's many political publications, his notes for a subsequent edition all through the book.

Finally, irritated by their scrawlings, I shelved the books.

Instead, I picked up Max's photograph album. Flipping through it, I gazed yet again at the numerous photographs of Seraphina, especially one taken in her boudoir—her hair long and flowing, pulled around to the front of her body, the Conclave's symbol tattooed down her back, the chalice stem following her spine; *A Posse Ad Esse*. There was one slightly fuzzy photograph of her in lamia form, perched high on a cliff looking out to sea. Her hair, still long and beautiful, rippled in the ocean breeze, while sand and grit clung to her scaly skin.

Mariah ...

I wondered how Max was using her now. Was he taking photographs of her too, as if she were a specimen?

My hand paused on the photograph of Mother painting in her small garden in Dublin. I'd always thought that she hadn't known that Max took the photograph. *But had she?* I remembered Wyatt's question: what was her relationship with Max? For the hundredth time since her death, I wondered if I truly knew her.

The clock struck midnight. Locking the library, I returned to my bedroom across the hall. William was sleeping in his bedroom two doors away from mine, and I peeked into Laura's small room. She was asleep, snoring softly.

I crawled under my covers, and soon the dream began.

I stood in front of a small church with a large clock perched at the top of its tower. Enormous oblong and square tombstones speckled the small lawn that stretched to the right of the church.

The church walls were made of stones, oblong windows cut into the sides. I heard the sounds of a train in the distance.

Suddenly I awoke, my heart pounding. I didn't recognize the church, but I'd had psychic visions and dreams in the past. I remembered the visions I'd had of Seraphina.

The church was small. Perhaps it was a chapel in one of the larger cemeteries.

The next day, as I accompanied William on his walks about the lawn and garden, I decided not to say anything about the dream. As always, I felt more comfortable discussing my visions with Simon.

"'Who are you?' said the Caterpillar."
     The next night, I sat with Laura in her bed reading aloud the scene in *Alice's Adventures in Wonderland* where Alice meets the caterpillar smoking the hookah. Laura had already fallen asleep upon my shoulder, her breaths feather-light.
     Simon had returned to Kennilworth just before dinner, but both he and William went to bed early. During dinner, Simon had seemed distracted, staring at William occasionally, lost in his own thoughts. I'd decided not to burden him with the details of my dream. It didn't make sense and, at this point, I felt too restless about the many pieces of the puzzle before us.
     "'Who are you?'"
     As I read the words, my mind returned again to Wyatt's questions about Max—his identity, my mother's relationship with him. These matters twisted through my mind like overgrown foliage. With a heavy sigh, I kissed Laura's forehead, pulled the covers up to her chin, turned out her lamp, and went into my bedroom through our adjoining door.
     As my eyes adjusted to the darkness, I saw that Miranda had recently brought new blankets and changed the sheets on the bed. Yet she had left the window open over the desk on the far side of the room. Although the night was warm and pleasant, some light rainfall had blown in, spreading like dew over my books and notes.

When I crossed the room to the open window I noticed, past the untended gardens, an old building—possibly a chapel or small cottage—with a forest stretching behind it.

I heard the scrape of a match, and a small flame shot out from the shadows about five feet from me.

Spinning around, I saw Max.

He was sitting in an ottoman near the window. How had I not seen him? His eyes glinted in the darkness. His face and his boots gleamed, slightly damp. His cigar glowed in the dark even as he put one finger to his mouth to silence me.

"Come sit by me, Abbie." He gestured to a chair near him.

"I prefer to remain here." I scanned the room for a weapon, as my bowie knife remained in my luggage at the bottom of my wardrobe.

"Are you looking, perhaps, for *this*?" Max pulled the knife from his belt.

"How *dare*—"

"You can't win this game, Abbie."

"You shouldn't be so certain. I won your other little game, in Orkney."

"Yes, and that was very well-played." He stood up and stepped toward me.

I fought my urge to attack him. It would be futile and too dangerous here—Laura was in the adjoining room. I suppressed a shudder as he approached.

He was wearing a white, loose-fitting shirt opened at the chest and black riding breeches. His boots were still wet, dried mud splattered about the soles. His hair spiraled dark and wild about his head and his eyes gleamed green in the darkness.

I recalled all of the attraction I'd felt when I first met him, before I knew that he was a murderer.

He leaned languidly upon the desk near me and tapped cigar ash on the windowsill. I recoiled as he pushed a lock of my escaped hair behind my right ear. The earthy scents of rain, grass, and mud lingered upon him.

"You know I've taken the elixir, Abbie. I have the formula even now. I will always—*always*—be swifter and stronger than you and any of your friends combined. I'm not like the others. They had no advantage upon you. They were old men, easy to kill."

"*You're—*"

"*Shhh!*" he hissed, laying a finger upon my lips as I started to retort. He took one more draw from the cigar and tossed it out the open window.

"This will end with your death, and the deaths of a great many of your loved ones along the way. Take the elixir and come away with me instead."

"With you and who else?" I hissed. "Who were those two men with you last week in Kensington? What are you doing to all of these corpses to make them alive?"

Max smiled. "Riddles, Arabella. I bring you many riddles. When you finally agree to take the elixir, I assure you all of your questions will be answered. You will be happy. You will strong. You will be free."

"At the cost of what?"

He groaned. "Oh dear God, not again. The woman moralizes."

"You have no respect for human life. You never cared

even about the Conclave's 'greater good.' You were just their assassin, their bodyguard and *bully*."

My mind scrambled with questions: What was his real name? What was his relationship with my mother?

"Who are you?" said the Caterpillar.

"Who *are* you, Max?" I demanded.

"Who am I?" He chuckled heartily. "*That* is a bedtime story for another time."

"Why me, Max?" I spat in a low voice. "Certainly there are other women you can convince to become immortal, even other psychic women."

He set his jaw harder.

Then my temper worked faster than my good sense. "Did you have feelings for Mother? *Did* you? If so, why the hell did you kill her?"

His face contorted in anger. In a split second, before I could react, he clamped his hand over my mouth and pushed me onto the desk with such force that I knocked over an ink jar. I felt the liquid seep through my skirts onto my sore thigh, still bruised from my fall from the swing. His face was so close to mine that I could see the crescent scar on his cheek from where I'd bitten him.

"*One* sound, *a single sound* from you, Abbie Sharp, and that little girl in the next room dies," Max growled. "If she comes in here, she dies. If she cries out, she dies."

I nodded.

"Good." He relaxed his grip a bit but kept me on the desk, his hand holding tight to my chin.

"You, Abbie, have been a very long project. The *only* reason your mother was allowed to raise you was because I pled my case to the others. There are not many truly psychic women, let alone young, intelligent, and free-thinking ones. Caroline Westfield, as such, was unique. When she was with child, we hoped that the child would have her abilities. I have followed you, saved your bloody hide from drowning, watched you over and over again through the years. I've seen your baptism, watched your knife-throwing tournaments in Dublin, your falls. *Everything.*"

He pushed me further, so that my back jammed hard against the wall. My knees bent up and he pressed himself into my spreading skirts. I beat him. Struggled to kick him. But he grabbed both of my wrists and twisted them against the wall over my head.

He kissed me, hard. Terror overtook me and I tried to fight him, but he was too strong.

When he pulled away, he was incensed. "I have waited years to have you with me, and I will not be deprived. I'm all the more determined after you defeated my feral mistress. *You* are the reason I murdered your mother. I would not have killed her otherwise, despite the Conclave's orders. You *are* her immortality. You look so much like her. I cannot—I *will* not—let you go."

I recoiled in disgust. Max had been obsessed with Mother, and I was an extension of his twisted affections for her.

Then he grabbed my skirts and pushed them roughly upward.

Biting my lip to keep from screaming, I kicked at him with both of my feet. But he only crushed himself harder against me. As I tried to fight him off, I heard fabric tear and, looking down, saw that Max had torn my petticoat up to my thigh, exposing the long thin scar I'd had since age eight.

"*Edinburgh*," he murmured. "You fell down the stairs at the back of the house. I watched. It was shortly before your move to Dublin. Caroline put salve on it and bandaged you—"

"How did you—"

But he grabbed my chin in his hands and kissed me hard once again.

"I have followed you for too long to let you get away from me, to let you grow old, wither, *die...* "

Tears streamed down my cheeks. Anger and confusion swept over me. "Did she love you? Did *she* love *you?*" I asked frantically.

"Enough!" he growled, shaking me until my teeth rattled. Then he stopped and pulled away, his breathing ragged as he struggled to control himself.

Grabbing my chin once again, Max pulled my face toward him, hard. "I'm losing patience, Abbie. I *will* see you again. Soon."

He started to climb out the window.

"Stay away from me," I whispered, wiping tears from my face and pulling my skirts down.

His answer was lost in the howls of rainy wind. I grabbed the bowie knife from where he'd left it on the ottoman and leaned out the window, the light rain falling on me, to see him crawl headfirst down the wall.

Then, with unbelievable speed, he ran toward the forest behind the small cottage. As I watched from the shadows just inside my window, I thought I saw a figure meet him near the edge of the woods, but the night was too dark for me to be certain.

Still shaking, I considered waking Simon.

It would do no good tonight.

Max had not said where or when he would see me again, but I knew we must return to London immediately. Wherever I was, Max would be near. What mattered now was getting away from here—away from Grandmother and Laura—as quickly as possible.

Eleven

I walked into the library at seven o'clock in the morning. I'd slept restlessly, and then awoken at six thirty feeling as if I had not slept at all.

Simon sat at a desk, several of the Conclave's books spread out before him. He looked up as I entered, alarm crossing his face. "Abbie, there are bruises under your chin. Did you fall out of bed?"

"No." I poured myself a steaming cup of tea from a tray upon the desk and slumped in the nearby ottoman chair. "I had a visit from Max."

"And you did not come get me?" Simon's voice was low with anger. "You know that you can summon me, day or night. I do not mind—"

"What could you or anybody else have done?" I rubbed my eyes, which were dry and sandy after my fitful sleep. "This is my battle. It's been my battle all along."

"You will never be in this alone."

I told him what occurred. How Max had a certain sick

obsession with Mother and now had an obsession with me. How he still hoped I would take the elixir. I also told Simon about the dream of the church.

The sun rose higher, breaking through the large windows, and I noticed then that Simon's face, normally perfectly smooth, appeared weary. Dark circles stood out under his eyes.

"We'll return to London today," he muttered. Carefully, he looked up from his desk at me, his mouth curved a bit into a smile. "I suppose there is still no possibility of keeping you here with Lady Westfield and Laura, or of having Richard sent here to protect you while I return to London?"

"Absolutely not."

He smiled and stood up from his desk. "I feared that would be your answer. When have you ever taken my advice?" He paced a bit. "William is up already. He's taking exercise in the gardens, but I'll fetch him. I have some ideas, some leads that I want to talk to both of you about. You and I can leave for London early this afternoon. William should stay here with your grandmother until Richard arrives."

I almost asked how he could be certain that Richard would leave Grandmother's house so readily. But I knew that Richard, if he knew that Grandmother was in danger, would choose to be with her.

"Also," Simon said suddenly, "I found Laura up early this morning, drawing in the parlor. Lady Westfield's idea to have her draw was brilliant. This is a way for her to communicate without speaking. But it's a bit compulsive at the moment. She's already drawn five sketches in the span of an hour."

"Is the compulsive drawing a problem?"

Simon drained his teacup and set it down lightly on the edge of the desk. As he looked out the window, his eyes rested on a sparrow's nest cushioned in the thick vines and ivy crawling up the side of the house. "I think we should let her do it now so long as she doesn't seem overly agitated. I have heard of conditions where traumatized people write compulsively."

"Write?"

"Yes. They will write stories, poetry, very bad novels, and even grocery lists of items they do not need. The hypergraphia, as it is called, ends at a certain point in the process, after days, or weeks, or years. I have not heard of compulsive drawing or painting, but I'm wondering if perhaps it is another form of the disease." He knitted his fingers together. "My hope is that Laura will do this until she expels like bad blood whatever it is that is keeping her from speaking."

"Do you think that will happen?"

"I'm hopeful." Then, looking down at his desk, I saw that he had Laura's five drawings in front of him. "She is drawing not fantasy, but the real scenes around her. Jupe, the maids in the kitchen, the dodos."

Simon caught my eye as he pulled a drawing from the bottom of the pile. "I thought you might not want Lady Westfield to see this one."

A deep blush burned on my cheeks. Laura had sketched, with startling accuracy, me kissing William on the bamboo swing the other night.

I stuttered, feeling my face blush to deep scarlet.

"Simon, I have … it isn't … "

I cut my gaze to him, but he had skillfully blocked his

expression, remaining gracious as always. He waved his hand slightly. "Never mind, Abbie."

By the time Simon returned with William ten minutes later, I had torn the sketch into little pieces and thrown it away.

William limped into the library without his walking stick. His face was red, flushed with exertion from exercising. Simon sat behind the desk while William sat on the sofa next to me, his brows furrowed in deep annoyance. "I'd like to know what's so terribly important that you had to interrupt my exercise—"

"Max was in Abbie's room last night," Simon said coldly.

William looked at me sharply, then reached out and lightly touched the skin upon my jaw. "These bruises—are they from him?"

I told William about the attack.

William swore a streak and stood up. "This has to stop. We need to find him!"

"Sit down, William. This is hardly helpful," Simon said strongly. "Abbie and I are returning to London today."

"The hell you are. One: she's staying here and I'm going back with you."

Simon's mouth twitched into a smile. "William, with that leg, you are hardly . . ."

"Two: I will not let the two of you go off again without me. Because I know that's just what you want, St. John."

"William, that's unfair!" I said sharply, standing to face him.

Simon remained seated behind his desk. "This bravado is not helpful, William. As of now, if the three of us leave together, the housemaids, a child, and an old woman are here alone and vulnerable. Not that you ... " He scanned his eye down William's leg.

"Careful," William growled.

"Not that you would be all that helpful," Simon continued, as if William had said nothing. "I'm going to ask Richard to come here as soon as possible and remain here during our absence. But—*sit down*—it seems to have slipped your mind that these matters and the decisions that have to be made are not all about *you*."

William glared at Simon, but remained silent and sat back on the sofa.

Simon unlocked a drawer from the desk and pulled out a large notebook. I leaned forward, recognizing the handwritten notes of Robert Buck.

"Not everything valuable burned with the Montgomery Street house," Simon said. "I found these the other night, mixed in with their books. Most of Buck's notes are mundane—pages about his attempts to breed the dodos, an entire notebook dedicated to herbs he collected in South America. But this morning I discovered his notes from the early part of this century, during the period when he turned Seraphina into a lamia. At that time, both Buck and Bartlett had developed an intense interest in cell structures. The notes here contain all of Buck's methods for developing the process. He thought that through inserting animal structures into the human cell, they could cure disease. The creation of a lamia was unexpected."

"We know all of this. You're not telling us anything new." William groaned and rubbed his eyes.

Simon continued, ignoring William. "*After* Seraphina's creation, Buck continued his research. Although Max told her that they were trying to find a cure for her, these notes indicate that Buck was only looking for 'new avenues' of research in cell transformation."

I walked to Simon's desk. Leaning across it, I peered anxiously at the notes. "Is the elixir formula in there?"

"No, I believe the formula was kept at the Montgomery Street house."

"But somehow Max has it now."

Both Simon and William turned their eyes to me.

"This spring, when he threatened me in that church confessional, he said he'd planned to kill me but then he 'located something of interest.' I've often wondered if he'd found the elixir formula. Also, last night he told me that he *has* the elixir."

Simon narrowed his blond brows. "Although we can't trust anything Max says, finding the elixir or the elixir formula would explain why he decided not to kill you after all. I think we can assume, at this point, that he has the elixir and possibly other formulas."

"Yet despite all these notes, we haven't found anything indicating that the Conclave was interested in raising the dead or creating cannibalistic revenants, as Max seems to be doing." I poured myself another cup of tea and glanced at William, who was sullen but listening.

"Actually, Abbie, they might have been," Simon said. "Robert Buck performed some grotesque experiments during this time period. After Seraphina's transformation, he tried to replicate the transformation upon many animals. They all died. He even had Max bring him a vagrant, a human who agreed to be experimented upon for money. Of course, they never planned to pay him, only to euthanize him in the end. Buck injected the same formula he'd used on Seraphina into the man; the same results ensued. Buck thus realized that there were unique aspects to human cell life, and he became obsessed with these processes. He had started reading the writings of Galvani and others interested in reviving the dead. His notes continue for two years, until this…" Simon lifted up the notebook and showed us how the last third had been torn out.

"And unfortunately," I muttered, "that might have been the *critical* portion of their notes."

"Possibly," Simon agreed.

"We can't waste our time delving into the details of these experiments," William said abruptly. "What does it matter that we know all of the 'science' behind their experiments? What I care about is knowing why there was a man in the menagerie who looked as if he might be my twin, and why it seems there are dead people attacking and eating Londoners. I also want to find Max and tear him apart limb by limb."

Simon cut him a gaze so contemptuous that I stifled a chuckle.

"William," Simon said, leaning forward upon the desk and folding his hands together. "I only called you to this meeting because I think you might be slightly relevant to these matters. What age were you when Dante Gabriel Rossetti found you?"

"Four years old, I believe."

"And you remember nothing of how you came to be on the streets?"

William's stony anger melted a bit. Although he never talked about it, I guessed that in his private moments he might wonder who would have abandoned him. He was a beautiful man, and I suspected he was a beautiful child.

"Where, specifically, were you found?" Simon asked.

"Just in front of Gabriel's home in Chelsea." William glanced sideways at me. "Jane Morris and Father went out on an evening walk. She was the one who spotted me first. What are you getting at, St. John?" he snapped suddenly. Then he glanced at me, reddening. "Christina has assured me many times that I am not my father's bastard. If you are trying to imply that Abbie is my half-sister—"

"That is *not* where I'm going with this, William. But we do need to know your origins. I think, based upon the letter we read in Orkney, that someone was concerned about your predicament this spring. Someone was giving Max orders to keep you alive."

William knew about the strange, water-ruined letter in Seraphina's album. We had never made sense of it.

"Who would write to Max about you?" Simon continued. "We need to know where you came from, and how you ended up wandering those streets as a child."

"How many times have I told you that I *do not know*? I was bloody four years old."

"There are ways of unlocking these memories, William."

William threw back his head and roared with laughter. "Please, Simon, don't waste my time with one of your harebrained schemes. Abbie, do you know that Simon has been trying hypnosis on patients at the hospital? *Hypnosis.* Did you know about this?"

"Yes," I said, looking down awkwardly. A memory of my own hypnosis experience with Simon flashed through my head.

"Hypnosis is in the same quack realm with mesmerism," William said. "Recently, Simon has started inducing 'hysterical paroxysm' in certain patients to alleviate hysteria."

"Hysterical paroxysm?" My mind spun, remembering its mention somewhere in one of my medical books.

Unable to recall exactly what hysterical paroxysm was, I moved on. "William, the hypnosis treatments are effective sometimes, particularly in pulling up memories."

"How would you know?" William asked, cutting me a glance.

"It doesn't matter, but I think you should—"

"Did you hypnotize her?" William asked Simon. "Did you bloody hell hypnotize her?"

"He did, William," I spit out angrily. "We did it to induce my visions when you were missing. I had seen you bloodied and hurt somewhere, and it was the only way that I could find you."

Simon waved his hand in the air to silence us, his face slightly red. Undoubtedly he felt the same unease I did in this moment, and it was best to divert the conversation. "William, you may join us in London if you wish. We won't talk about it anymore. But William, I would like you to consider the hypnosis experiment."

William looked from me to Simon and back, his face

burning with questions. My cheeks burned as I turned quickly away and looked out the window.

"Abbie, please go inform Lady Westfield of our plans to leave today," Simon said quickly.

I was all too eager to leave.

"But we only arrived a few days ago! How can you leave already?"

I sighed. I'd drunk two cups of tea before meeting Grandmother in the gardens as she walked Jupe.

"We must leave, Grandmother. Simon, William, and I have matters to settle."

The smell of the newly bloomed calla lilies was pungent and warm. I tossed a little ball for Jupe, just so I didn't have to look at Grandmother's expression. I could handle her anger better than I could her fear.

"These 'matters' have to do with that dreadful night," she said.

"Yes, they do," I replied limply.

"Please stay here with me. Simon can unravel—"

"No he can't, Grandmother." Thinking of Max in my room, threatening me, I squeezed my eyes shut to hold in the tears.

"Well," she said briskly, "what do you want from me now? My permission? You know I won't grant it. Yet I know that you'll return to London anyway."

A lump formed in my throat.

"I'm sorry that you had to be brought into all of this, Grandmother. I never intended—"

"Never mind that." She reached down and picked Jupe up when he returned with the ball. The blinding midmorning sun poked through a light cloud.

She peered at my face and I stared up at her, overwhelmed by her willowy height. I hoped she couldn't see the bruises from Max about my chin.

"Why are your eyes so red? Did you sleep well?"

"Yes."

She narrowed her gaze. "Please, Abbie, no more lies."

That hurt.

"How long will you be gone?" she asked quickly.

I shrugged. "I'm not certain. We will be staying at Simon's house, so write to him if you need us. Care for Laura while I'm gone, and please be careful." I paused, choosing my words carefully. "You will be safer with me gone, but there are real dangers even here. Please stay close to Laura. Simon will send Richard here. Also, William will leave you with one of his revolvers and also his dog, Hugo."

Grandmother waved her hand to silence me. "Yes, yes, of course, I'll be careful. Enough of that, Abbie. All that matters to me now is that you know my heart will break if something happens to you."

"Grandmother—"

"Don't give me any false assurances. It's the winter of my life. I have no one but you. Even my silly friends have kept their distance from me because of your bold behavior and your friendships."

I cringed. I hadn't meant to spoil her life so much. "I'm sorry."

"No, please, Abbie. No apologies. Oddly, this doesn't trouble me as much as it once would have. I could do without that Siddal boy in my cosmos, but you..." She scratched Jupe's ears and fussed with his collar. "Please don't break my heart."

I leaned up and kissed her cheek. I wanted to tell her I would be certain to return, but... no more lies.

"I love you, Grandmother."

After Simon put my luggage in the carriage, I went to Laura's room one last time. She sat on her bed, drawing. Three pictures lay around her, and I saw three more upon the faded carpet near her bed.

I had cut a few of the calla lilies from the garden to bring to her, and I placed them in a vase upon her dresser. "Laura, I want you to know that Simon, William, and I are leaving now, but you will have Lady Westfield here to take care of you. And, of course, Miranda and Bridget will be here."

She looked up at me, her eyes wide and dark, and expressionless now. The large ivory ribbon in her hair hung crookedly.

My mind fumbled. Then I knelt on the floor near her, brushed her hair, and straightened the ribbon. In addition to the Conclave's web and my conflicted feelings about my mother, this child was yet another puzzle I couldn't solve. After fixing her hair, I peered around at her face. Laura's brown eyes met mine blankly before she returned to her sketch.

I felt a touch of irritation at her silence; to withdraw inside of herself seemed like such a luxury to me, an easy way to deal with the past. But even as I thought this, I knew these feelings were unfair. Guiltily I turned and picked up the drawings lying on the floor.

Two of the drawings were mundane—Petey the tiger, stretching in his cage in the morning light; Simon, seated in the parlor reading. But my heartbeat quickened at the third one. The sketch was of a man, tall and imposing. His features seemed European, but he wore a cape and turban—so similar to the man I had seen in Grandmother's doorway the other night.

I picked it up and turned toward the child.

"Why did you draw this, Laura?"

Silence.

"Did you see this man?"

Silence.

"You *must*..." My voice came out harsher than I had expected. I took a deep breath. "You must tell me why you drew this."

She said nothing, but something shifted behind her dark chocolate eyes. Interrogating her would do more harm than good.

"Laura, might I please take this with me?"

She was silent for a moment before nodding slightly. She went back to a drawing of Miranda putting sheets over furniture in one of the unused wings of the house. I would show the picture of the turbaned man to Simon later; I remembered the figure I saw meet Max near the woods last night. Laura must have somehow seen the turbaned man on the property yesterday, or perhaps today.

"Thank you." Carefully, I kissed her forehead. She smelled vaguely of the rosewater that Bridget used to bathe her.

PART II

"But I don't want to go among mad people,"
  Alice remarked.
"Oh, you can't help that," said the Cat: "we're
  all mad here. I'm mad. You're mad."
"How do you know I'm mad?" said Alice.
"You must be," said the Cat, "or you wouldn't
  have come here."

  —*Alice's Adventures in Wonderland*

Twelve

The young man stared at the dark-haired girl in the cage. Her mouth frothed, and blood from her latest kill was drying upon her upper lip. Her eyes were no longer wildly beautiful, but entirely feral.

He watched her with indifference as she lunged at him, trying to rip out his neck through the wires. Calmly he adjusted his cravat, ran his hand through his dark curly hair, and thought of how much easier life was for him because he was beautiful. Many thought beauty didn't matter, but he and the other two—the three of them—were handsome, and their beauty brought others willingly under their power. Life for this girl, he had heard, had been better because of her beauty—her indiscretions more forgivable, her wit more alluring. Of all their resurrected, she had proved their best bait.

Beyond her snarls, the rush of the river continued. Its musty scent was overwhelming. He hoped that they would not have to live here much longer. Torchlight was the only lighting in this holding place; its sharp shadows fell upon the girl's fair skin, which was bruised and scratched from the inside of the cage.

His indifference turning to curiosity, he stepped closer, seeking some spark of intelligence in her eyes. But there was nothing. She only pressed her mouth further through the bars, gnashing her teeth and snarling, her eyes fixated upon the side of his neck as if she knew the exact location of his internal carotid artery.

She had looked at him differently right after her resurrection.

But now, in this state, she was no more use to them.

"A pity," Max said, from immediately behind him. "She was almost as charming after death as she'd been when alive."

"How long has she been like this?"

Max shrugged. "Since this morning. When I returned from Warwick and did not find her in her room, I went out searching for her. I found her like this near the river, devouring a vagrant. When she saw me and tried to protect her kill, I knew that the change had occurred. I locked her in here until I'd have time to deal with her."

Max pulled up his sleeve; a huge flesh wound was visible just above his elbow.

"*She* did that?" the young man asked.

"Yes. As with the others, it seems that any human acuity she previously possessed has disappeared into her appetite."

"Interesting. But she lasted so much longer than any of them. Six months. Why?"

"Why indeed," Max replied.

The man still stared at her, fascinated now.

Max smiled, his green eyes gleaming. "Yes, she has been our best so far. Which is why this is such a pity. Now stand back."

Then he stood back, just before the earsplitting blast. The girl's brains flew upon his freshly laundered jacket.

In the dream, the sun beat blindingly upon me as I lay on my back in a small skiff. Squinting, I shielded my eyes and noticed the sharp odor of lake water. I saw my bare feet before me, peeking out from under the hem of my nightgown. Propping myself upon my elbow, I peered over the side of the small boat and saw that I was floating in some sort of large lake. Expansive, still waters surrounded me with no shore in sight. Lily pads stretched out as far as I could see.

A warm body moved beside me. Startled, I turned so swiftly that the boat swayed unsteadily.

Mariah lay beside me, also wearing a nightgown.

"Mariah..." I murmured her name, lay back down, and touched her face. Now she had no cruelty, no hungry look in her expression. I ran my hand down her cheek again; her skin was warm. I touched her chest and felt no stitches through her gown.

She smiled her mischievous smile. "I don't have much time with you, but let's talk."

"Of what?"

She turned her face full up to the sun, closing her lids so that her lashes stood out black and feathery against her skin.

"Of nonsense. Do you believe in heaven, Abbie?"

"I'm not certain."

"I'm not either. But if it did exist, what would heaven look like to you?"

A lump formed in my throat. I couldn't speak, and I wanted to keep her here with me.

"Well, if you won't talk, Abbie, I will." She put her hands beneath her head. "My heaven won't have all of the blasted ridiculous angel fanfare. It will have books. In fact there will be no walls, only books. And I will have an eternity to write my own books. And when I don't feel like writing, I will have beautiful places to go, places I have never seen—jungles, the African savanna. Perhaps even the mountains in the American West."

She turned to me and opened her eyes. "And of course, you would be there."

"Mariah..."

Unsentimental, she turned her head back toward the sun.

"But never mind that. As I stated, it's probably all nonsense. Who knows what happens after we die anyway?"

"Mariah, why are you talking like this?"

She turned to me once more. This time she put her hand on my cheek and kissed my lips lightly.

"Goodbye, Abbie."

I awoke with a jolt. I was in Rosamund's old bedroom at Simon's house. Rose-lipped dolls from her childhood stared down at me from a shelf. I pulled my knees up to my chest, my stomach in knots. Intuitively, I knew that Mariah was gone. She had already been gone, but now I mourned her a second time. She never should have been brought back and made to live in that way.

I turned and buried my face in the pillow.

Max, those other men—had they killed her again? Or had she died quietly in her sleep, her risen body no longer able to sustain itself? It was a small gift to have seen her, as she had been, in the dream. I lay in bed, pulling from my memory all our good times together—playing archery, sipping too much elderberry cordial at Lady Violet's home. I wished that I had only those memories.

After a time, I dried my eyes and sat up in bed. Except for the outdoor sounds of horses and carriage wheels, the house was eerily silent. There was no rustle of maids' skirts, no soft clatter of dishes. When we'd arrived last night, Simon had immediately gone to Grandmother's house and dispatched Richard on the last train to Warwick. Simon's servants had all gone now, thinking that Simon was working on a book and could not be disturbed. His sisters, both married, didn't live at home, and his mother stayed mostly at their seaside residence for her health. William, Simon, and I had his entire Kensington house to ourselves.

Max had said that he would see me soon.

Where was he now?

I pulled myself out of bed, washed my face, and stepped into the hallway, almost colliding with Simon carrying a cup of tea into his study.

"Abbie, you look as if you've seen a ghost."

"In a sense I have." Standing in the early morning shadows of the corridor, I told him quickly about the dream.

"Of course, I can't be certain..."

Simon watched me. "It was only a matter of time. She couldn't possibly have survived long as a revenant. And..."

"And what, Simon?"

"If she faltered in any way, she would, of course, be disposable to Max."

"I know." My voice croaked with tears.

"Come," Simon said gently. "Perhaps work and study will help your mood. It always helps mine."

When I stepped into his study, I saw that he had some of the Conclave's books and notebooks on his desk, as well as an enormous map of London that had markings all over it. I remembered the large, marked map behind Inspector Abberline's office in Scotland Yard during the Ripper murders.

"It looks like you need this more than me," Simon remarked, handing me the steaming teacup. I didn't argue as I sat down. He seated himself behind his desk.

"Is William still asleep?" I asked. "I feel as if he should be here."

Simon's ice-blue eyes veiled. "William was up at four thirty this morning, walking and then running up and down the servant stairs in the back for exercise. I am surprised at his sudden determination. It shows fortitude I was not aware he possessed. I haven't said a word to him this morning, but while I was brewing tea downstairs, I heard him leave out the front door. It's now seven thirty, and he has been gone an hour. I have no idea where he went."

I tried to hide my smile. William's determination was so encouraging, particularly after this spring when he'd lost all self-control.

I felt Simon's eyes on me. Quickly I looked up at his face. With the large window looming behind him, he looked like my angel of judgment.

"Don't look at me that way." My retort came out sharper than I intended.

"Abbie, you know how I feel. I don't want you to be hurt. William is—"

"William is many things. I can't help but love him." I looked away, ashamed. I was so disciplined in everything else, and yet I couldn't control my feelings for William. Taking another sip of tea, I turned my attention to the map spread out between us.

Simon gave the faintest sigh before leaning forward, focusing.

"We do not know exactly how many revenants there are, or how they are created. But we do know that the attacks, with the exception of Kensington and Covent Gardens, have occurred in and around cemeteries. We have, here, six of the main cemeteries around the city: Highgate, Abney Park, Tower Hamlets, West Norwood, Brompton, and Kensal Green. I'm wondering if Max and the revenants might have a central location near one of them."

I looked at all the marked places on the map.

"But wouldn't that be too obvious? Wyatt's men have been all around these cemeteries and would have found it already. Also, the Conclave had many residences. If Max is following the same pattern, he might have more than one home base, even here within London."

"True," Simon replied, furrowing his blond brows. "But also, I've been thinking about your vision of the small church. I can't think of any London church that meets that description, so I was wondering, perhaps, if it might be a chapel in one of these cemeteries."

I stared at the map. "I also thought it might be a cemetery chapel. But I still think Max might have several concealed locations. The attacks all seem to have been carefully planned. First, they occurred in cemeteries, the Conclave's chalice symbol drawn upon the graves to draw attention to them. Then the killers become more brazen—the revenants eluded and even killed some of Wyatt's men. They have carried out two attacks now in Kensington, as well as the one in Covent Gardens. My concern is *why* they are doing it."

"Indeed. We must know Max's motives. And we must discover who the other men with him are. William…"

"What about William?" I asked urgently, although I knew it would do no good to probe Simon about his suspicion that William somehow factored into Max's game.

"Abbie." He stood. "I must go to the hospital. We have several women who are due to deliver at any moment, and I will need your assistance."

"What about William? He'll be worried if he doesn't know where we are when he returns."

Irritably, Simon stated, "I'll leave a note for him."

"Thank you."

Simon watched me carefully. "Abbie, on our way to the hospital, we must stop at Lady Westfield's house. There is something that you must see."

"Max and those creatures were in *here*? They were in my room?"

Simon had taken me back to Grandmother's house. As

soon as we went upstairs, I saw that everything in my room had been torn apart. My mattress was slid somewhat off the bedframe, the covers disturbed. Someone had stabbed a knife through it and the pillows, leaving down feathers strewn about the floor.

"Late last night, when I stopped by here to speak to Richard about the arrangements, he told me this happened that afternoon while he was out. Knowing a bit about what we were caught up in, he didn't contact the police. He wanted us to see it first, in order to determine if anything specific had been taken."

I ran to the trunk in my closet where I kept many of Mother's books and mementos. The trunk was emptied out, her possessions cast all over the floor.

"Mother…" I murmured as I began rummaging through the mess. I found I still had many of her books. Rossetti's portrait of her as a lamia remained on my closet wall, although it dangled sideways.

"What was Max looking for?" I muttered.

Simon walked over to my desk, papers and books scattered about its surface. "Can we assume that it was Max?" he asked.

"Who else would it…" My mind spun, trying to take in every detail of the mess at once. Nothing seemed to be missing.

Simon walked over to my wardrobe, where several dresses I had left behind lay tossed about on the floor. "It might have been Max or someone in league with him. But why would the intruder have waited for Richard to leave? Max would be more likely to cut his throat and then search the room at his leisure."

"True…" I pushed a desk drawer back into place. Thoughts pressed upon my mind, but I was weary. After the trip yesterday from Warwick and the dream of Mariah, exhaustion was taking over my bones; my mind didn't feel clear.

Then, as Simon lifted up a pinstriped dress and put it in the wardrobe, I said, "Abberline! This might have been his work. Or Wyatt's."

Simon's eyes glittered. "Perhaps. We can't make too many assumptions now, but I think it's safe to say that we may have pursuers from many sides."

I groaned. "What jolly fun."

Thirteen

We arrived at Whitechapel Hospital in the early afternoon, delivering two infants within our first hour there. Another woman, only thirty years old, was laboring with her seventh child. As Simon expressed concern about the stability of her womb, William stepped into the curtained first floor delivery area.

Both Simon and I looked up at him, surprised, but neither of us spoke. William hadn't entered the hospital since his depressive bout this spring.

He looked darkly at Simon and me. I knew that it irritated him to see us working together like this.

Simon ignored William as he wrote notes. "She'll more than likely be fine," he said quietly to me. "But tell Nurse Josephine to watch her in the postpartum ward for signs of hemorrhaging."

William was behaving as if he hadn't been away from Whitechapel Hospital for nearly three months. He crossed the delivery area with only a small limp, cleaned his hands in the lime solution, and rolled up his sleeves.

Simon finally looked up from his notes, surveying William shrewdly from head to toe. We had to be careful with what we said, as the patient lay on the bed before us, groaning from her contractions. I wiped her face with a wet cloth.

"It's nice of you to join us, William," Simon remarked coolly. "Where were you earlier?"

"Walking," William said with great control. "And since when do I answer to you?"

The woman yelled loudly, purple veins popping out on her pale forehead. She clutched at the bedsheets.

"Are you ... ?" Simon murmured to William.

"Yes, *yes*. I'm quite sober."

The woman moaned again. I blinked, my eyes dry as sandpaper.

Dirt and perspiration clung to the woman's face. I dipped a sponge in the washbasin, then saw that the water needed to be changed. Lifting the washbasin, I started to take it from the delivery area, but I stumbled, almost dropping it. William caught my wrist and took the basin from me. "I'll call Nurse Josephine to assist. You're tired. Go upstairs. Rest."

"No ... "

He smiled, beguiling. "Do as I say just this once, please. There is a small couch in Simon's office. Nurse Josephine can cover for you down here."

I couldn't object.

I climbed the stairs to the fourth floor and found it dark and gloomy as usual. Unless one of the nurses needed something from the pharmacy in the laboratory, only William, Simon, and I ever came up here.

I entered Simon's office near the stairs and lay on the small sofa, right under the unnerving gaze of Robert Buck's taxidermied owl, which perched on a shelf high above the desk. Ignoring the owl, I rested my head upon the moldy-scented pillow and promptly fell asleep.

The dream of the church began again. The same small stone building rose before me, and I saw again the tower with the great clock upon it. Large tombstones stood about the grounds.

I tried to pull the vision toward me, but it was weak, pulsing a bit and then evaporating quickly.

When I awoke, I found dried spittle on my cheek. My limbs were achy and stiff from the deep sleep.

I sat up, rubbing my eyes and wondering why this dream had reoccurred. According to a small clock on Simon's desk, it was five in the afternoon.

I had been asleep for three hours.

I stood, numb, my mind caught in the dream. Vaguely, I thought I should return to work downstairs.

I stepped out into the hallway, which was dimmer now than when I'd started my nap. The laboratory doors were still closed. A bit of waning light came out from behind William's half-opened office door at the end of the hallway.

Just as I was about to go downstairs, a man's figure crossed the doorway of William's office, briefly obscuring the escaping light.

"William," I called down the hall.

No answer.

The hairs upon my neck stood up.

Chastising myself for my jittery nerves, I walked down the hall. Perhaps in my groggy state I had imagined seeing the figure. Perhaps no one was in the office.

"William," I said again firmly, refusing to let my imagination cave to nonsense.

No answer.

Pushing open the office door, I stepped inside quickly and scanned the desk, the grinning skull, the nearby bookcase.

Empty.

The drapes were pulled away from the window. Crossing the small room, I peered down onto busy Commercial Street, staring at the crush of carriages. A ragged lamplighter lit streetlights below. Perhaps, in the early evening's mottled light, I had only seen an elongated shadow cast from below.

Then the office door behind me groaned as it shut. I froze, holding my breath, and then spun around.

A man stood just in front of the closed door. He must have been hiding behind it when I entered.

"William!"

In the dark office, the man certainly looked like William. He had dark curls about his face and well-chiseled features. Then my eyes adjusted. I blinked.

He *wasn't* William. This man's dark eyes sparked with a cruel glint and I tensed, horrified. His clothes looked neater, less rumpled than William's typical attire. He wore perfectly pressed trousers and a double-breasted jacket. A silk cravat pressed up at his neck.

"Abbie..." he said, smiling. His voice came out slightly huskier than William's voice.

Max's web was closing in upon me. My mind raced for answers—I would have to catch on *quickly*.

"You…you were one of the men in my house that night in Kensington," I said. "Who are you?"

"Someone very interested in you. Someone you will know very well, if you play along nicely." He clucked his tongue and cocked his head. "Unfortunately, I've heard that you don't always play nicely."

He took a step toward me. There was only the desk between us. He was blocking the door, and escape through the window wasn't an option as it was a four story drop to the ground.

I needed a weapon.

Grabbing the skull on the desk, I clutched it tightly.

The young man paused and arched his dark brow in amusement, an expression uncannily like William.

But there was something in his cold demeanor so similar to Max—that same inhuman expression that Max and the other immortals of the Conclave wore.

Was he as fast and strong as Max?

It was time to tell.

I threw the skull hard at his head and dashed toward the door. He ducked, but not fast enough, and I heard the loud smack of the skull hitting his forehead.

"*Bitch!*" he yelled, clutching his head as the skull fell to the floor, shattering.

Throwing all of my weight upon him, I tried to push him out of the way. But he grabbed my wrists, twisting and pinning them above my head, against the door, with one hand. He wasn't as formidable as Max, but he was still young and strong.

I kneed him, hard, but he pushed against me violently

and my head hit the door with such force that my teeth rattled and I saw stars.

His infuriated face was inches from mine now. I remembered kissing William in this office. At this close proximity, I saw that my attacker wasn't *exactly* like William—his eyes were a bit rounder, his nose more Roman-shaped.

I kicked upward to break a rib, but he blocked me. Then he squeezed my neck hard, keeping his grip on my wrists above me. I struggled and fought against him; I smelled a musty odor, like foul water, upon his clothes.

"*You . . .*" he hissed against my ear. "I'm still trying to figure out what's so very special about *you*. I'm not as sold on you as Max is. You look to me like a silly girl, and I'm told that you're nothing more than the bastard of some whore."

He had all of my limbs pinned, but I couldn't let him get by with saying *that*.

I spit in his face.

He pulled me forward and slammed me back again. Blinding pain shot through my head.

"Careful," someone else's voice said, from the other side of the door.

The voice didn't belong to Max. It sounded genteel, like antiquated Scottish—rather similar to Seraphina's accent.

"I warned you how this meeting might go," the voice added.

The man in front of me narrowed his eyes; it seemed he was exercising great restraint to keep from murdering me. With one final thrust, he slammed me back against the door.

After that, all went black.

Fourteen

Is that what you want me to admit? That I'm a *bastard*?" William's angry words jarred me as I regained consciousness.

I felt sensation first in my fingertips. Then severe pain bloomed from the back of my skull throughout my head.

"I'm simply saying that she was attacked while we were only one floor away. I've already told you that her room was ransacked. If you are a key to this puzzle, and if you love Abbie as you say you do, then I don't understand why you resist this treatment." Simon's voice was loaded with disgust.

I opened my eyes and Simon's office slowly came into focus. I was lying on the couch, Simon and William arguing from where they stood nearby.

"Your *idiotic* practices—" William began.

"Be quiet. She's waking up."

"Abbie, did Max do this to you?" William asked, kneeling beside me.

As I slowly sat up, my vision refocused. I couldn't pull

my eyes away from William's face. "No..." I murmured. The resemblance between William and my attacker was uncanny.

"Abbie. Are you hurt?" Simon asked, leaning against his desk.

"No, only a splitting headache."

"I'll bring you some absinthe," Simon said, leaving the office quickly.

"He was like you, William."

"What?"

"The man who attacked me, he looked like you."

William's eyes narrowed.

"He wasn't you, but he looked as if he might be your twin brother. And there was another man. I didn't see that one, but I heard his voice through the door. His accent was Scottish, genteel Scottish."

I closed my eyes, my headache like fire.

"And the man who looked like me," William whispered. "Was he also Scottish?"

"No. He spoke as if he was from London."

Simon returned with the absinthe and handed it to me. As I took the first burning sip, William growled softly, "I'll do it, Simon."

After checking on the women in the postpartum ward, Simon instructed Nurse Josephine that we were not to be disturbed on the fourth floor. He closed the door of his office and turned off the lights. The absinthe had started to take effect and my headache had dulled a bit. While I remained seated on the sofa, Simon asked William to sit in a chair in front of his desk. Simon opened a small drawer, bringing out a teacup. It was white, with a bold painted chain of red roses just under the rim. Then he lit a small tallow candle and placed it near the teacup.

"This is probably a worthless endeavor," William growled.

"Possibly," Simon said dryly. "It might work differently for you than it did for Abbie. With her, we were trying to pull out her visions so that she could find you, see a place she'd never seen before. Presumably, since you are not psychic, your results will be much more mundane. Your brain will simply be trying to surface a repressed memory that you might have closed and shelved like a book."

"Excellent," William said wryly. "I hope that you find my simple brain to your liking."

"William, what I'm doing here is attempting to strip your mind of any senses, sensations, or protective edifices you might have erected to prevent early memories from surfacing. Specifically, memories from the time of your abandonment."

"Enough … *enough* … just get on with it. And for goodness' sake, please don't summon a specter or anything like that!"

William's hypnotism took longer than mine had. He had difficulty focusing on the illuminated teacup pattern for very long and he cursed frequently, wanting to give up. Simon displayed an enormous amount of patience, his voice soft as down as he urged William along, reeling his attention repeatedly back into a state of concentration.

Finally, after no less than half an hour, William slipped into the hypnotic state, his eyes steadying upon the cup's rim. Simon met my eyes across the candle flame, a small smile on his lips.

Then he turned his attention to William. "How do you feel?"

"Cold..." William murmured. "Very cold. Someone is carrying me."

"Who?"

But William was consumed by the memory. "I'm wearing dirty, torn clothes. I'm uncomfortable." His faraway look intensified. "I'm wearing torn clothing, and he...he is not."

"Who is *he*?" Simon asked.

"I cannot see. He's holding me. We're in front of a house with many bright windows. A door at the house starts to open. He's leaving me. I'm crying, so cold. I don't want him to leave me."

Then William stared silently at the teacup pattern. I caught Simon's eye and he shook his head a bit, unworried. I reminded myself that he had performed this therapy numerous times.

After about five minutes, William continued. "I'm running after him."

"What is he wearing?"

"Gentlemen's clothes. I'm running after him, crying. But he steps into a carriage, leaves me."

"What does he look like?" Simon asked through gritted teeth.

"Oh..." William's face whitened and his body jolted, skidding his chair away from the desk.

The trance broke and William stared, pale as a ghost, at Simon. "Might I have a bit of that absinthe?"

Simon poured a small decanter of the absinthe and passed it to William. "*Who* was the man in your memory?" he pressed impatiently.

"My great uncle, John Polidori."

Fifteen

Simon extinguished the candle, opened the door, and turned on the nearby lamp. I wiped William's face with a handkerchief and led him from the chair to the more comfortable sofa.

My mind raced back to the portrait of Polidori displayed in Christina's parlor.

My attacker... now I began to see shared characteristics between him and the portrait.

But it was impossible.

Simon seated himself at his desk, his face thoughtful.

William leaned forward, his head in his hands.

"Your great uncle, William, died decades before you were born," Simon said. Yet there was something encouraging in his voice.

"In 1821, to be exact," William said. "As I've told you, I grew up learning the story. He was Byron's physician. But he was also a writer. He wrote the ridiculous novella 'The Vampyre.' Weighed down by gambling debts, he killed himself with prussic acid at his childhood home in Soho. The family pressed for the official report to say that he died of natural causes. We know now, of course, that he was killed by Max."

"The Conclave. He was connected to the Conclave ... " I murmured. My headache, and now the absinthe, worked to fog my brain.

Simon looked up at the ceiling. "More specifically, Polidori was interested not only in medicine, but in more obscure areas of science such as somnambulism, which is a very real condition. But I've discovered through my research that some of his colleagues found his scientific experiments and interests unorthodox. However, I can't find any *specific* evidence about what these experiments and interests were. I've found only brief statements, quotes about him in the British Library's reading room."

William watched Simon warily. "You know more about him than I do. Why have you taken such an interest in him?"

"I am keeping an open mind since the attack at Lady Westfield's residence. Pursuing many paths."

I was more certain by the minute that my attacker tonight was Polidori, yet I struggled to believe my intuition. "Is it possible, Simon, that William might have *imposed* his uncle onto his memory? That he inserted him there, in the place of the actual person who abandoned him?"

"Anything is possible, Abbie. But I have never read about such an occurrence, nor heard of it at any medical conference."

William's face blanched even more as he took another sip from his glass of absinthe. "Abbie, you've seen the portrait of Polidori in Christina's house. Did the man who attacked you have *any* resemblance to the man in that portrait?"

"Yes."

"William. Was the man you saw in the menagerie that night possibly John Polidori?" Simon pressed.

"Yes, but..." William stood up and threw his glass onto the floor. Simon's lip curled in disgust as glass shattered everywhere.

"Why would he look so much like me?" William snapped. "I'm not blood-related to him."

Raising an eyebrow, Simon said, "If Polidori somehow got hold of the elixir—if he was practicing experiments similar in nature to the Conclave's experiments—there might be a great many possibilities. I have heard that some scientists are interested in replicating cells of one organism in order to make an identical one..."

"Are you saying he might have *grown* me, as one would grow a tree? Cultivated from the cells of a human being?" William growled.

Simon, slightly exasperated, replied, "As I said earlier, we must keep an open mind, pursue all paths—"

"What we must first do," William exclaimed, interrupting Simon, "is find out whether Polidori is dead or alive. Whether he is truly buried."

"Do you know where he is buried?" Simon asked.

"Of course I do. On the grounds of St. Pancras Old Church."

"Abbie—I hadn't thought of St. Pancras Old Church!" Simon exclaimed. He pulled out paper and a pen. "Draw the church that you saw in your dreams."

Rapidly, I begin sketching the church, its stone walls, the bell tower.

"What is he talking about, Abbie?" William demanded.

"I've had dreams recently about this church." I glanced at Simon. "I had the second one just this afternoon, while napping."

William peered over my shoulder. "Yes, that's certainly St. Pancras Old Church." He paused. "My great uncle is supposedly buried there."

Simon and I looked at him sharply.

"Many of those graves were destroyed," Simon explained quickly.

"What do you mean?" I asked. I had never even heard of the church.

"Last year," William said, "shortly after you came to London, there were extensive renovations done to the church. The bell tower was rebuilt. But long before those renovations, in the 1860s, there was a famous little uproar when a railroad was built that sliced straight through the back part of the church's cemetery. The workers initially showed no respect for the dead. Bones and skulls were sticking up from the ground, pushed aside during the construction. One of the architects tasked with correcting the affront put the tombstones around an ash tree. But our family knows exactly where Polidori's grave is. It's in the far back, just at the edge of the railroad. It's in awful shape—broken, covered by lichen, sunk into the ground—but I've seen the gravestone. Both Gabriel and Christina took me there on at least three occasions."

Simon remained quiet a moment, and suddenly I felt queasy at the turn the conversation seemed to be taking.

Then Simon spoke, clearing his throat. "Of course, because of all the railroad work, there might be no coffin under the gravestone."

William arched his eyebrow and looked at both of us. "My aunt said that Polidori's grave was spared. If there is a coffin, and it is empty, that would be the best way to know if there is any credence to our speculations."

Simon turned and set his teacup aside. "Then we must go. We should be prepared and conceal our tools."

"What if we're followed? Wyatt..."

Simon glanced at me. "We'll be discreet. I'm not convinced Wyatt is as much of a problem as we think."

"What do you mean?" I asked.

"Now is not the time to discuss it," Simon said cryptically, standing. "Come, let's go back to the house. We should take dinner before we leave."

William, Simon, and I took the carriage to Pancras Road, then walked toward the church. William had carefully packed shovels and a pick from the garden shed at Simon's house while Simon and I prepared a quick dinner. It was now close to midnight as we walked silently through the warm shadows.

This area was relatively quiet tonight. The road curved so sharply I didn't see the church until we were almost upon it. It rested upon on a small patch of land. I saw the sides of worn brick buildings rising up further down the road, overshadowing the church.

"Workhouses," Simon said quickly, nodding toward the buildings.

A large iron fence enclosed the property. At the front

gates, Simon glanced about, crouched, and began picking the lock with a thin metal tool, his elegant white fingers working swiftly.

William shifted the large canvas bag of tools that was slung over his shoulder. "Where did *you* learn how to pick locks?" he asked haughtily.

Simon finished with the lock in a matter of seconds. He silently opened the gates. "I *read*, William."

For once, William chose not to retort, and Simon closed the gates behind us while leaving the lock still open. We were all very alert, trying to watch everything at once. A large stone tower with a black-faced clock rose from the right side of the small church; an archway framing the wooden front doors stood immediately before us. Small patches of drooping fox-gloves spread about our feet, their closed petals still in the breezeless night. Except for the distant rattle of a train, all was calm and silent.

"It's this way," William said, cocking his head toward the far corner of the churchyard. "It's beyond the clock tower, near the fence bordering the railway."

I followed William, stepping between several very large lichen-covered tombstones. Sensing that Simon was not behind me, I turned and saw him staring intently at the church building.

I continued after William, who showed very little sign of his limp now. I wondered yet again why I couldn't cast aside my feelings for him and love Simon instead. Simon was undoubtedly better for me. I thought of that night in the menagerie, of how unruly my feelings for William had been. A reckless part of me wondered if I should even try to rule them.

Then I looked back; Simon was still watching the church. Laying my hand on the cold side of the nearest gravestone, I called softly to him.

He snapped out of his reverie and followed me quickly.

We made our way to the back corner of the grounds. Polidori's grave was certainly well concealed. The tall fence bordering the railway towered above us, covered in thick foliage. I turned to my left, surveying the scene behind us. In the darkness, I observed the ash tree by the church, its spindly branches stretching upward like fingers, clusters of headstones around its base.

I stepped closer to Simon and William, tripping over a small branch. Simon caught my arm to prevent me from falling. But as he lifted me, he pulled me close and whispered, "Careful, Abbie. I don't trust this place."

I glanced up at him quizzically, but his attention was on William.

In the back corner, we were fully in the shadow of the railroad tracks. The tangled overgrowth offered us a natural cover, and we stayed within its shadows. Although the church had seemed empty, there was a light in a window of the small brick rectory.

This would all have been easier with a lantern, but of course that was impossible. We only had small dashes of moonlight breaking through the clouds.

William peered into the darkness. Several waist-high headstones stood stacked like dominoes. "No, not those," he said, walking past them. "This one."

A lone headstone stood, its lowest quarter sunk into the ground.

"Are you certain, William?" I asked. "How many times have you been here?"

"Twice with Gabriel, once with Christina. The last time was when I was thirteen. This is the tombstone."

"Are you truly sure this is Polidori's grave?" I asked. The stone was worn as if sanded, the lichen covering it thick as wool. I could not make out any letters. "This is completely unreadable. I cannot tell if these engravings are numbers or letters."

I knelt down, my kneecaps under my skirts sinking into the soft ground. "Here, Simon, pass me the paper and charcoal."

As William and Simon crouched beside me, I placed the paper over the indentions and rubbed the charcoal. Very soon, as my eyes adjusted in the darkness, I saw the end of the name: *olidori*.

"It's his. It is his grave."

William began pulling the shovels from the bag. Simon started to take out a pick, then paused, laid it down, and crouched at the other side of the headstone.

I watched as he separated the long grass at the base and ran his fingers along the stone.

"William, did you ever notice these words on the back of the stone, near the ground?"

"No. And why should I care? It's likely some Bible verse. Doesn't every dead Londoner have one chiseled on his tombstone?" William rolled out a small canvas to lay our instruments upon. I knelt in front of Simon, held the paper over the lettering, and began rubbing it with the charcoal.

"Simon," William began, "you can either stand there

examining the verse, bloody translating it from Greek, or you can help—"

"Wait," I muttered irritably as I rubbed at the letters. "It's a single word."

Simon peered over my shoulder and read it: "*Resurgam.*"

William paused, mildly interested now.

"I've never seen this on a tomb," I whispered. "But I remember it from somewhere … perhaps from a book."

"*Jane Eyre,*" Simon said quickly. "When Jane's best friend Helen dies, *Resurgam* is carved upon her tombstone. It is Latin for 'I will arise.' Many early Christians had it on their graves to signal belief in their bodily resurrection."

William walked to our side of the stone, his shirtsleeves rolled up. "If we're going to find out if it has any significance, we need to dig the rummy fool's coffin up." Then he chuckled. "I always thought I was more sane than other members of my family, but now here I am, stealing into a churchyard at midnight to exhume a body. I'm just like my father. Perhaps even a bit *more* mad. At least he had others do the exhumation for him." He thrust a shovel into Simon's arms. "Abbie— you stay close, where we can see you."

"You didn't bring a third shovel?" Simon asked.

"No. Why should I?" William plunged his shovel deep into the dirt.

I crossed my arms angrily. "Because I *told* you that this would get done a lot faster if the three of us worked together. I'm not afraid to get dirty…"

"You were attacked today. You're not working," William said calmly, as if the matter was settled. And I supposed with only two shovels at our disposal, it was.

I looked at Simon.

His mouth curved into a smile, and I scowled. He was too much of a gentleman to hand over his shovel and make me work.

William and Simon dug at a furious pace, and I stayed in the close vicinity. After an hour, they were waist-deep into the hole. At some point, the light in the rectory went out.

All was still dark, quiet. I wandered a bit away from them, looking at the old, large tombstones closer to the church.

As I traced my finger along an *M* upon a tomb, a soft footstep sounded nearby.

Tensing, I pulled out my bowie knife and looked around in the darkness.

Nothing.

I turned my attention back to the letters. Then, seeing movement in my peripheral vision, I spun around.

A little girl about seven years of age, her face shaded by a dark hood, stood near the front doors of the church. She wore a ragged dress and was barefoot.

I stared at her, but she remained absolutely still.

"'elp me ... " she murmured softly.

I glanced back, unable to see William and Simon now. "What do you need?" I whispered.

"'elp me."

She turned and walked into the church.

Due to her hood and the darkness of the place, it was almost impossible to tell whether she was one of the revenants. The workhouses loomed in the distance; the more likely scenario was that she was one of the neglected child factory workers who needed food.

Carefully, I stepped into the church.

There was a tiny whitewashed entryway, with a twisting, narrow stairwell winding upward to my left. I didn't see the little girl.

As I walked into the nave, I heard only the sound of my boots on the stone floor. The inside walls were either stone or whitewashed, and there were no pews, only small chairs in neatly lined rows. The altar was quite large, disproportional for this small church, and stood immediately behind the open communion rail. To my right, a small altar stood within a little alcove, the interior of the bell tower.

My eyes adjusted and I looked all about for the girl. When I was halfway up the aisle, I heard the lock on the church doors behind me click into place. Swiftly, I turned around, but I could not see anything.

A noise startled me, and I saw the girl near the altar. She was facing it, her back to me.

"Can I help you?" I asked, stepping forward.

I thought I heard a rustle behind me, near the bell tower, but when I scanned the nave, I saw nothing.

Moonlight broke through the stained-glass window over the altar and I saw the dark, tweed fabric of the girl's hood. I clenched my knife, trying to see all around me at once. Perspiration dripped down my forehead.

I tried to bury the bowie knife's blade in the folds of my skirts.

Then, all at once, the girl turned, her teeth gnashing at me.

I screamed and pushed her down. She was very thin and

pale. She had that ghost-white appearance the other revenants had, with dark purplish circles under her eyes.

She lunged at me again, and once again I pushed her down, cringing as I heard her fall hard against the stone floor. Her hood fell away. I saw the oily, sandy-colored locks of blond hair.

How could Max do this to a child?

She came at me again, clinging to my arm when I tried to push her down. I had the knife in my hand, but I couldn't use it, not against someone so small. Growling like a savage kitten, she kept flinging herself against me with surprising strength. She bit my forearm and I cried out, twisting my body so hard that I flung her past the communion rail onto the floor.

I had never treated a child this way, and tears fell down my cheeks. I trembled all over, horrified at the sight of the girl before me, at what I had done to her.

She lay stunned on the floor, then righted herself, reminding me of Mariah crouching like an animal in my bedroom.

"Enough!" a man yelled from the back of the church.

The girl froze in her stance.

The man stepped into the main aisle, walking slowly toward me.

Keeping one eye on the stilled child, I stepped back, bumping against the altar.

It was the turbaned man who had been at Grandmother's that night. The man in Laura's sketch. But tonight, he wore no turban. He was dressed in the evening attire of a gentleman.

"Dear God..." I muttered. The moonlight fell upon his face as he approached me.

At this close proximity, I saw that his head was covered

in short hazelnut curls that hung about his high forehead and well-chiseled cheekbones. His bluish-green eyes gleamed sharply; his chin jutted out a bit, a thin moustache above his lip. He wore high Hessian boots over breeches and a long gold-and-green smoking jacket covered with intricately embroidered designs. A knotted silk cravat rested at his collar, pinned with a ruby brooch. Like Polidori, he was beautiful, stunning.

"Excellent work, Martha," he said with a light Scottish accent, and I knew instantly that he'd been the man on the other side of the door this afternoon.

Martha still looked at me, her little lips curled up in a snarl. The man placed his fingers gently on her head.

"No!" I cried. As he twisted her neck sharply, a sickening crunch sounded.

She slumped to the floor. He picked her up and slung her lifeless body over his shoulder.

"Never fear, Miss," he said glibly to me. "Her time was up anyway."

Not only his bearing but his voice was genteel, aristocratic. I backed away, put the altar between us. It seemed impossible... yet, if the other man was Polidori...

"Who are you?" I asked, clutching my knife in front of me.

He leaned forward across the altar, his demeanor full of wry and charming irreverence.

I froze, unbelieving. He was even more beautiful than he'd been in the illustrations in Mother's poetry books. Although it was widely rumored that he had a deformed foot,

I had not noticed a limp as he'd walked toward me, only his perfect form.

"Lord Byron," I muttered hoarsely.

"Yes, it's me." He bowed, the dead little girl's hair swinging behind him. "*Mad, bad, and dangerous to know…*" As he leaned closer to me, I saw the cleft in his chin, the ruby brooch glittering beneath it. His eyes glinted as if he were holding back the most marvelous secret, and then he glanced sideways. "Do they still say that about me?"

"What are you doing?" His spell upon me broke and I tightened my grip on my knife.

He cut his gaze to the blade and shook his head. "I wouldn't do that, Miss Sharp. You're in *our* territory now."

"Why are you here?"

He chuckled. "With you so close to our lair, I had to see you."

"Your *lair*? Where is it?"

I heard the rattle of the lock on the church doors.

"Shhhh…" He leaned across the altar, laying one heavily ringed finger on my lips. "You'll know soon enough. *Soon enough…*" There was a terrible gleam in his eyes.

Someone banged on the doors. "Abbie!" William's voice echoed through the darkness. "Abbie…where are you?"

I froze as Byron leaned across the altar, pulled my chin toward him, and lightly kissed my lips. Then he disappeared, melting into the darkness to the left of the altar, still holding the girl. I heard the soft grind of stone sliding upon stone, the rustling of other feet in the darkness.

Still reeling from what happened, I tried to run after him.

I ran into the sacristy, but there was nothing there except for a credens to store vestments.

Where had he gone?

"Abbie!" William was running toward me now, Simon just behind him. "Are you all right?"

"Yes...yes..." I muttered, stumbling back into the sanctuary, stunned, still trying to put together the pieces of what had just happened.

"We heard you scream." William moved toward the altar with his revolver out, looking behind it and all around in the darkness.

"Children...they are resurrecting *children* now," I stuttered.

Simon stared about the sanctuary, his gaze taking in everything.

"There was one out there in the graveyard, a little ragged girl. She said she needed help, so I followed her in here."

"Of course you did," William said irritably. He shook my shoulders gently. "What were you *thinking*? Why didn't you stay near us?"

"Be quiet. He killed her right in front of me!"

"Who is *he*?" Simon asked. "Polidori?"

I tried to answer, but I was having trouble catching my breath so I shook my head vigorously.

Simon said nothing, just looked around again. Tightening his lips, he pushed me gently toward the nave, away from the altar. "Polidori's coffin was empty, Abbie. We need to cover up the grave and leave. We're not safe."

"*Who* did you see in there?" William demanded as we ran

out of the church. We closed the doors; Simon secured the lock again.

"Lord Byron," I said breathlessly. "Lord Byron is the third man involved here."

We all said very little as we quickly filled the grave again and returned to Simon's house.

I took a long bath, immersing myself in hot soapy water, feeling the dirt and the smell of grass wash away from my body. Unfortunately, I couldn't rid myself so easily of the image of that girl, the sound of Byron snapping her neck with as little feeling as if he were crushing a spider.

Her nightmarish white face, her dead eyes, also burned in my memory. How she'd lunged at me like an animal.

I wondered what possible use a child could be to them. Perhaps as a lure. Mariah, a beautiful woman, worked well as a lure for their victims. A child, particularly a child in need, would draw the attention of empathetic adults.

The whole business was gruesome.

Finally, I surfaced and stepped out of the bathtub.

I glanced at my body in the mirror. My skin was too pale. And so many scars.

A few old scars stood out amid the many I had accumulated this year. I turned slightly and saw, in my reflection, the whitish, crescent-shaped scar on my thigh from my childhood fall down the stairs in Edinburgh. I saw the scar from my fight with Seraphina, snaking from a small curl at the base of my throat into a straight slash across my left shoulder and breast. Wryly, I thought it resembled a crochet hook. My other shoulder displayed the ugly remnants of Simon's stitches on Mariah's bite.

I dried my face and body with a towel. Casting one last look at the scars, I wondered vaguely if life would ever feel normal. If *I* would ever feel normal.

The clock in the bedroom struck two o'clock in the morning.

I dressed again, knowing that this would be another sleepless night. Simon, William, and I were to meet in the parlor to discuss the happenings at St. Pancras Old Church.

Sixteen

I reached the parlor just as Simon brought in a tray of tea and biscuits. I slumped onto the sofa next to William. Simon sat across from us, his back perfectly straight in spite of our exhausting night.

As I poured myself some tea, William spoke. "So it seems possible that my great uncle, John Polidori, is alive. Although he would be almost a hundred years old by now, he appears to be about my age. And if he is indeed alive, it seems he's cavorting about London with Max and Lord Byron." He chuckled darkly, rubbing his eyes. "It's like a terrible opera."

"Lord Byron ... *mad, bad, and dangerous to know*," I murmured into my tea. Knowing the reference, Simon met my eyes and smiled.

William turned to me quizzically.

"It's what one of Byron's lovers, Lady Caroline Lamb, famously said about him," I explained.

William shook his head in disbelief. "So are we assuming

that Max has done to them what he is doing to the others? That he has somehow resurrected them?"

"No," I said quickly. "Neither of them have that deathly paleness of the revenants, the dark shadows under the eyes. They do not appear to be resurrected as the others are."

"Then, how?" William stuttered.

"I believe Max lied about killing Polidori years ago for finding out about the Conclave. For some reason, Max might have given both Byron and Polidori the elixir, and they've been hiding in London or abroad for all of these years. They are immortal, like him."

"Then it must have been Max or one of them who took the Conclave's notes away before the Montgomery Street fire," I said quickly. "Perhaps Polidori, as a scientist, has been creating other formulas, perhaps one that brings the dead back to life."

"I'm concerned, William," Simon said carefully, "about what *your* role is in all of this. Based on that letter about keeping someone alive, I think Abbie might not be their only interest. These other two men, presumably Polidori and Byron, want *you* for some reason. Perhaps your great uncle—"

"But Simon," William snapped, "why would Polidori 'create' me—if your ridiculous theory is true—and then abandon me, and then want me again?"

"That is what we are trying to determine," Simon said dryly. "I will surmise at this point that Max might be trying to create his own Conclave."

"If that's the case, and he's somehow in league with Polidori and Byron, then he must have been planning this for decades," I muttered.

I glanced at William. He seemed extremely agitated.

Simon stood suddenly from his desk. "It's late, and I think we should all go to bed now. I'd like to have another look around the church interior. We'll return to St. Pancras in the morning."

Seventeen

I entered the dining room to find Simon alone, sitting and reading through a very large book. Steaming coffee and a plate of toast sat on the table.

"Is William still asleep?" I asked, spreading marmalade on my toast.

"No. He left before even I was up. I can only assume that he's out walking again."

I stared at the heavy velvet drapes. With the servants gone, a thin film of dust now covered the folds.

"William was so agitated last night," I said quietly. "Of course, it's understandable."

Simon looked up from his book for the first time. "Yes." He pushed the book away. "I wished to speak to you alone about a matter. I have considered another possible explanation as to why William looks so similar to Polidori."

"Other than the replication of cell structures?"

"Yes. Even if you have not acknowledged it, I'm certain that another possibility has crossed your mind."

I paused, knowing exactly what he meant. "That John Polidori is actually William's father?"

"Precisely. The more I read about cellular replication, the more unlikely I think it is that William was 'created' in that way by Polidori."

"Why?"

"With cellular replication, the new organism is identical, a perfect mold, as if it is cut by the same cookie cutter. Even the fingerprints match."

"And there are slightly different physical characteristics between William and Polidori," I said quickly. "The shapes of their eyes and noses. The resemblance is more as if they are brothers, or father and son."

"Yes." Simon took a sip of coffee. "I think their being brothers is completely impossible. If Polidori took the elixir at the time he presumably 'died,' any brother of his would be deceased by now. Of course, theoretically, William could be a natural brother whom Polidori gave the elixir to yearly, preventing him from growing or aging for sixty years until leaving him with Rossetti. But if that were the case, William would have decades of memories, which he simply does not have."

"And it seems like rather a lot of trouble."

"Which is why I think it is more likely that Polidori is William's father. He could have naturally conceived a son at any point during the past sixty years."

"So why did you want us to have this conversation away from William?"

"Because..." Simon drummed his fingers on the lace tablecloth. "I don't believe that William is ready to admit this possibility even to himself. During the hypnosis session, even as William experienced all the feelings of abandonment and saw Polidori as a father figure, he still only referred to him as his great uncle. I am theorizing that the last part of the edifice he's constructed in his memory blocks any acknowledgement that Polidori is his father."

My mind tried to wrap around this. Perhaps I too had tried not to consider this, as it meant that William and I were related—albeit distantly.

"Should we bring up this possibility to William?"

Simon shook his head. "Not unless it becomes absolutely necessary. But I feel that it will not be long before he figures it out."

I sat in silence for a few minutes, considering all the questions and conflicts I had about Mother. William would certainly have a heavy burden to bear if Simon's theory was correct. At least Mother had never abandoned me.

I finished my coffee, peering at the open pages of the book Simon read. The book displayed an odd map; rivers twisted across the pages like ribbons.

"Why are you reading that?" I asked.

Simon poured more coffee into his teacup. "You mentioned last night how Byron called the church his 'lair,' and I'm wondering if the church might be one of Max's main residences."

"But it's so small."

"Wyatt's men have investigated the *main* cemeteries. A small, less conspicuous location like St. Pancras Old Church could be a perfect place for Max to house his undead."

"Again, *where*? That seems a bit absurd, as the church is so small."

"According to this book, the church borders the River Fleet, and some of its tributaries run very deep beneath the church."

"So you think the 'lair' is actually an underground place."

Before Simon could answer, a loud knock sounded at the front door. He stood up and left the dining room.

Too weary to follow him, I listened to the low murmur of voices and pulled the open book about London's underground rivers closer to me. The concept of underground rivers as a place to hide fascinated me. But in my mind, I had difficulty picturing it. All I saw was running water and darkness. I couldn't possibly imagine it as a hiding place for an entire group of people.

Simon returned to the dining room, his pale face smooth in the dim light, his lips tight.

"Abbie, Wyatt is waiting in the parlor. He wants to speak to us both."

I sighed.

"I share your sentiments," Simon whispered. Then, catching my sleeve as I exited the room, he added, "Don't tell him anything that he doesn't already know."

I nodded.

Wyatt sat in the parlor alone, just under the portraits of Simon's two beautiful sisters. Their faces, pale as porcelain, were a dramatic contrast to Wyatt's own odd ruddy complexion.

Simon did not offer him coffee or tea.

"You're probably wondering why I'm here," Wyatt began.

"Not at all," I muttered wryly, noting that Wyatt appeared even more gaunt then he had at his flat.

Simon's mouth curved into a smile, and Wyatt cast me an expression of deep annoyance.

"Five more resurrection men were discovered dead this week," he announced. "Two murders happened near Brompton Cemetery, and another triple murder occurred in Nunhead. All the victims were cannibalized."

"We have nothing to offer," Simon said quickly.

Wyatt watched me as he spoke. "I'm not certain about that. Miss Sharp, why didn't you notify me after the attack upon Lady Westfield's Kensington residence? You must have known that Scotland Yard worked on the case."

Simon spoke quickly. "I told you at our last meeting that we don't have anything to offer. We fulfilled our obligation by reporting the crime to Scotland Yard, but we are under no obligation to work with you."

Wyatt bit his lip so hard that I saw a hairline trickle of blood, which he wiped off with a handkerchief. His face turned three shades more red, although I wouldn't have thought that possible.

"A murder of a housemaid so vicious that Lady Westfield leaves London for a time?" he asked, his eyes boring into mine.

"Leave her out of this," I said sharply.

"Oh, I have no intention of picking the brain of a wealthy Kensington woman. Although there *are* curious aspects of that household—why is it that your butler for the past several years, a Richard Smith, apparently once worked for the Secret Service Bureau?"

"I knew him," Simon said quickly. "He assisted me when I became ill at Port Francqui. The position with Lady Westfield was a returned favor upon his retirement. He knows nothing about the Conclave or their matters."

Simon and I both knew that Richard would have the good sense to lie if ever questioned by Wyatt.

"A happy coincidence," Wyatt remarked.

"Yes, it is," Simon said, his gaze icy.

Wyatt opened his pocket watch, his fingers trembling so violently that he struggled to undo the clasp. After checking the time, he snapped it shut. "I'm almost finished imposing upon your time."

"And this will be the last time you ever will," Simon said.

Wyatt glared at both of us. "The elixir is what kept the Conclave alive for all these years. It represents not only immortality but power. Dr. St. John and Miss Sharp, I want to ask both of you if you've indeed been forthcoming with me about the elixir."

"What are you implying?" I asked.

"I'm implying that if you possess any of the elixir, I would like you to give it to me now."

I chuckled, astonished at his request.

"Miss Sharp, my suspicions are not entirely absurd. The elixir, as I said, is a source of power, and it should not be released. You should turn over any of it that you possess. Now."

I found this request bizarre; I thought Wyatt was more concerned with finding Max.

"Thank you," Simon said, ushering Wyatt to the door. "Miss Sharp and I have work today. And, as I said, this will be our *last* meeting with you."

After Wyatt left, Simon and I watched him walk toward Kensington Road.

"That was odd," I said quickly.

"Indeed."

"Yesterday, you said that Wyatt may not be as much of a problem as we think. Why?"

"Come. I'll tell you on the way to the church."

"Did you notice his trembling fingers?" Simon asked once we were settled in the hansom cab.

"Yes."

"I've discovered that Wyatt is an opium addict. His tremblings, his manic behavior—perhaps even his bold request for the elixir—indicate to me that he was heavily under the drug's influence this morning."

"How do you know this?" I asked, incredulous.

"I first became suspicious that afternoon at his flat." Simon stared out the cab window. In spite of our terrible evening and our bizarre morning, the day was unfolding sunny and beautiful. I wondered vaguely if I would ever enjoy a day like this by strolling through the park, perhaps buying pineapple ice from a street vendor. It seemed so much more appealing than chasing revenants and immortals through London.

"As you know," Simon continued, "I've been pursuing many threads in these matters. After you and William went to bed last night, I decided to visit some of the more famous opium dens in the Limehouse district."

"How do you know where they are?" I smiled at the thought of Simon in such a seedy place.

He smiled back. "I assure you, it was the first time I had stepped into an opium den, but I knew from my travels that opium addiction is a particularly common vice among government workers abroad. Those who frequent these dens are often regulars, so I thought that there might be a good chance, if Wyatt was an addict, to see him in one. My premonition paid off when I found him unconscious at a notorious little den on Narrow Street."

The cab turned onto Pancras Road.

"So why would this make him not a problem?"

"Perhaps I should restate that sentiment to say that I think we should worry about him both more *and* less. He might be following us, although I haven't seen evidence of that lately. But if he is reliant upon a drug, then he is likely to be inattentive in other matters. His thinking will be muddled. On the other hand, muddled thinking might also make him more dangerous. More volatile. You saw the sharp stops and starts of his moods just now. He'll make his duties less about the monarchy and more about himself. He will lose focus and grasp at goals like possessing the elixir for himself—which is exactly what I think he was trying to do, in a very foolish and sloppy manner."

"So how exactly should we proceed with him?" I asked as Simon helped me out of the carriage.

"Mindfully and cautiously."

Many used the church grounds as a dog park, and the area now seemed very different than it did last night. A nanny pushed a perambulator past the Burdett-Coutts memorial sundial. A young man walked his two terriers in the lawn near the rectory.

"Our grave exhumation last night seems to have gone unnoticed," I remarked as my eyes swept over the cemetery toward the forlorn, far-back border of the churchyard.

"*That* place in the cemetery is so untended, I'm certain no one will notice or even particularly care. As you saw last night, those graves are terribly neglected."

Simon and I walked through the front doors of the church, which were unlocked this morning. One middle-aged female parishioner in a plaid shawl knelt at the communion rail in prayer. Otherwise, the place was empty. We walked quietly down the far left aisle, our footsteps echoing off of the stone floor. I scanned the nave in the daylight. Most of the walls were whitewashed, with the exception of the nearest wall, which I saw now was merely exposed, rocky stone.

"Norman era," Simon said quietly, nodding toward the wall. "I was up reading about this church last night." He chuckled. "After returning from the opium den, of course."

"Do you ever sleep?" I asked quietly, running my hand over the old rock surface.

"Never." He smiled. "This is supposedly the oldest Christian church in England. This building itself is *very* old. Renovations have uncovered Norman structures within the walls and Roman tiles in the foundation."

We sat quietly in chairs near the left front side of the church, near a statue of Mary bolted into the wall above a votive candle rack. As we waited for the woman at the front of the church to leave, I tried to take in every detail: the Stations of the Cross, the large altar surrounded by memorial plaques to famous parishioners, a stunning gold-plated, tri-fold image of the crucifixion on the ledge of the center window immediately behind the altar.

"Do you think William is working at the hospital?" I whispered, suddenly wishing he were here helping us.

"I don't think much about how William spends his time."

Finally, the parishioner stood and left.

Simon whispered, his lips like moth wings against my ear, "I'm particularly interested in the sacristy."

"Where Byron disappeared," I murmured.

"Come along," he said, standing.

"This feels entirely irreverent."

Simon cast me a small smile as I followed him toward the altar. I wondered what he was looking for. Simon had an uncanny ability to see what I could not.

Glancing behind us, Simon stepped through the open gate of the communion rail. He walked to the wall left of the altar and began running his fingers along it. "As I told you this morning, I'm very interested in what is underground here."

"But what would be underground other than the river?" I asked, keeping one eye toward the front doors of the church.

Now behind the altar, Simon ran his fingers upon the wall directly beneath the tri-fold image. "The construction of our underground railway system has exposed much about the world of ancient London. Yes, it's all a complicated webwork of tributaries and distributaries branching out from the main river, but it also teems with life."

"Life?"

"Well, life and death." Simon crouched on the floor behind the altar, considering each wall. I tried to see what he was looking for, but the rough stone patterns covered with the memorial plaques and artwork all seemed uniform. "Often, as they dig deep beneath the city, construction workers find mass graves of plague victims. In terms of life, there are rats and stray dogs, but also bizarre rumors of underground colonies of people who have never seen daylight, living deep within the city's bowels."

"That seems impossible."

"Of course, the colony stories might not be true," Simon said, his eyes pausing on the doorway to the sacristy. "But it does raise questions about what might be underneath here."

He walked to the wall bordering the sacristy and placed his hand on a long seam, which was merely a darker area of plaster on the wall. He ran his fingers along the seam, considering it. "Workers throughout the city have discovered crypts and arched corridors from the Roman era. Pagans and early Christians created healing wells, and many of these wells are now merged with the city's culverts and draining systems. Considering the ancient history of this church and what you saw last night, I'm wondering if such a place exists deep beneath here."

We heard the front doors open, the echo of footsteps.

With a quick brush against my wrist, Simon led me through the door into the sacristy. It was mostly empty, as it had been the night before, except for the credens and some unlit votive candles.

"You mentioned you heard a sound like stone rubbing upon stone?" Simon asked quietly.

I followed his gaze to three seams in the wall. One ran five feet up from the ground, four feet over, and then descended to the floor again. A straight hairline crack ran neatly inside the seams.

"It's a door," I exclaimed under my breath. "I never would have noticed it."

"We see what we wish," Simon said wryly. Then, glancing about us, he pushed the stone to one side and, with a low grinding noise, it swung open a few inches. Simon crouched, and I peeked over his shoulder to see a dangerously narrow set of twisting stone steps descending into darkness.

An unpleasant dank smell blew out at us. Disturbed dust marked each of the visible steps; cobwebs draped from the stone walls like torn lace.

Simon quickly closed the door.

I cast him a quizzical glance as we silently left the church through a nearby door. We walked over to stand by the ash tree with the tombstones.

Simon sighed, looking toward the back of the cemetery. "I'm surmising that the stairwell links the church to underground structures. It might be very deep, although we cannot know for certain."

"Why is it hidden? The priests must know of its existence."

"Yes, they probably do. Although they very likely have never been down there, as it is of no use to them anymore. This church, like others, was forced to hide valuable relics and altar pieces during the Reformation when Puritans ravaged them. Those steps probably served as a hiding place for the old relics. I'm guessing, though, that it is much more extensive. Perhaps there are deeper caverns than the Reformation-era priests knew of, or wished to explore."

Wind blew lightly against us as we walked past the looming ash tree into the graveyard again. A train raced by with such a roar that we didn't speak as we approached Polidori's gravestone.

In the daylight, I saw that Simon and William had indeed smoothed the ground almost perfectly around the grave, and no one would likely notice that the area had been disturbed. The plot was neglected in any case, abounding in overgrown weeds. Even in the daylight, the lettering on the stone was indecipherable. We turned and stared back at the tree and the church behind us, seemingly so harmless on this summer morning.

Simon broke the silence after the train passed. "If that stairwell does descend as deeply as I suspect, it's a perfect spot for Max to house his revenants."

"A 'lair' is what Byron called it."

"*Lair* is perhaps the best term," Simon said, his gaze steady upon the church.

"I wonder how many revenants they've created."

Simon shrugged. "There is no way to know. I must read a bit more about subterranean London. I think you and I should continue scouring the Conclave's notes at night. Perhaps William will eventually decide to help us."

I ignored the bitter tone in his voice.

Thinking of that stairwell, I felt more of an urge than ever to end this uncertainty. I thought of Mother, of Mariah, of that little girl last night. "When can we go down there?"

"Not now. With as little as we know, it would be too dangerous."

"But they might come for us."

Simon's gaze darkened as we walked through the cemetery toward the front gates. "I think *that* is inevitable."

Eighteen

Over the next two weeks, William, Simon, and I fell into a wearying routine. Simon and I left for work at Whitechapel Hospital every morning, and William continued to depart early to walk about London for half a day of exercise. He would join Simon and me at the hospital by one o'clock every afternoon. Then, each evening until the early morning hours, the three of us read and re-read the Conclave's notes, looking for any clues about Max's project.

Each night, I tried to read the materials in a new light, remembering what Simon had said to me when we discovered the hidden staircase in the church: "We see what we wish to see."

Yet even Simon agreed that when it came to the Conclave's notes, he saw nothing new. The only thing we noticed was that there were more pages missing than we had previously thought.

"Probably the pages that we need," William muttered grumpily late one night. "I don't understand why we don't storm down there with revolvers or dynamite."

"Because we will die," Simon said flatly. "At this point we don't know why Max, Polidori, and Byron are doing what they're doing, or if St. Pancras is even their only location. After all, the revenants have been hunting in other boroughs of London. We need more information before we do anything else."

The corpse lay on the operating table unconscious, the top of the skull removed.

The air in the laboratory was almost as musty as their subterranean residence, but it was suffocating with the odor of formaldehyde mingled with the blood. As his gaslight burned nearby, Polidori wiped perspiration from his brow. He cursed silently under his breath while examining the brain contents under the microscope.

A stream of light poured down the long staircase. He heard the lithe footsteps of Byron stepping leisurely down it. Byron was wearing a turban and his oriental robe, and holding a glass of brandy in his hand. It was close to two o'clock in the afternoon, and he was only *now* getting out of bed.

"Is he restrained?" Byron asked as he reached the bottom step.

"No need for that. He's dead."

"Where is Bartlett today?" Byron asked, tightening his robe and taking another sip of brandy.

"In the caverns."

"How long did it take for this one to degenerate?"

Polidori furrowed his brows and pulled the gas lamp closer

as he peered through the microscope lens. "This one, only two weeks, and I even used the revised formula."

"Still no progress," Byron murmured, disappointment thick in his voice.

"Yes. I *see* what's happening in every undead autopsy, but I don't know why the results are so unpredictable. I don't know exactly why some degenerate so quickly, while others take so long. I have my theories, of course. But this revised formula made no difference."

"Science is but the exchange of ignorance for that which is another type of ignorance," Byron said, draining his glass.

"Strange words from someone who is still alive *only* because of science."

Max started slipping through the window into her bedroom at night. Simon St. John, for all his protective measures for the girl, couldn't keep him out. Locks, latches, bolts; he could always find a way in. Sometimes he sat by her bed. Sometimes he would lie, light as a phantom, on the bed beside her.

Caroline.

He always thought of Caroline when he watched her. He saw the same dappling of freckles across her nose. So imprudent in the sun, just as her mother had been.

When he was close to her like this—her defenses down, surrendered to sleep—he could feel her energy more strongly. It curled about her like a stream of smoke, and he could feel it dance, coil with his own energy on these nights.

She had no idea how, with the elixir, her mind, her body, would burn with this energy. It all lay tragically untapped.

Since discovering the hidden stairwell with Simon, my sleep became fitful, strange dreams playing out in my head like streams of running water.

Some dreams were particularly vivid.

In one, I was eight years old again in Edinburgh, blind-folded as I chased friends in a meadow. Giggling, I lunged toward the sound of a child's laugh, but he leaped away, out of my reach. My heartbeat quickened, and I laughed as my hand brushed the folds of a girl's skirt just behind me, but as I spun about, my arms swung through air. I felt a stick poke me, and I twirled so fast that I tripped and fell lightly into the grass. As I stood up, the children's laughter rose, then dissipated. The sun beat down hot upon me and I almost removed the blindfold. But then I would lose the game. Their silence *must* be a trick.

"Hello!" I called, but I received no response. Someone was near, though, and I smelled the thick scent of an Oriental cigar before awakening.

Another night, I dreamed that I was back in the Kennilworth menagerie on the bamboo swing with William, kissing him as I had before. There was no gaslight, only a bit of moon streaming in from beyond the monkeys' cage.

The sensations in the dream were frighteningly real, and a fire unleashed inside me that I couldn't quell. I leaned back upon the side of the swing as William's body pressed upon mine; my left arm twisted about the suspension rope above me. William kissed my ear, my cheek, my throat.

The animals were unusually quiet.

Over William's head I saw, in the gleam of moonlight on a high branch, the crouched outline of a small spider monkey, his hands over his face like Mizaru of the three wise monkeys.

I pulled my arm away from the suspension rope, letting my hands wander about William's hard chest as I pulled him closer to me. A dark cloud passed over the moon. Our kissing became more urgent; my fingers fumbled with one of his shirt buttons, and I hesitated. The cloud passed, and moonlight spilt upon us once again.

Then I smelled something strange and slightly rancid. William moved his mouth from my throat to my lips. His lips, his touch, his chest upon mine were suddenly cold. I pulled away; his eyes held the milky shine of the revenants. His face was dreadfully pale. His expression was predatory.

I awoke on the floor, having fallen out of bed. Every limb of my body was trembling.

A summer wind had blown my window open, and the gauzy curtain billowed out about it. I latched the window and returned to bed, but I was too frightened to sleep.

According to the clock over the fireplace, the time was nearing four o'clock in the morning.

I curled up in bed, still trembling from the nightmare.

As on most nights during those two weeks, I'd gone to sleep at one o'clock, far too late. The nightmares were likely from the stress of studying the notebooks and trying to solve the massive puzzle we faced while still working exhausting hours at the hospital.

I felt continuously on edge, uneasy. It was a sensation like walking on a tightrope between two tall buildings. Max had said, the night he attacked me in my bedroom at Kennilworth, that he would see me soon. Simon, William, and I had been back in London for several weeks now; I felt better that Grandmother and Laura were away from me, but no one I loved was safe while Max lived. I remembered what Simon had said, that morning at St. Pancras Old Church—that it was inevitable that they would come for us. And I believed him.

I was surprised to see both Simon and William downstairs at breakfast. William's face was flushed deeply. They seemed to have been arguing. But this was nothing new, so I poured a cup of tea and slumped into a seat at the dining table.

"You look awful," William exclaimed. "As if you didn't sleep at all last night."

"I *didn't* sleep well." I took a long sip, and hot steam burned my nose. "Frankly, I'm frustrated. The notebooks didn't help us at all. I agree that we can't go into that underground place without knowing more about it, but we need to put these pieces together. So far, Max is trifling with us, and everything seems to be playing in his favor."

"Abbie," Simon began, "you should eat some—"

"She's right." William cut Simon off. "In fact, Simon and I were just arguing about that."

"William wants to go into the cavern below the church and blow it up with dynamite," Simon said flatly.

"Exactly!" William exclaimed.

Simon sighed. "Apart from the fact that all three of us are probably inept at handling dynamite, *we cannot* act brashly, as I stated the other night. It could be disastrous."

William groaned and pushed back his chair. "What you don't seem to understand, Simon, is that they are *always* ahead of us. Max just because of who he is. As long as he takes the elixir, he will be invincible to *anyone.*"

I chuckled darkly into my teacup. "So what are you saying? That *I* should take the elixir so that I might be like him?"

William's eyes brightened momentarily. "It's an idea."

"Never," Simon and I muttered simultaneously. "That's complete nonsense, William," Simon added.

William pulled his jacket off the back of his chair. "I'm going out. When you come up with a plan that's better than mine, do please let me know."

The front door slammed, hard, as he left.

Simon and I sat in frustrated silence for a full five minutes.

"Abbie, I almost forgot. A letter from Lady Westfield has arrived for you."

Taking the letter immediately into the parlor, I began to read.

Dear Arabella,

I wanted to write to you to let you know that Laura is SPEAKING now.

After you left, I let her draw as much as she

wanted to. She drew pages and pages, hanging them about the walls of her room.

Arabella, I wondered if I should have allowed this—her drawings grew darker by the day. One day, she drew a picture of a dead duckling we found in the gardens. She painted a hawk with a rabbit in its mouth, and a dead hare that Bridget was about to stew.

Her paintings then turned away from the present, back to her life in Scotland. She drew moors, the rocky shores of Orkney, a small cottage.

Then yesterday, I went in to call her to tea. Her window was open and wind blew through the room, rattling the drawings upon the walls and ceiling. She was kneeling, her back to me. I half wondered if I had been right to indulge this drawing obsession of hers.

Then, still turned away from me, she said, "I am finished."

Just like that.

I stepped near her, shocked when I saw her final drawing. It was that lamia you described to me. The monstrous creature looks like something out of a book.

She stood and turned to me. Her face was pale, but some type of edifice had come down. She embraced me, and I was quite startled. I'm fond of her, Arabella. This is perhaps the worst place to make this confession—in a poorly written letter while you have so many other matters on your mind—but I never hugged Caroline. Never.

Laura began talking then, and I'm finding

(apart from the vile dialect) that she is quite like you.
You will have to come soon to see her improvement.

Her picture of the creature haunts me, and I
know you gave instructions to the maids not to enter
the library, but, well, I'm the mistress of the house
now, and I unlocked the library, looked through some
of the books.

I looked through Dr. Bartlett's very large photo-
graph album, and I was filled with regret. I'd been
so blinded, blinded by his scientific knowledge, the
prestige surrounding him. I feel quite terrible that I
put you in his path.

Please come back to me. I meant what I said
that day you left. My heart will break if I lose you.

While you're in London, please do fall in love with
Simon St. John. William Siddal is like an untrained
pup. Pretty in the window of the pet shop, but he will
do you no good in the long run.

—Your loving Grandmother . . .

I sat in silence, listening to Simon clear away the breakfast dishes in the next room. It was a small grace to know that
Laura was talking now, and I couldn't wait to share the news
with Simon. Regarding Grandmother, it was difficult to believe
that this was the same woman who had brought me back from
Dublin after Mother's death. She was still indomitable and
maintained many of her flourishes, yet her Kensington soul had
melted a bit. And I loved her more.

PART III

"Why, sometimes I've believed as many as six impossible things before breakfast."
            —*Through the Looking-Glass,*
                and What Alice Found There

Nineteen

L ater that afternoon, Simon and I washed surgical instruments in the laboratory after completing an appendectomy. The hospital had been relatively quiet that day, the summer heat extending through the building like a blanket—and heaviest on the fourth floor, where we were. Yet more weighed upon our minds than the heat, and beyond discussing Laura, we said very little.

Suddenly we heard a great thumping noise upon the upper part of the stairs, and William promptly burst through the laboratory doors pulling a small cart covered with a thick canvas. His face was flushed, his shirt rumpled and unbuttoned to the chest, the bottom part of his trousers dirty and torn. His expression was strangely triumphant.

"William, you were scheduled to help me in the appendectomy. And what are you doing entering the hospital in such disarray?" Simon asked flatly.

"Simon, even *you* will be happy about what I've been up to this morning." Excited as a child, William pushed the cart near the dissection table. He pulled off the canvas, and I gasped.

"Dear God," Simon muttered.

Curled inside the cart was a young man, about twenty-five years of age, who had the distinct face of the other undead—purple circles like bruises lay under his eyes. A thin trail of brown, oily blood seeped out of a neck wound and pooled at the bottom of the cart.

"How did you?" I stuttered as Simon and William lifted the body out of the cart and laid it upon the table.

William ran his fingers through his hair and went to fetch his notebook from a drawer. Simon was already pulling over the medical trolley of instruments. I tied an apron about my waist.

"I had an appointment in Cheapside with our family solicitor this morning when I saw *this* fellow following me as I left. Although he blended in with the crowds, I knew immediately that he was a revenant. He followed me into the East End, where I pulled him into a nearby alley to confront him. Once we were in the alley shadows, he was much less well-behaved than in public. He kept lunging for my neck. He either wouldn't or *couldn't* tell me why he had been following me. I'm not certain if he could even speak. I think we all know who sent him."

"Max," I muttered.

"Or Byron or Polidori," William said quickly. "He wasn't armed, but unfortunately for him, I was. So I cut his throat."

William paused, staring down at the cart. "I bought the cart and canvas for a ridiculously high price from a nearby shopkeeper so that I wouldn't have to walk down Commercial Street with a dead body over my shoulder."

"Yes, that might attract attention even in *this* neighborhood," Simon quipped dryly.

After quickly shaving the corpse's head, Simon selected the skull saw and began cutting into the top of the skull. The peculiar, oily brown blood seeped down onto the table.

William stood nearby, sleeves rolled up. He scowled, probably irritated that Simon was making the first incisions. Yet he said nothing. Although it was unspoken, we all knew that Simon was the better physician when it came to performing autopsies.

While Simon worked, I pulled out a syringe and drew a sample of the blood. As I filled the vial, Simon glanced up at me. "I'm assuming the blood is brown from oxygen depletion. The oily consistency—I'm wondering if that has something to so with whatever formula is being used to resurrect them."

After Simon neatly removed the top of the skull, I helped him extract the brain. Once the organ had been entirely removed, he began slicing thin layers of brain matter for the slides. By then, both of our hands were slick with blood.

William, restless, began cutting off the corpse's shirt. After he'd removed it, I saw a small bullet hole in the lower abdominal wall. William took the nearest scalpel. "At least we know how he died."

While Simon and I washed the blood off our hands to begin preparing the slides, William muttered, "I hope they haven't started using means other than grave robbing to find corpses."

"I wouldn't put anything past them at this point," I said.

171

While Simon and I worked on four slides, placing tiny samples upon each glass with tweezers and staining them with a drop of iodine, William opened up the corpse's chest cavity to take a look at the other internal organs.

Simon looked at each slide under the microscope. He took his time. There was no sound now except for our breathing and the cracking of rib bones in the background. In the warm laboratory, perspiration ran down my face like tears. After several minutes, Simon retrieved the first slide and returned it to the microscope.

"Interesting."

"What do you see?" I asked, standing beside him.

William chuckled behind us, blood smeared up to his elbows as he worked deep within the corpse. "Perhaps evidence of a soul."

Ignoring him, Simon invited me to look into the eyepiece. "What do you notice about this sample?"

I peered into the microscope. "It looks normal. The spindly threadlike neuron structures are all strong and unbroken."

"And this one?" He placed another slide onto the stage.

"The threads here are broken, less stable. More like frayed thread."

"My thoughts exactly. I would surmise that the cellular structures in this portion of the brain, the cerebral cortex, only work sporadically, while in the other, deeper portions of the brain, the connections are particularly strong."

William paused in his examination, listening to us.

"Abbie, how much neurology have you covered in your studies so far?" Simon asked.

I tried to remember my notes. "A bit. The cerebral cortex,

some believe, controls the reasoning portion of the brain while the hypothalamus deals more with appetite."

"So it would seem," William said, wiping blood from his forearms with a towel, "that the more disintegrated portions of this brain are those that control choice and reason."

Simon peered back into the microscope. "That is what I'm beginning to think."

"Cerebral specialization," I murmured.

Simon started to quickly sketch the cell appearance in his notebook. "Yes. It goes well beyond phrenology. There *is* substantial evidence that certain parts of the brain control certain behaviors."

"There was that case of the American railway worker," William said, walking over to the washbasin to clean the remaining blood off of his hands. "He lived, after an accident sent a spike through his brain that destroyed much of his frontal lobe. But for the last twelve years of his life, he struggled with impulsive behavior and difficulty controlling his temper." William chuckled. "Although I've never heard stories of him cannibalizing anyone."

"But there's another school of thought that I think might be more appropriate to this situation," Simon said quickly. "Some think that the earlier, less evolved portions of the brain are located deeper within it. In these samples, it is the deeper portions of the brain that are more stable."

"So when Max, Polidori, and Byron revive these corpses, the strongest surviving portions of their brain are in fact the 'least human' portions," I muttered.

"That's precisely what I'm thinking. Perhaps these revenants do not 'live' forever after they are revived, and I'm wondering, based on the tissue breakdown of the frontal lobe, if they become increasingly animalistic the longer they survive, as the cerebral cortex eventually disintegrates completely. I certainly see this pattern within these four slides; the neuron fibers gradually weaken upon progression to the frontal lobe."

I bit my lip. "Byron did say something the other night, before he killed the little girl, about her time being almost up."

We stood in silence near the microscope.

"Of course," Simon said, "these conclusions are based only on samples from one revenant. But it might explain why the revenants seem to function at different levels—how Mariah could speak, how she could remember people from her life."

"But they *all* eventually degenerate back into a completely predatory state, most likely," William said.

"I wonder how long the process takes. What's the timeline?" I asked quietly, trying not to think about Mariah.

Simon shrugged. "The corpses would have to be taken fairly soon after death for there to be any revivable brain matter. Mariah died in November, and she attacked you in May, so at least six months. But it's almost impossible to tell at this point. I'm assuming that the different physiological makeup of individuals affects the outcome."

"Perhaps, in the same way the elixir affected Max differently from the other Conclave members, these experiments might have varying results among the revenants." I struggled to wrap my mind around these matters.

William stepped around us to peer into the microscope.

"Do you see the pattern?" I asked.

"I do."

After looking at the last slide, William began writing down

some notes. "I should probably tell you about my errand in Cheapside today. I visited my aunt this morning. I don't want to involve her more than necessary, but I asked her about our family's past, particularly more details about my great uncle. She suggested that I visit our family solicitor this morning. We rarely use the firm anymore, except to handle wills or legal matters pertaining to my father's art. But they have all of the known legal documents surrounding our family."

Simon listened silently.

"According to our family solicitor," William continued, "Polidori's home on Regent Street was not his only London residence. He had purchased a modest house in Highgate, bordering the cemetery, in 1821, just before he supposedly died. For unknown reasons, Polidori did not want the property's existence known to relatives or included in his will. Because of the decades that have passed, the solicitor relented when I coaxed him a bit, and gave me the spare keys to it."

"It is rather puzzling that he would make a purchase in such secrecy. And where did he get the money? He had so much debt," I mused.

William arched one eyebrow as he pulled a small key ring, holding two keys, from his pocket. "That is why we're investigating the property tonight."

Simon stared at the eviscerated body on the table, the slides spread out in front of us, sighed, and nodded.

The bell at St. Paul's Cathedral tolled the ten o'clock hour as Simon, William, and I rode back to Kensington to eat quickly and retrieve a few weapons.

The night was dark and moonless.

As the carriage lurched upon the cobblestone streets, we discussed the news from Grandmother's letter about Laura.

"What happens to her now that she's talking?" I asked Simon.

"She's peeled away the layers of memories to the root of her trauma. It was a process, like peeling an onion apart to reach the core. Now she tries to cope with the memories, to live in the present alongside her unpleasant past."

"She tries to be normal," William said suddenly. "As we all do."

"I hope that she and Grandmother are safe," I said worriedly, remembering the drawing she had made of the three men.

Simon's eyes met mine. "Richard is with them."

"And Hugo," William said.

"Also, *I'm* away. Everyone is safer away from me," I said dryly as we rode past Kensington Park, the palace rising like a little brick dollhouse in the distance.

Simon smiled quietly from his seat across from me, and it was like a downy touch.

Twenty

The three of us were so tired we didn't see her until we reached the little gate in front of the St. John residence.

Simon saw her first and pushed me behind him. William almost stumbled over me.

"Damn it, St. John, *what...*" Then William stopped, frozen.

In the shadows on the front doorstep sat a young girl, her face covered by a hood. I stared quickly about us, wondering if there were more—if the child was perhaps a decoy. But I saw no movement, only night shadows.

Then the girl raised her head and the hood slipped away.

"Laura!" I exclaimed. I saw her small bag on the ground beside her.

"Laura, did you come here by yourself?" William demanded angrily.

"Ah wan tae help," she said meekly.

"Lady Westfield does not know that you're here?" Simon asked quietly.

"No." She looked down at the folds of her skirts, ashamed. "Ah dornt think sae. She went tae bed early and Ah walked tae town, took the last train."

"She'll be beside herself, Simon," I said quickly. "Can you dispatch a telegram to her immediately?"

"The Paddington office should still be open," Simon said, his ice-blue eyes watching Laura carefully.

Then, under my breath, I said to both William and Simon, "We can't go to that Highgate property tonight. We need to get her back to Warwick immediately."

"I fully agree," Simon said. "I'll return as soon as possible."

Simon left while William, his face flushed in frustration, unlocked the front doors and stepped inside. "We can't take her back tonight. It's almost eleven o'clock. There are no more trains to Warwick."

"Ah wan tae help!" Laura pleaded again, looking up at me.

"Nonsense," William growled. "You have no idea what we're doing here."

"William, I think we should listen to her."

William's expression softened. As I removed Laura's cloak from her, he suggested that they play a game of dominoes.

By the time I entered the parlor, setting a tray of sandwiches and milk upon a small table, Simon had returned. Laura giggled as William let her knock down a long line of dominoes stretching from some potted plants near the fireplace to the wall just under Rosamund St. John's portrait.

I handed Laura a sandwich as she sat on a nearby chair. Then I sat next to William on the sofa while Simon leaned against the wall near the front door. All of us were very tense.

"Please tell us why you're here," Simon said to Laura.

"And *how* you left and boarded a train alone," I added.

She took a sip of milk, a small frothy line above her lip. "Ah know it was wrong, but Ah took th' money fram Lady Westfield's writin' desk. Ah walked tae town, paid fur mae ticket, sayin' that mae mum was awreddy on th'train. He didne ask nae questions."

"I believe her," Simon muttered. "The Warwick station is particularly inept."

"That was wrong to take money from Lady Westfield for your fare. And what you did, traveling alone at night, was very dangerous," I said to Laura.

"Seems rather like something *you* would do," William whispered.

Ignoring him, I asked, "Why did you do it, Laura? You keep saying that you want to help, but why do you think we need help?" Remembering her drawing of Byron, I felt a rising uneasiness about how much she knew of our current troubles.

After a few moments of silence, she answered.

"When Ah saw mah sister git killed"—a tear fell down her face—"a lump formed in mah throat that Ah couldn't git away. Ah couldn't spick. It was awful."

She stopped, put her hand to her throat.

"Lady Westfield taught me tae draw. Th' lump lightened every day until one day, it was gone, an' then Ah could spick."

We listened silently.

She stopped and took another small bite of sandwich. Her brown eyes watered.

"Lady Westfield has bin kin tae me. Ah don't want tae worry 'er. But Ah 'eard you talkin' in the library about bad men who wan tae 'urt you and Ah wan tae help!"

William leaned forward and sighed loudly, putting his head in his hands.

"Does that man Ah drew in the picture hae anythin' tae do wi' mah sister's death?"

I didn't know how to answer her. William still had his head in his hands. I looked to Simon for help. I'd told him about Laura's sketch of Lord Byron, but we both assumed she might have seen him somewhere on the estate before Max attacked me. Now, I wondered why she thought he might be connected to her sister's death.

"Laura, you are a brave girl, but this is not your problem," Simon said solemnly.

"But it is. Ah've lost mah grandmum, mah sister, 'er betroth'd."

"Oh, dear heavens, she *is* just like you. The fearless avenger." William groaned. "God help us all."

"Laura, you must go to bed soon," I said. It was nearing midnight. "But I must ask you about your drawing of that turbaned man. Where did you see him?"

She paused, looked from me to Simon then back to William as if ashamed.

"Laura, you can tell us."

"Ah saw 'im in mah head. And two others as well."

I met Simon's eyes.

"Two other *men*? What do you mean, Laura?" I asked.

"Sometimes when Ah'm doing somethin' else, drawin', walkin' in th' gardens, Ah see three men in mah head."

William pulled his head up from his hands.

I promptly dropped my glass of milk upon Lady St. John's carpeted floor.

My mind still reeling from what Laura had told me, I said very little as I took her upstairs to my room. I opened her bag and saw, lying on top of her clothes, *Alice's Adventures in Wonderland.*

"Ah thought if ye 'ad time ye might reid it tae me."

I smiled, slipping the nightgown over her head. Her mouth opened a bit to reveal her teeth; they were uneven, as her adult teeth grew in large. I had a sudden flashback to when I was her age and my teeth grew in the same way. Mother called them my "jack-o'-lantern teeth."

"Lady Westfield tauld me she didn't like th' nonsense. She read me books about manners and grammar. But Ah like *Alice in Wonderlain* better."

"As do I."

I pulled the covers up to her chin. "Laura, I'll be in here with you shortly, but I wanted to ask if you have ever had visions before?"

She paused, looked up at the ceiling. "Nah, ne'er. Only after comin' tae Kennilworth."

I kissed her forehead, then pulled down one of Rosamund's china dolls from the shelves and gave it to her.

She held it in her arms and said quietly, "Can Ah stay 'ere wi' ye?"

"We'll have to see about that."

I met William and Simon in the study. Simon now sat at his desk, writing.

"This adds a new element to everything," William said as I sat down next to him. He took a long sip from a glass of water.

Simon poured two brandies from a nearby decanter, handed me one.

"I wonder if Max knows about her?" William asked.

"She told me just now that she never had the visions before she came to Kennilworth. *I* never had one before coming to London." A headache began just behind my eyes and I drained my glass of brandy. "I'm assuming, unfortunately, that Max tapped into her gift."

"She cannot go back to Kennilworth," Simon said strongly. "Which is why I'm writing to Lady Westfield to let her know that Laura will stay here, safe."

"But she is not safe," William said, chuckling a bit maniacally. "And what now? Is Lady Westfield going to show up on our steps with that damnable little dog and her trunk of petticoats?"

"Laura is *safer* here with us," Simon replied wearily. "In my letter, I'm also instructing Lady Westfield to under no circumstances come to London yet. In fact, I'm dispatching another telegraph in the morning to make certain that she does not."

"Simon, you have done so much; I could have written to her," I said.

His mouth curved into a smile. "Yes, but she will listen to *me.*"

William set his glass down on a nearby table and began

pacing the room. "This business is going to be much more difficult to navigate with an eight-year-old on our hands. Am I supposed to pack milk and biscuits along with revolvers as we venture into the bowels of St. Pancras Old Church?"

Neither Simon nor I answered.

William spoke again, suddenly. "He wants you, Abbie, because of Caroline. Would he want Laura *only* because of her gifts?"

Simon finished his brandy and stood up. "These are questions we cannot answer now. We should go to bed."

Simon rubbed his eyes. "We have three surgeries scheduled for tomorrow. We'll go to the Highgate property tomorrow evening after work."

"And what about the child?"

"For now, she stays with us at all times."

Near three o'clock in the morning, Laura awoke.

She heard Abbie breathing evenly in the bed beside her.
What had awakened her?

She clutched her doll, stared at the ones on the shelves above her, each one dressed in lace and finery. She loved dolls, but tonight all of their painted white faces made her uneasy.

A flame flickered from the shadows near her bed.

She sat up, startled, and rubbed her eyes. One of the men from her visions—the one with the spirally black hair and bright green eyes—sat in a chair nearby smoking a cigar.

"Shhhh..." He laid a finger on his lips.

She rubbed her eyes, pushed her hair out of her face. "Ur ye bad?"

"Very."

They sat in silence, staring at one another, his cigar glowing in the darkness. She thought of the glowworms behind her grandmum's house in the late summer, and a knot tightened in her stomach.

As he continued to stare at her, taking long draws from the cigar, she trembled.

When she had been unable to speak, others sometimes forgot when she was present. She had listened through the doors of the library at Kennilworth. She couldn't hear everything, but she knew enough from listening to the bits of conversations between Abbie, Dr. Siddal, and Dr. St. John that there were other bad people behind the monster who killed her family. She felt as if the people they sought might be these three men she had seen in her head.

The cigar smoke, wafting through the room, turned her stomach. It wasn't comforting like the scent of smoke from her grandfather's pipe had been.

In her imagination, she had always pictured herself attacking this man with her nails, maybe little knives like the ones she'd seen Abbie throw at a target in the gardens. But now, as she clutched her doll, she shook violently. He was so large. His eyes gleamed a strange shade of green in the darkness. She could never make anything that shiny and green in her drawings. The hue seemed impossibly bright.

As her trembling increased, Laura dropped the doll, which

fell onto the floor. Abbie stirred beside her and rolled onto her side, but did not wake.

"Why ur ye 'ere?"

The man smiled widely, then stood up and gave her back the doll.

"I'm trying to decide what to do about you," he said.

She froze, terrified.

What could he do to her?

He stood above her bed, smiling strangely. Then he laid one finger over his mouth. "Don't tell Miss Sharp that I was here tonight."

That was all he said, but there was a terrible edge in his voice.

She wouldn't tell Abbie in the morning.

He went to the window, the cigar still in his mouth. Silently, he slipped over the ledge, pulled the window closed, and disappeared.

Twenty-one

While William and Simon went to the hospital to perform the scheduled surgeries, I took coffee with Christina and Laura at the Jamaican Wine House. The pub, located inside St. Michael's Alley, was crowded yet full of private tables. My head ached; I was frustrated by what we had learned about Laura last night. My night had been another continuous stream of fitful dreams, lingering so vividly in my mind that I feared I smelled the sweetish smell of Max's cigar when I awoke this morning.

Christina slid into the chair across from me while I sat next to Laura. I drank a second cup of coffee while Laura nibbled at a tart. Christina ordered hot tea, then stated bluntly, "You look as if you haven't slept in days, Abbie."

"I haven't. Actually, I have, but not deeply. I never feel rested in the morning. And now, well..." I glanced down at Laura.

Christina nodded discreetly. She knew what we had discovered. William had stopped by her house to tell her about Laura, and also about Polidori's secret house. He hadn't yet told her that her uncle was still alive, although I knew that if we survived this muddle, he would tell her.

Christina had been surprised to learn about the Highgate residence. She called it an "economic waste" to have had a residence all these years that could have been sold or used as another home for her "friends."

Tears pricked the corners of my eyes. William talking to Christina this morning, me meeting with her here—it was all so selfish of us. But she was like a mother to William and me. "We shouldn't be involving you," I mumbled into my coffee cup.

She hushed me and began making conversation with Laura.

While they talked, my mind wandered. I watched the many customers around us. A middle-aged woman with a small hat of faux violets sipped a cordial near me. A young man with a very thin moustache wrote vigorously in a notebook as he sipped tea. Old men in suits, with neatly trimmed beards, took a late luncheon at a large oblong table across the room; bankers, possibly solicitors.

I scanned the sea of faces neurotically, half expecting to see the pale face of a revenant.

"*Abbie.*"

My thoughts refocused. Christina was watching me worriedly from across the table.

She tightened her lips and glanced down at Laura, who was trying to make an origami swan out of her napkin as Christina had shown her. "William said that you are going to investigate that Highgate property this evening."

"Yes. It's likely empty."

"But it might not be," she muttered, glancing toward Laura again. "Why don't you leave the child with me tonight?"

It sounded like a wonderful idea, but I couldn't do that— leave Christina unprotected with a child who might be targeted by Max. Scenes from the attack at Grandmother's house unfolded in my mind.

"No, I won't involve you any more in this." My words came out sharper than I had intended.

She stared at me pityingly from under her spectacles.

"I'm sorry," I muttered. "I'm rather snappish today."

Christina eyed a large window nearby. "There's a little flower stand at the end of the alley. Let me take Laura there for a few minutes, give you time to finish your drink. Perhaps eat something."

"I can't let her away from me."

"Abbie," Christina said firmly. "It will only be for a few minutes. The streets are crowded now, and I will keep her arm linked with mine. No harm will come from it, I assure you."

I stuttered.

"I insist," she pressed.

After Christina left, I ordered more coffee and began to finish the last tart on Laura's plate. I thought of my medical books, out on my desk at Simon's house. I had rarely looked at them since returning to London. This life—always looking over my shoulder, worrying about those I loved—this wasn't the life I wanted to live. I wanted to be a physician. But *that* life now seemed elusive as a faraway star.

And Mother...

If I could have fifteen minutes with her. Only fifteen minutes to sit across from her at a table like this one, talk to her knowing what I know now. She had been Rossetti's lover, beguiling enough that the man I'd thought was my father, Jacque Sharp, married her. If I had her with me now, I would ask her how many times she'd fallen in and out of love over those years. And I would have to summon the strength to ask her if she'd ever loved Max.

"Miss Sharp."

Startled, I jumped a little. It was the sound of Inspector Abberline's voice.

"Dear God, it's you," I groaned. My reaction was certainly rude, but I had more important things on my mind than making a show of good manners to Scotland Yard.

"Might I sit here?" he asked, pulling out Christina's chair.

I shrugged. Although I still didn't trust him, his voice was gentler than usual.

He sighed. "Miss Sharp, I feel a bit like we're old friends."

I took a long sip of steaming coffee. "Funny, I don't share those same sentiments."

He removed his bowler hat and fumbled at the rim awkwardly. In the dingy light of this room, I noticed many more lines upon his pale face.

"Did you know, Miss Sharp, that many years ago I was a clockmaker?"

I watched the door. How long had it been since Christina and Laura left? Certainly a bit longer than fifteen minutes now. If they didn't return soon, I'd go looking for them.

"You should go, Inspector."

"Probably I should leave you alone. But I wanted to have a word with you first."

I glanced up sharply and peered at him in the dim room, stuffy now with pipe smoke.

"Clockmaking is such satisfying work. Sometimes I wonder why I never just stayed in that business. There's such an order to clockmaking: the balance wheel must be round, all of the gears must work properly. It's detailed work, *difficult* work in fact. But there is always a finished project."

I glanced at the front doors. Still no sign of Christina and Laura.

"I was working at the Metropolitan Police Station here in London when my first wife died, only a few weeks after we married. I channeled my grief into my work as I advanced through the police force. I married again, several years ago, and I solved most of my cases like I used to finish a clock. Solving a case became a need for me, like water. The Ripper case was the most perplexing case I'd seen. Now I have another criminal case on my hands. A...grand mess over on Cleveland Street."

"Why are you telling me all of this?"

He paused and looked away.

"This isn't actually about your investigations, is it?" I asked.

Still not looking at me, he shook his head. "My niece..." His voice cracked and he stared down at the stub of his finger. "She died this past weekend. Drowned. She was your age, Miss Sharp."

Abberline took out a handkerchief and wiped perspiration off of his face. "I've taken account of my life, and I find that I'm lacking. I have neglected my wife. I have often neglected the basic rules of kindness due to those around me. Strangely, I've thought of you." He paused. "I know you know more than you've told me about the Ripper murders."

"I'm not talking."

"I'm not asking you to talk. Rather, I'm making you an offer."

"I don't understand."

"I'm still an Inspector. I still want to solve my cases. But I'm *weary*, Miss Sharp. I'm middle-aged and I'm weary. The Ripper case will remain open, but I'm stepping away from it for now."

"Is this an apology?"

"Of sorts, and a confession. I simply want you to know that I will be of assistance if you need anything. But I will not bother you anymore. That is my offer."

"Thank you, Inspector," I muttered hesitantly.

He started to stand.

There was still no sign of Christina and Laura. Still, as long as I had him here, I thought I would see if he would make good on his offer.

"I have to go soon, but I want to ask you quickly if there have been more grave robberies."

He lowered his voice. "More than reported."

"How many?"

"Five in the past two weeks. And there have been more reported murders of vagrants and gravediggers. But the Queen's Secret Service Bureau has taken over dealing with them now. Scotland Yard is supposed to report everything to the Bureau and leak nothing to the public."

He stood up and put his bowler hat back on. "All in all, I

want you to know that you have my assistance if you need it, and I hope that you might eventually consider me a friend."

That seemed a bit far-fetched. Nonetheless, I thanked him and wished him well.

As I hurried out the front doors, very anxious now, I almost collided with Christina and a very happy Laura—two small roses tucked behind her ear.

Laura followed me around Whitechapel Hospital, helping me carry laundry away to wash or give medicine to patients. We always kept her near. The fourth surgery of the day, a hysterectomy, proved more difficult than usual, and the medical students who were supposed to assist Nurse Josephine that evening arrived late. We didn't get a chance to leave for Highgate until eight o'clock.

Located very close to the cemetery, Polidori's house was at the end of an abandoned stretch of row houses, ivy curling like gnarled fingers about every edge and chimney. Broken windows marred the front of many of the homes, and ravens nested abundantly throughout the chimneys. The night was quiet with very few carriages passing through the streets.

No light shone from any windows.

"Careful," Simon whispered as William unlocked Polidori's front door and we stepped inside. My bowie knife was in my boot, five throwing knives in my belt; both Simon and William had revolvers at their waists. We'd decided not to light our two torches unless necessary, so as not to attract attention.

A musty smell assaulted our noses as we stepped into the parlor. The house was seemingly unlived in—sheets covered the furniture, cobwebs draped from the ceiling.

"Upstairs first," Simon said.

As we followed Simon's tall figure up the stairs, Laura pulled at my sleeve and whispered, "Is this place haunted?"

"Let's hope not," William murmured lightly, behind us.

"No, it isn't," I said quickly. "There's no such thing as a haunted house." But Laura's eyes stayed on William.

The three bedrooms on the second floor were mostly empty, unfurnished except for basic wardrobes and beds. The bedcovers of two of the rooms were rumpled, and when Simon opened one of the wardrobes, three ornately designed smoking jackets hung within.

"This is very at odds with the rest of the house," I murmured.

"Indeed," Simon said quietly.

"I think we might have found Max's other lair," William said.

"Yes." Simon bit his lip. "But they don't seem to use it often."

We continued up the small staircase, which narrowed as it neared the third floor.

"This is quite different," William murmured as we opened the single door on this floor. This room was more furnished than the others, with a small desk and chairs. A decanter of brandy rested upon a tray on the desk. Faded green-and-burgundy-striped wallpaper covered the walls, heavy drapes covered the windows, and books, both new and old, lined the shelves. A pale green porcelain clock displaying the correct time rested upon the mantelpiece. A human skull grinned next to it.

Keeping Laura near us in the dark room, Simon and I browsed the bookcase as William peered through the drapes. Many of the books upon the shelves were anatomy books. Simon pulled one off the shelf and arched an eyebrow in the darkness. "Someone here was an admirer of Luigi Galvani."

I peered at the shelf, seeing at least five books about Galvani and his bioelectrical experiments.

"And also of black magic," I said as I found three books on the German occultist Heinrich Cornelius Agrippa. I pulled one from the shelf, opened it, and saw John Polidori's name neatly signed on the title page.

"What have you found?" William asked, turning away from the window.

"Only some books owned by your rather odd family," Simon murmured, gently taking the Agrippa one from me and flipping through its pages. Polidori's handwritten notes appeared in the margins of nearly every page.

"You forget that they're my family too," I remarked lightly.

"I *always* forget that," Simon said, smiling.

William, though, seemed to be only half listening to us as he explored the room, running his hand over the desk near a small inkwell and writing quill. "This must be some sort of study."

"But this can't be the only reason they keep this place— as a place to study and read," I murmured. "There *must* be more here."

Simon took one more look at a page and carefully closed the book. "I agree."

After descending the stairs again, we walked back through the dingy parlor into an unused, outdated small kitchen.

A large sturdy door stood at one side.

"For some reason, I don't think this leads to a regular cellar," William said as he took out the key ring.

When the key to the house didn't fit, William inserted the second key and turned the heavy lock. The door swung open, revealing a long flight of stairs. A slightly acidic and rancid odor wafted up to us.

Simon quickly lit the two torches, taking one and giving the other to William.

We started down the stairs, Simon and William in front, their revolvers out.

A snarling sound came from below.

"Get back!" William yelled, the torchlight swaying wildly.

I pushed Laura back up into the kitchen, tumbling over her. I tried to pull her up, expecting a great swarm of revenants to come up from the depths at any moment.

But as I spun around, Simon yelled from below, "Wait! Don't fire, William. It's caged."

I saw only the shifting light of their torches, heard what sounded like the lone snarl of a revenant.

"Stay here," I said to Laura, seating her on the top step. "Don't follow me downstairs or move away from here. I'll be back shortly."

She nodded. To my knowledge, she did not yet know of the existence of the revenants, and I didn't want her to see whatever was down there.

Hurrying down the steps, I found myself in an underground laboratory. It seemed rather like a darker version of the laboratory at Whitechapel Hospital.

As Simon held the torch in front of us, I saw the revenant behind the steel bars of a cage. A thick auburn beard flared out from the lower half of his face like a mane. His eyes blazed hungrily at us as he reached through the bars of the cage. He pressed his mouth through them, snapping his broken teeth at us. His gaze locked upon my throat.

I stepped away. Now, safely able to observe a live revenant, I felt fear, pity, and curiosity.

Two cages stood open and empty beside his.

Simon stepped as near to him as possible, just beyond the reach of the man's dirt-stained, grasping fingers. "I think that our assumptions might be correct. This seems to be the stage where they completely degenerate. He is nothing more than a beast now."

"It's cruel," I said, "how they keep them locked up like laboratory mice."

"I can't stand it," William said, lifting his fully cocked revolver.

"No!" Simon hissed. "It's too loud. We don't want to use them unless absolutely necessary."

"Stand back," I said. As both William and Simon stepped behind me, I threw the bowie knife hard between the bars, into the revenant's heart. Still snarling as he fell, he vaguely grabbed his chest, oily brown blood seeping from the wound. The snarls died down, and then he was silent.

After waiting to make certain that he was dead, I reached through the bars and pulled the knife from his chest.

"Sometimes you frighten me, Abbie," William said with a smirk as I wiped the blood off the blade with my skirts.

"Good," I said, grateful for his levity.

"Laura," William called, peering back up the stairs. We could see the soles of her boots. "Are you all right?"

"Aye."

William, Simon, and I walked about the room. Jars and jars lined the shelves with strange preserved jellyfish and odd creatures I'd never seen before. I stepped back and almost collided with a preserved chimpanzee's head floating in a large glass jar near me, its eyes milky white.

Simon waved the lamplight about a large dissection table in the middle of the room, and I shuddered. Steel clamps protruded from its sides.

"This looks rather more like a torture device," William said, staring at the clamps.

"In a sense, it is," Simon muttered, staring at the table.

This dissection table seemed more crude and not as clean as our dissection table at the hospital. It was stained with blood. I cringed, trying not to think of the experiments they conducted down here.

"Polidori—he's the physician, the scientist. He's likely the one who works down here most of the time," I muttered.

"Undoubtedly," Simon replied. "And it's conveniently close to the cemetery, where they could find specimens."

"Laura!" I called up the stairs. "We'll be up shortly."

No answer.

I walked closer to the stairs, and I couldn't see her boots.

"Laura!"

Quickly, I ran up the stairs, William and Simon close behind me.

When I reached the parlor, I saw the front door wide open; the cobblestone streets beyond were empty. "She's gone!"

Twenty-two

"She can't be far," William said as we ran out the front door into the night. Simon and William had their torches in their hands, revolvers still at their waists.

Swains Lane was empty. The only sounds were distant carriage wheels, a barking dog.

As we ran, I scanned the streets—they were heavily lined with large, knobby trees. A tall wrought-iron fence stretched beside us. White tombstones stood out behind it, ghostlike among the foliage.

"There!" Simon said, pointing ahead.

In the darkness, far down Swains Lane, I saw the figures of two little girls. I recognized Laura's dark brown hair even from this distance.

"Laura!" I called, but a sudden summer wind rushed hard at us, carrying away my voice.

"They're going through the entrance," William murmured.

"Which should be locked," Simon said, slowing his pace. He pulled out his revolver, kept the torch out in front of him.

"I can't believe the gates are unguarded after all of the murders," I hissed under my breath as we ran full-speed toward the gates, which were slightly ajar.

As he ran, Simon said, "Wyatt is low on men. There are six main cemeteries to guard. I'm not surprised by this. In fact, as all of the cemetery casualties have been resurrection men, I'm certain that Scotland Yard, or the monarchy for that matter, sees very little need to protect them."

Breathless by the time we reached the gate, I heard the giggling of girls inside the cemetery.

"She's in here," I hissed.

"Wait!" Simon whispered. With lightning speed, he extinguished the torches and placed them in the bag slung about his chest. "I'm certain there are revenants here, and we will be spotted immediately if we wander through this place with torches. We'll keep the revolvers out, but William, *do not* fire unless absolutely necessary. We certainly don't want the police arriving and bungling matters for us."

We stepped through the gate, near the main chapel, and scanned the area.

"That other child must be a revenant," I whispered, listening again but hearing nothing.

"I can almost guarantee it," William said, running ahead of me toward the stone steps leading up into the cemetery.

A small streak of moonlight poured down the steps.

"Careful, William," Simon said from behind us.

Once fully in the cemetery, we ran along the path, past two large tombs shaped like animals and into the curve ahead.

"Stop," I said, grabbing William's sleeve in the darkness.

Somewhere ahead of us, the laughter of little girls rang

out. But an eerie rustling sounded throughout the bushes around us, reminding me of that night this spring when I had pursued Mariah through this same cemetery.

Then I saw the girls, kneeling in a patch of pink foxgloves between two tombs. Their backs were turned to us, but I saw Laura pick one of the blossoms and hand it to the other child.

The other child, a bit younger than Laura, was not tattered like the revenant girl in the churchyard had been. Seemingly affluent, she was dressed like a doll. She wore a well-tailored, lacy, dark violet dress. Her black hair hung long down her back, tied with a large silk ribbon.

As we watched, her back stiffened, and then she turned. Moonlight struck her face, and I saw the feral gleam in her eyes. Suddenly she snarled, her little white teeth bared.

Laura screamed and fell back just as the little girl lunged at her, teeth aimed at her throat.

William pulled out his revolver.

"No!" I yelled, part of me horrified at shooting a little girl even if she was dead. But then her teeth locked at the base of Laura's neck and I leaped upon them both, prying her strong little body off.

At least ten revenants ran at us from the bushes.

Simon swiftly put away the revolver, pulled a knife from his waistband, and began slashing at the three men who advanced upon him.

William fired his revolver, blowing a hole in the abdomen of one of the revenant men, who promptly fell to the ground.

"William!" I shouted as four others advanced upon him, knocking his revolver into a thick patch of ivy. Quickly I tossed William one of my short-bladed knives.

But then three others—a girl of about thirteen, a woman with milky white eyes, and a man—turned toward Laura and me as I struggled with the little revenant girl. I covered Laura with my body and saw the wound bleeding just below her throat. The revenant girl, set upon her prey, lunged repeatedly at Laura, her teeth biting into my arm. Just before the male revenant fell upon me, I swiped at the child with the bowie knife, cutting her throat.

Thrusting her limp body away, I stood up and with a clumsier strike cut the revenant man's arm so that he fell back two steps.

I heard William cursing loudly in the background. Simon yelled out in pain.

Jerking Laura to her feet, I backed her against a large tomb behind me and faced the three undead. Simon swung and fought hard against two revenant men; a third lay dead, a large bleeding gunshot wound at his chest.

I snapped my eyes to William. He had killed one of the revenants, but the other three continued attacking.

I turned, acting quickly. With my free hand, I grabbed a short-bladed knife from my belt and threw it hard into the chest of the girl. As she fell to the ground, I pulled the knife from her and sliced the revenant man's throat.

Laura sobbed behind me, clutching at the bite wound in her neck. As I backed against her, I felt her fists grasping the folds of my skirt.

The woman with the milky eyes was stronger and more strategic, not quite as disintegrated as the others had been. She lunged at me and held my wrist in her cold grip so that

I dropped the throwing knife. I still had my bowie knife, but the woman pushed me and I lost my balance.

Laura screamed as I fell back against her, smashing her hard into the monument. Simon freed himself from his attackers and ran toward me as I struggled with the revenant woman.

"Laura! She's wounded!" I shouted at him, and with a burst of energy, I cut the revenant woman's throat.

Simon scooped Laura into his arms, his eyes on me. A bony revenant woman came at him from behind and I threw another knife at her, stabbing her in the neck. She fell back, and I heard her head strike a tree trunk with a sickening crunch.

"Laura's bleeding. We need to get her out!" I yelled to Simon, stabbing his last attacker just as William slammed one revenant's head against a rock. The body slumped to the ground. William's shirt was torn, a long scratch cut across his neck. William must have lost my knife in the struggle, but he fought well.

Laura's sobbing eased off as she went limp in Simon's arms. Simon lifted her wrist and felt her pulse.

"She's fine," he said breathlessly. "The wound missed her carotid artery. But we need to get her to the hospital *now*. She's losing too much blood."

I rushed in and stabbed one of William's attackers while he broke the neck of the last revenant.

Within seconds, we heard more raspy breaths and saw seven more white figures crashing toward us from the darkness beyond.

"Dear God," I murmured. "We can't fight all of them now. Run!" I hissed to Simon. "William and I will give them chase in the other direction. Get her out now."

"No," William said. "*I'll* give them chase. You're leaving with Simon."

"No! I'm not leaving you," I snapped.

I had never seen Simon look desperate and indecisive. But now he stood frozen, his ice-blue eyes locked onto mine.

"Go!" I hissed. "We'll lead them away. She'll *die* if you don't get her out now."

Still, he hesitated.

"I'll return for you later," he said quickly. Then, taking the revolver from his waist, he tossed it to William and turned and ran at lighting speed, back toward the entrance.

But we were too late. We had hesitated for too long. As William ran with me down another path, toward another part of the cemetery, only half of the group chased us. The others ran after Simon.

"He's unarmed!" I yelled.

"We can't help that now. Simon's fast. And I'm pretty certain God's on his side," William said breathlessly, flashing me a half-smile as we crashed through foliage, narrowly missing running into gravestones.

I clenched my bowie knife, pulled along by William. He veered us off the main paths, through tiny trails between plots; the crinoline under my skirts weighed me down, and I stumbled twice. William pulled me to my feet within seconds. I remembered that day I had collided with him as he tended to Elizabeth Siddal's grave, and even here, in this place, I felt warmed. He knew this cemetery well, and I trusted him.

As we ran, twisting in and out around mausoleums, at some point we lost our pursuers.

We stopped to catch our breath near the front of an enormous mausoleum that had lion's head door knockers bolted to its front doors.

All was silent about us.

"I can get us to the entrance," William said quickly.

I nodded.

He grabbed my hand, and we continued running at a breakneck pace until we reached the stone arch that framed the stairs descending toward the large entrance gates. Hearing the shuffled heavy breathing of the undead, we peered down toward the chapel, where six of the undead crouched near the closed gates, grasping through it.

I saw Simon just beyond the gates, running fast with Laura in his arms down Swains Lane.

"He's eluded them," I whispered with great relief. "It must have been a very close call."

"Unfortunately, he had to shut the gates to get away. He must not know that they lock automatically," William grumbled, running his hands through his hair as he looked about us. "Now *we* need to find a way out of here."

So far, the revenants at the gate had their focus upon Simon. Many of them were still reaching through the bars, staring in the direction Simon had gone.

Someone jerked me up by my hair; my neck twisted painfully and I stifled a cry. A white-faced revenant man, completely disintegrated, tried to bite my neck. I grabbed the bowie knife from my belt just as William threw him to the ground. William punched him three times hard in the face until he lay still, either dead or unconscious.

"So much for hiding," I murmured, pulling William up by his arm.

In my peripheral vision, I could already see the others running up the stone steps behind us.

I grabbed William's hand, my other hand hard on my knife, and we ran along the rough cemetery paths, avoiding sagging tree branches in the darkness. We were both exhausted. I tripped and fell hard, hitting my head against the sharp side of a large white tombstone. Hot pain seared through my head; I was dizzy and saw stars. Warm blood seeped down my face, but William jerked me up and pulled me along behind him.

Glancing behind us as we ran, my head still spinning, I heard the sounds of the others coming, their low snarls, their footsteps. One of them, a barefoot young man with torn clothing, was within sight of us.

William pulled out his revolver and tried to fire, twice, but both times the gun misfired.

"Damn!" he shouted, dropping it on the ground.

"Leave it!"

We continued running.

"This way. We might hide in here," William whispered, pulling me sharply to one side.

We ran through drafty, dark Egyptian Avenue, a light wind sweeping downward against us, soothing my bleeding temple wound a bit. When we reached its end, William jerked me hard right into the Circle of Lebanon and pushed our bodies into the corridor's shadows. We both were breathing hard, and perspiration ran down William's flushed face.

The wind blew stronger now, sweeping through the mausoleum-lined corridor. The leaves of the giant Cedar of Lebanon tree loomed above us, rattling violently.

We heard the crowd of revenants go by, running past us at the Egyptian Avenue entrance.

But then, as I sighed in relief, a raspy, wheezing sound started and William peeked around the corner.

"He's coming!" he hissed. "But we can't keep running. I think we should hide until this one passes and then work our way back to the entrance."

We heard the young revenant man's footsteps in the corridor now, slow at first and then faster as he began running clumsily toward us.

Desperately, William and I ran up the row, pulling at the doors of the mausoleums. I finally found an unlatched one. The heavy door stuck as I pulled it, so I pulled harder, feeling as if my fingers would break.

"It's too late!" I said, still trying the door.

The man had already rounded the corner; his teeth bared as he snarled loudly and ran toward us. I heard the crowd of undead in the distance.

"The others are coming back!" I hissed.

William punched the revenant just as I burst the door open. The man fell hard, into the mausoleum.

We heard the others at the entrance to Egyptian Avenue and darted inside the tomb. William tried to roll the revenant's body out.

"There isn't time, William. Shut the door, *now*."

William silently and firmly popped the door into place just as the revenant man started to stand. In a single movement, I cut the man's throat. He slumped heavily against the closed door, and then down to the floor.

I staggered back, my heart pounding in my chest. Only

then did I notice that my dress sleeve had been torn all the way up my arm. The wound at my temple throbbed.

The shuffle of footsteps sounded outside, the snarls and growls of the other revenants as they passed by. But all was dark inside, and the door was shut. William and I stood absolutely still, waiting.

"Is the door latched?" he whispered.

"I believe so, but I don't think we should test it yet. I don't want to rattle it if any of them are still in the corridor."

William fumbled in the darkness and lit a match. The flame lit up the small room eerily. We both looked as if we had been in battle—William was dirt-streaked and the scratch on his chin bled a little. He crouched down by the revenant man's body at our feet, the oily brown blood dripping from its neck wound.

I pulled my arms around my chest, feeling somewhat indecent about my exposed arm, and made futile attempts to hold the torn material together. I shivered. The temperature felt so much cooler in here than outdoors. The smell of decay and rot lingered in the air.

"It's unbelievable that even though the coffins are enclosed in cement, these rooms still smell as they do," I muttered.

"Good God, Abbie, your temple."

"It's nothing." Although now that I had stopped running, the pain intensified. I touched my temple and felt wet sticky blood on my fingertips.

Still holding the match, with his other hand William pulled out a handkerchief. Stepping forward, he dabbed it lightly on the wound. His face was close to mine, and the pain of the wound faded even as he gently rubbed away the drying blood. He moved the handkerchief down near my right eye, then onto my cheek. The goose bumps on my exposed arm disappeared, and I felt pleasantly warmed even in this place of death.

He met my eyes, inches from my face in the darkness, and smiled a little.

Nervously, I took the handkerchief from his hand and stepped away, dabbing the wound myself while clutching again at my torn sleeve.

Still smiling but taking the hint, William lit another match and waved it about us. The room was no more than ten feet deep, with shelves lined with coffins like dusty books in the bowels of a library. But the coffin near the back wall appeared to be new. A small bouquet of calla lilies rested upon the floor near it. We peered through the little cut-away window to see the decorative velvet enshrouding the coffin.

"These little windows, for the family to see the coffin, are rather silly and morbid, don't you think, Abbie?" William asked.

"Quite. Why would someone want to dress a coffin up like a present?"

"Yes," William agreed. He stared at me. I saw a streak of dried blood through his torn shirt, but I felt too shy to acknowledge it. In the flickering light, his dark eyes bore into me.

My hand trembling a bit, I pulled the handkerchief away from my temple and nervously fumbled with the stained material.

"Abbie..." William said suddenly. The match burned down; he lit another and leaned against the wall. "Do you think that I'm good for you?"

"What do you mean?"

"It's a straightforward question. Do you think that I'm good for you?"

I couldn't answer. I wanted him, I loved him—but this was a question I'd skirted around, never addressing head-on.

He stared down at the floor, pushing his boot through a thin coat of dust. "When I was kidnapped this spring, you and Simon got along perfectly well together. Yes, of course, I despise him utterly. But to tell the truth, he is a better man than I. He would be better for you, Abbie. You deserve better. I'm a lost soul." William chuckled. "We're not even certain who my father is..." His voice drained away.

This was something we had not yet discussed.

"I think *I* should determine who's good for me," I said briskly. My irritation was unfair, but I resented William for trying to make me answer this question. Grandmother had told me in her letter to love Simon. Even now, my own good sense sat on my shoulder like a rosy cherub advising me to abandon my reckless love for William.

The match flickered out, and we stood in complete darkness.

"Perhaps if we can't see each other, we might be more honest," he said.

Dear God.

"Why do you love me?"

I paused, then after a moment said, "I don't know. Perhaps you aren't good for me. You might wound me deeper than anyone else in the world, and I still couldn't let you go. It's ridiculous, really. It's like..." I chuckled; it seemed so sentimental, so silly, but the complete darkness did somehow make this honesty easier. "It's like you're a part of my blood."

"That's because we might be related," William muttered wryly.

I shook my head. "*Not* as brother and sister. It would be more distant."

"Perhaps."

Why did I love him?

"We should probably try to slip out of here," I said after a moment. "I'm certain they're gone now."

I walked toward the door in the darkness, carefully sliding my feet along the floor so as not to trip over the dead revenant. I leaned against the door and put my ear to the cold stone.

Why did I love William?

My memory of first meeting William flashed through my mind like a photograph. When he'd stepped behind the delivery curtain at Whitechapel Hospital, his presence had jolted me as never before in my life. He had been so rude, so overly flustered by the delivery. He'd run his hands through his dark curls, as he did now. He had terrible control of his emotions, of his appetites, and yet, these past weeks, he had tried to conquer his sanguinity as never before. Something stirred within me, always and persistently, whenever I was with him. If we were related, perhaps our shared blood pulled us close like a magnetic pull.

Leaning into the door now, I rested my whole cheek upon it. I moved my hand down slowly to the latch. "I don't hear anything," I whispered. "It should be safe to leave."

"You haven't answered my question," he said softly.

With my face against the door, I confessed. "Quite simply, it's like I told you in the Orkney Isles. I cannot *not* love you. That's my most honest answer and I'll say it hundreds or *thousands* of times until you finally believe me."

I turned the latch and pushed at the door.

It didn't budge.

I tried again.

Then William was immediately behind me. I felt the warmth of his chest on my back. He reached around me, his arms encircling me.

The situation here, inside the tomb, was becoming more dangerous by the minute.

He rattled the door a bit. Chuckled. I felt his breath on the back of my neck. "It appears that we're locked in."

I didn't respond, just leaned my whole forehead against the door.

"If you cannot *not* love me—if I'm a need to you, like water—then perhaps the matter is settled."

I remained facing the door. Afraid of him, but more afraid of myself. If I should turn around, face him ... then, well, I would be far too close. It would be like thrusting my hand into a fire.

"Yes, William. The matter is settled. I love you in spite of good sense."

He kissed the back of my neck. "Then please, let's not be sensible right now."

I should run; I should put as much space as possible between William and myself. I remembered a line from *Alice's Adventures in Wonderland*: *"She generally gave herself very good advice (though she very seldom followed it)."*

"Abbie." William kissed the back of my neck again and I closed my eyes, shivering with pleasure.

He kissed my earlobe.

I had kissed William many times before, but here, trapped in this place, all rules might break.

I turned to face him, feeling more than seeing his face in the darkness. I reached up and felt his curls with my hand, his sandpaper jawline. I wondered if he could see me smiling. I would choose this any time over good sense. I felt him hesitate for a second, and then he kissed me passionately, pressing me up into the mausoleum door.

We were enclosed in this place, cocooned with the dead. The only sound was our breathing, the rustling of my skirts as he crushed against me. He groaned softly, deepening the kiss. His hands traveled up my back, along the buttons of my dress. His mouth left mine, traveling feather-light up my jaw, and he lightly kissed my cheek, my ear, and then my wound.

I clutched him to me as we kissed, and we slid awkwardly down the stone door's rough surface. I felt a few buttons tear off, heard the fabric of my dress grind against the rough stone; the sleeve of my dress tore further up my shoulder, and yet I did not care.

Vaguely, I thought that I should stand, to make our situation more proper. But I did not have such willpower, so instead I remained against the wall as he knelt before me, kissing me. As he leaned into me, I slid sideways and bumped against the dead revenant slumped nearby in the darkness.

I giggled at the absurdity of the situation.

"This won't work," William murmured against my lips, smiling.

Quickly he pulled away, removing his torn shirt.

"What are you—"

"Shhh..." he hushed me as I started to stand.

Before I could care about propriety again, William lifted me gently, lightly, away from the door and laid me down on the floor, his shirt like a small blanket underneath us, blocking the dust a little. He lay beside me, propping himself up on one elbow and lightly stroking my face.

Then his hand wandered from my face, lightly down the side of my body. I pulled his face down, kissing him, feeling the scrapes and cuts from tonight upon his bare chest. He groaned and rolled a bit on top of me, propping his weight up on his arms. He kissed my face, my neck.

He touched the bare skin of my exposed arm and I shivered. His fingers ran lightly upon the hardened scar from Seraphina. I didn't stop him as he ran his finger along the curved top of the scar, then traced it slowly down from my shoulder to the top of my breast. He paused, caressing the long scar lightly as if it weren't rough but the softest, fleshiest part of my palm, or the curve of my neck.

Transported, I arched up against him, deepening the kiss. He pulled the pins out of my hair and it fell around me like a pillow. The heat inside of me became a small fire, and suddenly my fear returned as I thought of the consequences. I was past caring about blemishes to my virtue—rather, I had too many memories of all of those women, my age and younger, on delivery tables at Whitechapel Hospital and at New Hospital. My unexpected arrival had impoverished and complicated Mother's life more than it had been already.

William sensed my tension and pulled away a bit. "I'll never leave, Abbie. I'll always love you."

"I believe you." This was the truth. William might not always be "good" for me, but my worries about his constancy had vanished by now. Still, whatever unfolded tonight, even if William remained with me, *I* would be the one to shoulder the consequences.

As if reading my mind, William rolled off of me and chuckled; he ran his fingers through his hair. "This is precisely why you shouldn't be with me."

"This is why I *want* to be with you. But tonight...well..."

"Yes, yes..." he murmured, in light bitterness. Playfully, he leaned over me again and coiled one of my hairs around his finger. "Speaking of not going away, have you noticed that we've been circling one another like stars around a planet our whole lives?"

I smiled. Even on this cold dusty floor, I felt happy, languid. "My mother was your father's lover; you and I collided in Whitechapel. The man who adopted you is my father. Now here we are, and it seems that you're as tied to this Conclave matter as I am."

"My point is..." William kissed my forehead lightly as he continued weaving my hair in his fingers. "It seems as if you will continue to fall into my wayward path, so perhaps you should fall into it permanently."

I tried to focus on his face in the mausoleum darkness, my heart pounding, elated. "Are you asking me, *here*, to marry you?"

"Yes, I am in fact." He chuckled. "I didn't think you were the sentimental type."

"No, not sentimental." I smiled, happily thinking of a lifetime ahead with William—if we ever escaped this Conclave mess.

"You haven't answered me yet."

"Yes," I said quickly. "But not tomorrow, of course. Certainly, though, after the Conclave is behind us... and then there's medical school."

"Of course... of course..." William said. "I just wanted to secure your promise here."

"You have it." I pulled his face to me again, kissed him. "I'm quite happy."

We lay peacefully in each other's arms. We talked about our childhoods, similar in their eccentricities and abundances of art. The engagement created a new intimacy between us, and more barriers of propriety slipped away. William laughed heartily as he told me about walking in upon his father making love to a model in his studio. He had been twelve at the time. I told him how Mother would sometimes have a vision and then paint all night until dawn. I told him how she often looked desperately lonely.

At some point, after talking for so long among the dead, we fell asleep.

A deafening jolt sounded throughout the mausoleum. Blinding light burst in upon us as we lay on the floor, me asleep on William's bare chest.

I sat up, startled. Facing the blinding light, I felt about the floor for my bowie knife. Grabbing it, I cursed as I realized that I'd lost the throwing knives during the chase last night.

Just outside the mausoleum door, in the early morning light, Max, Byron, and Polidori stood staring down at us. The revenant's corpse had fallen backward at their feet, its dull milky eyes facing up toward the sun.

"Well, *this* is a sight," Max said, staring at William and me in cold amusement as we scrambled to our feet. I quickly tried to clutch the torn top of my dress about me, feeling humiliation amid my fear.

Byron looked stunningly handsome in a well-cut jacket and trousers. He smiled widely. "What is this? A love nest with a corpse."

"Yes," Polidori cooed, taking out a handkerchief to cover his nose against the dead man's odor. "This seems to push the limits even for *you*, Byron."

Byron laughed, still watching William and me.

Max stared hard at William. "Abbie, how often have I told you that your taste in men is deplorable?"

"What do you want?" William demanded, pushing me behind him protectively. His eyes were locked upon Polidori.

Then, before I could react, William snatched the bowie knife from my hand and lunged out of the mausoleum toward Polidori.

"William, *don't*!"

William and his damn temper. We were outnumbered, and this could end badly.

Max and Byron merely stepped aside for William, nasty smirks on both of their faces.

William pushed Polidori against the stone wall of a nearby mausoleum, the knife pressed into his throat just above his silk cravat knot. I lunged forward to stop him, but Max grabbed my arms and held me tightly.

Although the air around us was slightly chilled, bands of sunlight spread throughout the Circle of Lebanon corridor and I could clearly see the uncanny resemblance between Polidori and William. They might have been twin brothers.

Polidori smiled brilliantly over the blade of William's knife, unafraid. William trembled with a bewildering rage.

I fought against Max as he held me, but I couldn't free myself from his grip. Calmly, he brushed my loose hair away from my ear and whispered, "Temper, Abbie. Let this one play out."

William pressed the knife harder into Polidori's throat. His hand shook upon the knife handle and perspiration dripped from his forehead, running down his cheek.

"William," I hissed through clenched teeth, keeping my eyes upon him.

Byron pulled his pocket watch out, clicked it open to check the time, and then sighed loudly before returning it to his pocket.

"*William...*" I hissed again.

He paid me no heed.

Once again, I tried to pull away from Max, but he only held me closer to him, my back against his hard chest. I shuddered as he brushed my hair aside again and kissed the dried blood at my temple. "Did one of my pets wound you, love?"

I elbowed him sharply and he responded with a low chuckle.

Polidori, still smirking at William, slid his eyes downward to the curved knife blade. "I don't think you want to do that."

I saw the glint of a knife blade in Max's hand, near my waist. Whatever link William had with Polidori, I sensed that Max didn't share it.

"Careful, William," I muttered again under my breath.

Only then did I see Byron standing nearby with a bottle and a wet cloth.

"Watch out, William!"

But Byron had already slipped the chloroform-doused cloth over William's mouth and nose. Polidori whipped the knife from William's hand and swung him about hard, so that William stumbled forward onto his knees. Polidori held him in a vise-grip while Byron continued to press the cloth on William's face until he slumped forward, unconscious.

"No!" I yelled, kicking back against Max. "What are you *doing?*"

"Sorry, love," Max said from behind me as he placed a wet cloth over my own mouth and nose. I tried to fight him, but my world quickly spun about me.

Then all was darkness.

Twenty-three

As I awoke, a splitting headache began. My vision blurry, I blinked away film from my eyes. I had a lingering sickly sweet taste in my mouth from the chloroform. The headache spread, and my stomach reeled.

I was going to vomit.

A washbasin. I needed a washbasin.

Or I should run outside. But I couldn't move. My arms, my legs, wouldn't work.

My vision came into focus and I realized that a rope had been tied around my hands, ankles, and waist, restraining me to a chair.

We were in that upstairs study at Polidori's house. The door was shut, the drapes pulled with only a small amount of light working through the cracks. As my eyes adjusted, I saw William tied up in a chair beside me, his head flopped forward, still unconscious. A tiny stream of light rested on the half-empty decanter and brandy glasses nearby; the clock on the fireplace mantle ticked away, showing that it was nearly six o'clock. Although whether it was morning or evening, I couldn't tell.

My stomach churned again. Before I could stop it, I vomited, my stomach contents falling onto the faded carpet in a large puddle.

I heard a door swing open heavily, far below. Some murmured voices. Then heavy footsteps on the staircase.

My stomach relaxed, but I felt weak and dizzy.

William's eyelashes fluttered. His finger twitched.

Suddenly the door swung open. Max entered with a tea towel in his hand, which he snapped hard against William's face to wake him. Max looked as if he had been working outside. His shirt was unbuttoned, dried mud splatters specked his boots, and perspiration dripped down his face.

William's eyes blinked open just as a red welt spread rapidly across his cheek.

Max knelt in front of me. He smelled of wet grass and mud.

"Untie us," I demanded.

He only met my eyes and smiled, his green eyes glowing. Gently he wiped vomit off my lips and chin. I shuddered as he wiped the stains off of my chest; the top of my dress was torn so severely that my corset was exposed. Finally, he slid his hand away and sopped up the bit of vomit from the floor.

Polidori and Byron stepped into the study. Byron poured himself a glass of brandy from the decanter and leaned against the fireplace, watching me with his green eyes. His hazelnut curls, manner of dress, and finely chiseled features made him undeniably alluring. I saw now how he had been able to seduce women throughout England and abroad.

Max sat down on a chair at my far right, but I felt his eyes upon me. I heard the strike of a match and smelled the scent of his cigar.

I tried to put together pieces in my still-swirling head as memories of last night and this morning came flooding back to me.

"Where have you been?" I demanded, turning to meet Max's gaze.

"Taking care of some matters."

Polidori and Byron chuckled simultaneously.

"Bastards!" William yelled suddenly, pulling hard at his restraints. His chair rocked dangerously. "Untie us now!"

"No," Byron said, draining his brandy and pouring another one. He snickered as he stared at me, his eyes sweeping about my loose hair, stained skirts, torn dress. "I'm still having difficulty seeing precisely what you see in her, Max."

I glared back at him.

William swore a streak as he continued struggling against the ropes that bound him. I shot him a look and he settled a bit. Still, his expression remained incensed.

Max chuckled and blew a cloud of smoke about him. "You never met her mother."

I glanced at him, but Max cut his gaze to the men. "Our young Abbie will be brilliant under the elixir's influence. She will shine like me, and prove quite useful for us."

Polidori stepped forward and lightly touched a lock of my hair. He coiled it about his finger as I tried to pull my head away.

"Leave her alone," William growled.

"No," Polidori muttered, keeping his hand tangled in

my hair and casting an amused expression at William—as if he were nothing more than an angry puppy. Then he stared down at me again and turned to Max, sighing loudly. "I don't understand, Bartlett. Why don't we try it *now*? It would be so easy. Just force it down her—"

"No. I've told you," Max said. "It won't work that way. We must have her *will* or she will be useless to us."

Byron spoke up loudly. "I'm rather in agreement with John. I don't see why—"

"I'm not against heavy coercion, blackmail, or murder," Max said. He glared at me as he tossed his cigar stub, still smoking, into the nearby ashtray. "But even I have my limits. We must not only have her. She must *want* to join us."

Byron started to retort, but Max gruffly cut him off. "Surely, Byron, you of all people know about women and wills."

Before Byron could argue, Polidori's expression brightened, a ripple across a pond surface. He removed his hand from my hair and waved his fingers dismissively at Byron. "Yes. *Yes.* Of course, we must have her willfully."

He stepped back, turning his attention to William. My mind spun as I tried to figure everything out as it happened.

Polidori glanced at me curiously, as if I were some sort of specimen. "Women and their wills are important in these matters. We all remember how badly matters went, Max, when your mistress went feral in Orkney."

Byron chuckled. "She sounded like a spicy one. I wish I'd had a turn with her."

William couldn't contain his rage a moment longer. "What *is* this game you bastards are playing at?"

Polidori stepped back and poured a glass of brandy. Taking a sip, he leaned against the desk. "Bastards?" he repeated, his tone mild. He took another long sip and smiled. "Such disrespect, dear boy, for your *father*."

William's face paled. For a few moments there was only the ticking clock.

"I'm not your bloody son."

"Ah! But you are!" Polidori exclaimed gleefully, his dark brown eyes shining. He set the half-empty glass on the desk. "And it's time we spent some time together, *son*. But you've seemed so ... *angry* lately. Trying to dig up my empty grave, attacking me with a knife." Polidori shrugged and threw his hands up in the air. "Poisoning you with chloroform and tying you up here was the only way to make you hear me out."

Byron chuckled.

Max remained absolutely still.

It seemed too cruel for William to learn this here. I shuddered, watching him carefully.

"How can I possibly be your son?" William snapped.

Polidori laughed hard, throwing his head back. I began to wonder if he was sane. "Oh yes, we've never had *that* talk. Suffice it to say that your mother was smitten with me."

"My *mother*?"

"Yes, an adorable little Austrian actress."

"Wise choice of a mistress," Byron muttered, taking a long sip of brandy. "Those French ones, they're *never* faithful."

"But it wasn't a *woman* I wanted. There are many of those to be had," Polidori continued. "And during the past decades, no woman could ever know my real name, of course.

But after forty years as an immortal, I became slightly bored. I thought a child to take along with me would be interesting."

"And my mother?" William growled.

Polidori sighed and leaned upon a nearby desk, pouring himself another brandy. "When I took you and left, she killed herself with prussic acid. You were raised by a series of nurses. But I found it quite cumbersome traveling with a small child and silly middle-aged women, constantly hiding my studies and experiments from them. You belonged with family."

"So you abandoned me in London near the Rossetti house," William said flatly.

"Yes. I left you with my grand-nephew." He chuckled. "And thus my poor, *troubled* grand-nephew raised his own distant cousin. It's better than a novel." He smirked into his glass.

William's hands trembled as he stared hard at Polidori, visibly shaken by this news.

I pitied him, but I couldn't let William lose his temper before I had certain questions answered. Choosing my words carefully, I asked, "Might we go back a bit? I'm assuming that you both took the elixir. I would like to know when and how." I glared at Max. "*Someone* here told me, Polidori, that he killed you because you'd discovered Dr. Buck's notes and learned about the existence of the elixir."

Polidori's eyes gleamed. He looked from Byron to Max and drained his brandy glass.

Max's deep voice echoed in the small study. "A few decades after I became part of the Conclave, I began to feel a bit like a—"

"Gamekeeper?" William spit out.

Max stared icily at him. Yet again, I wished William would be quiet. If Max intended to make me his immortal mistress, William would, for obvious reasons, be in the way.

Max stretched his heavy, mud-stained boots out in front of him. "I believed in the causes of the Conclave; I murdered for them, managed their projects and animals. But I wanted more. I thought it couldn't hurt to have a few projects of my own going on. In 1821, when I was sent to assassinate Polidori for discovering Dr. Buck's research, I found him too interesting to kill. He had scientific knowledge that I did not. So, Polidori—and then a few years later, his friend Lord Byron—"

"Who did *not* die on the way to fight in the Greek Revolution," Byron said, flashing a roguish smile. He opened a cigarette case and took out a cigarette, then offered another one to Polidori.

"Why did you need *him*?" I asked. "He's not a scientist; he's a poet."

Byron glared at me, but Polidori shrugged. Inhaling from the cigarette, he continued lightly. "Science can be learned, and I needed a partner in my studies, of course. A partner with a sturdy soul, exceeding amounts of curiosity, and freedom from tedious morality."

"So both Polidori and then Byron took the elixir," Max said. "I was curious to see what projects Polidori would pursue on his own, so I smuggled the elixir to him, as well as copies of the Conclave's research notes. This proved difficult at times, as I was extraordinarily busy with their projects."

"Yes, your schedule was chock-full with murdering whores, wasn't it?" William spat out.

"Watch your mouth, Siddal," Max muttered through clenched teeth. "You're certainly not here because *I* want—"

"Careful," Polidori murmured lightly under his breath, tapping his cigarette gently against an ashtray.

I watched, trying to figure out the dynamics among the three men.

"We worked from the Continent," Polidori continued. "Then, more recently, in London under different names. We worked together to evolve the elixir."

"But what about the papers that *you* wrote?" I asked him. "The papers that you sent to the family's French solicitor in Avignon? William found those papers."

Although Christina knew of the papers, I was careful not to mention her name.

"Of course, I wanted my son to join me when he was of age," Polidori replied. "I didn't place my papers in the Avignon safe until after your birth, William. They were my way of ensuring that you would be prepared, that you would know a bit about my history before I sought you out. The papers were sealed, only to be opened by you when you reached the age of twenty-three. And it worked brilliantly, as I am to understand that you indeed found them."

I breathed a sigh of relief and hoped that William wouldn't say anything foolish. It didn't appear as if Polidori knew that Dante Gabriel Rossetti had discovered his papers first and shared the information with his sister. Christina would be safe.

"Our experiments went on for decades," Lord Byron said. "In fact, Bartlett here was becoming bored with them."

Max smiled. "So I carried out the East End project with more flourish than Julian had hoped for."

"So you did." Byron shook his head and exhaled a long stream of smoke. "That mailing of the kidney to the police was a bit much." Then he resumed the narration. "Although we finally discovered a new formula that would regenerate dead tissue and raise an animal from the dead, we had more trouble reviving *people*. Our first successful case was last summer. Remember that night in the Alps when it finally happened?"

Polidori smiled fondly. "I was ecstatic. We'd been missing a vital protein. After all those decades of experimentation, Max brought us a soil extract that Buck had brought back from the Easter Islands. Of course, we had more work to do to perfect the formula, but that addition to the elixir was our breakthrough. Our very first revenant was around for two days before expiring."

Although horrified, I was equally intrigued by the scientific process. "Only two days? What was wrong with the formula?"

Max's eyes gleamed bright as a glowing ember at my question. He was still hoping I might want to join them.

Polidori paced a bit. "After we altered the elixir to revive dead cells, the formula's effects would not last as long as we'd hoped. I've improved it, but so far I've been unable to perfect it."

I thought of that brain in the corpse, of how Simon had noticed that the brain slices seemed to degenerate. I glanced sideways at William, but his expression was stony, unreadable.

"There are good and bad consequences of the formula," Polidori added quickly.

"The good consequence," Byron said, "is that when the patient is revived, which must be within twenty-four hours after death, the corpse completely imprints upon us. He or *she* will do whatever we want. The other, somewhat fortunate consequence is that the creature craves blood, making it dangerous to everyone else."

"We speculate," Polidori said, "that this has something to do with the quick decomposition of the frontal lobe. The revenants are thus revived in their original primitive, predatory states, their only 'moral reasoning' being to eat and to obey us. What is 'right' for them is simply what we tell them to do."

I remembered Simon's conversation with me about the ambiguity of death. I thought of how Mariah had stood before me—herself, yet so far from her old living self. She had wanted to rip my throat out, and she had cowered to Max upon his arrival.

"Unfortunately," Polidori continued, "the patient eventually degenerates into a non-reasoning predatory state, losing *all* ability of speech, restraint, or reason. It is at this point when they become useless to us."

"What do you do when they are no longer of use to you?" I demanded.

Polidori smiled. "Why, my dear, we kill them. A blow to the head is most efficient. Or we cut their throats. It's much quieter if we have to kill and bury several in one of the cemeteries at once."

William chuckled bitterly. "You're insane."

"Is that what you did to her? To *Mariah*?" I demanded, straining against the ropes.

Max's mouth curved into a smile. "Your friend. I enjoyed her company very much before her ... untimely death."

I remembered how Mariah was infatuated with Max before her death, how she had known him merely as "Charles."

"She wanted to be a writer ... " I said quickly, tears in my eyes.

"Indeed," Max said. "While most of those we've revived have been indigents taken from common graves—alcoholics, prostitutes, those who nobody would miss—last autumn we became interested in the effects that the formula might have on the body of an independent, well-educated woman. When we revived her soon after her burial, she was everything I had hoped for. Intriguingly, she lasted much longer than the others. Most of our undead are of use to us for only a few weeks, a month at the most, but her mind fought degeneration. She was with us for six months."

"And what a wonderful six months it was. Why, I never thought that a revenant—" Byron began.

"You killed her!" I shouted at Max. "You *killed* Mariah that night in the attic just so you could experiment upon her!"

"Of course we did," Polidori said. "And she was our most delightful revenant of all."

"After that," Max said, "we began experimenting on more professional, educated Londoners."

"And *children*," I said icily.

"Children have their purposes," Max uttered, his eyes locked upon mine.

Thinking of Laura, I panicked and took the conversation in a different direction. "So ... " I tried to keep my voice controlled. "You dig up bodies to create these revenants. When they start to degenerate, you shoot them in the head." I looked at the mud stains on Max's boots. "That's where you've been, isn't it? You've murdered and buried those revenants from last night."

"That's *one* place I've been today," Max said cryptically. "Their time was up. But your arrival here has provided a frightful diversion."

"What are you talking about?" William asked.

Polidori smiled. "We have ways, through the underground, of reaching most areas we wish, particularly cemeteries. We had to cull seventeen undead last night, which is why I had them in the cemetery. When George here"—he nodded to Byron— "saw you breaking into my house, Max thought we might have a bit of fun. So we lured your friend there via the little girl revenant. I was assured, Abbie, that you are a good fighter, and I have to say, even from a distance, I was quite impressed."

Byron snorted. "Of course, we lost track of you when we unleashed the second group upon you, but Max here is good at tracking. He located you this morning after we'd culled all of them."

"You're all lunatics," William exclaimed suddenly. "These revenants—creating them, having them do your bidding, keeping track of them, and then killing them—it seems like far too much trouble. What is your purpose in doing all of this?"

Max uncrossed his legs and stood. "Clearly, Siddal, you haven't inherited your father's intelligence."

Byron flicked open his pocket watch and glanced at the time. Polidori's mouth curved into a smile.

"I had powers that Julian, Marcus, John, and Robert never could attain," Max said. "This was quite galling to me, as I always had to do their bidding. They"—he nodded toward Byron and Polidori—"represented my hope to break away, to cut out with my own Conclave."

"Where even the 'greater good' would no longer be a factor," William growled.

"Precisely," Polidori remarked glibly, smashing his cigarette into the ashtray. "It's only about power at this point."

Lord Byron exclaimed giddily, "We're an immortal establishment with a revenant army to do our bidding. Do you realize what we might *do*?"

I thought of how the monarchy had trodden lightly in their relationship with the Conclave, and of the Secret Service Bureau's handling of Case X. Public knowledge of an elite group with immortal powers—one member of which also had frightening mental and physical powers—could uproot the entire structure of the nation. My mind scrambled to wrap itself around the many possible chaotic outcomes that would occur if this *new* Conclave's existence became known, if Polidori, Byron, and Max multiplied their revenants to terrorize London. I remembered how the Ripper had struck such fear in the Whitechapel district that it had incited a mob. The stakes here were much higher.

"I had considered many options throughout the years," Max said. "I had considered leaving the Conclave, going out on my own. I had considered demanding that the Conclave evolve a bit, to elevate my position and include Polidori and Byron. But I had not yet decided how to proceed. I stayed with the Conclave as they began entertaining your mother, Abbie. Then, when we discovered your psychic abilities—that you were like me—it complicated my own project further."

His eyes gleamed at me. "Fortunately, although the little fire that you started at the Montgomery Street house destroyed valuable information I needed to continue making the formula, I found what we needed in the Conclave notes in Orkney. In the end, you actually performed a great service for me. It was the open door that I needed to continue with my project."

"So why are you holding us both here?" I demanded. "You already know that I will not take the elixir."

Max said nothing, but Polidori played his card. "Now that we are reunited, *son*, I thought that you might join us."

"Never," William muttered.

Polidori sighed lightly. "We had anticipated this, but I would advise both of you to not be foolish. Bottom line, while the revenants are invaluable to us, we need a larger Conclave. We are offering the two of you something together. Miss Sharp, you will presumably become like Max once you take the elixir. That would help us. *I,* for one, have a particular interest in my son."

"As do I," Byron said, his eyes resting upon William.

Polidori cut him a wry sideways glance before continuing.

"Abbie and William, you clearly have an interest in one another. With the elixir, you could be together without the whole 'till death do us part' pledge."

Byron was watching me, and then looked at Max. "Although there might be *complications* ... I mean, with all of these crossing threads."

Polidori smiled. "As if anyone expects—to use an awful zoological term—*monogamy* from any of us."

"You're all not merely bastards, you're *bloody sick* bastards," William retorted.

My mind spun. I still had more questions. "How do you control the revenants? Where do you keep them?"

"They're all at different stages," Polidori said. "Some are in cages; we are running experiments upon them. We used to keep them in the laboratory here, but at the beginning of this year it proved too dangerous—far too small—so we located a different place to keep them. They have another home now... but I think you've found it."

St. Pancras Old Church.

"Your actions are wrong," I retorted. "You can't use people, living or dead, in this manner."

"*Oh bloody hell,*" Lord Byron exclaimed. "She's going to drive me insane in the coming decades." He finished his cigarette and tossed it in the ashtray with Polidori's, then glared at Max. "*You're* the only aberration under the elixir. Even if she is psychic, we cannot be certain that the elixir will have the same effect on her that it has on you. I still think that we should just make her drink it. We already have it prepared. She's restrained. Then we—"

"She will do it *willfully.*" Max clenched his jaw.

Cold anger marked Lord Byron's face.

Max walked to the door. "It is time for us to leave. We have other matters to attend to."

"You can't leave us here!" I yelled, pulling at the ropes again.

All three men turned to face us. Max spoke first. "You killed my lamia, Abbie—I think you'll find a way to free yourself. But time is up. The elixir is waiting for you and William downstairs, in the laboratory. Consume it, then come meet us at ten o'clock underneath St. Pancras Old Church."

"Or don't," Byron said lightly, "and we'll find *you.*"

"Oh, I think they'll join us even if they don't take the elixir," Max said, his eyes locked upon mine. "I have a small incentive for them."

Laura. Simon.

"What did you *do*?" I yelled, incensed, pulling at my restraints.

But Max only smiled. The other men chuckled and they left, shutting the door behind them.

Once they were gone, leaving us in darkness, William muttered, "They have to die. *All* of them."

"That goes without saying." My eyes searched the room for something sharp. Guiltily, I wished that Simon was here. He would be much more help at finding a way out of these ropes than William.

The knots were strong. We both tried to untie them for the better part of an hour.

"We need something sharp," William muttered, perspiration running down his face.

I wanted to weep in angry frustration when I felt wet blood upon my wrists. "I'd better get my bowie knife back after all this," I growled. I hadn't seen it since we'd been kidnapped from the cemetery.

A door opened somewhere downstairs.

"Damn it!" William growled. "They cannot be back already."

We heard footsteps upon the stairs. The lock clicked, then the door slowly opened.

"Simon!" I exclaimed as his tall figure stepped into the room, brilliantly pale in the darkness. He was holding a pistol in his hands, and a large gash bled at the top of his head.

"You're injured, Simon!" I cried.

"They have Laura," he said quickly, kneeling behind me. I heard the click of a pocketknife and he began cutting the ropes around my wrists, ankles, and waist.

"Oh my God, I feared that." Quickly, I told him everything that Max, Polidori, and Byron had talked about—how they'd mentioned that they had an "incentive" to lure us to St. Pancras Old Church.

Having freed me, Simon quickly handed me his jacket to cover my exposed chest and began to work on William's restraints.

"When I left you last night, I took her straight to the hospital to attend to the wound at her throat. I was going to leave her with Sister Josephine and return to you. But as I attended to her, someone struck me in the back of the head and I blacked out. When I awoke, three hours ago, she was gone."

"Max must have gone to the hospital after culling and burying the revenants," I gasped, rubbing my bleeding wrists.

"So if Max found you, why are you still alive?" William asked Simon, leaping up from the chair the moment he was freed.

"The more people I love, the more leverage Max will have over me when we reach that church," I said quickly, looking around for my knife. "Damn it. They took my bowie knife."

"They left it for you," Simon said, pulling it off the mantelpiece.

"At least they play fair," I muttered wryly, taking it from him. "How did you find us here?" I asked as we hurried down the stairs.

"I found a piece of your dress fabric near the entrance to

Egyptian Avenue, and I panicked. I looked everywhere but could not find you. I searched that area; I even searched the east part of the cemetery. I broke into three mausoleums. It was only half a hour ago that I decided to try the Highgate house. I picked the lock."

"We need to get Laura," I said quickly.

"Yes," Simon said, three steps ahead of me, his pistol out. "But first we need to destroy the elixir that's in the basement. And I'm rather inclined to think we should destroy the whole laboratory."

"Now you're thinking like me," William said.

"That's twisted," William remarked as we reached the laboratory.

The Conclave's chalice, with *A Posse Ad Esse* inscribed upon it, rested on a tray with a small bottle behind it. A thin ribbon had been tied around the neck of the bottle with a little message attached: *Drink me.*

I reached forward and touched it, fascinated. I picked it up. The liquid was clear, like water, yet *heavier* somehow. I spun the bottle between my fingers. The surface of the liquid glittered in curious sepia hues.

"This must be destroyed as quickly as possible," William said, taking the bottle from me.

"As does this place," Simon said quickly. "We can't let these cages, these trappings of terrible experiments, stand."

William and I quickly began helping Simon dump out

formaldehyde jars, even inside the empty cages. The revenant's corpse had been removed.

"This area will burn quickly, and by the time the rest of the house catches fire, we'll be gone," Simon said.

Careful to keep the chemicals off of our clothes, we spread the formaldehyde over the counters and flooded it upon the floors, from the back of the room to the base of the stairs.

"Go on!" William shouted at Simon and me as he lit a torch. "I'll finish this up."

As I clutched Simon's jacket about me, he pulled me upstairs. I heard the roar of the fire just as William joined us, and we ran out the back door.

Twenty-four

Once we reached Simon's house, Simon exchanged his pistol for a better revolver while William retrieved his other revolver. Opening my case of short-bladed knives, I placed five into my belt and the bowie knife in my boot; I'd changed into a pair of Simon's trousers, rolling the bottoms up inside my boots. It was close to eight o'clock now, and night was falling. I pinned my hair tightly behind my head. I was grateful for the growing darkness, as I hoped no one would notice my improper attire.

Alice's Adventures in Wonderland lay open on the bed. I knew Laura must be terrified, in the bowels of that church with Max and the others. I hoped they were just using her as a lure for us, but I wasn't certain what card she represented in the game they were playing. Possibly she was my replacement, and I needed to protect her from them.

When I reached the bottom of the stairs, I nearly collided with William. He held a plate of bread and cheese and a small glass of wine.

"Come eat something, Abbie. You're very pale."

Although I started to protest, not wanting to stop to eat, I knew he was right. I ate the bread and cheese quickly, at the base of the stairs.

William stood in front of me, watching me oddly. "Are you afraid?" he asked.

I hesitated. "Of course I am. I just want this all to be behind us, but it seems impossible." I remembered the scene in *Through the Looking-Glass* where the Queen told Alice that she sometimes believed *"as many as six impossible things before breakfast."*

I finished the plate and lifted the glass of wine. "Here's to impossible things."

"Yes indeed," William said, his eyes shining upon me strangely.

Leaving the empty plate and glass with William, I hurried to meet Simon. I found him packing our torches in his bag. He had his revolver and a small knife at his belt.

"I would ask you, Abbie, if you would like my spare pistol, but I know that you prefer knives."

"Always."

I saw the outline of bandages on Simon's chest, over the wound he'd received in the cemetery. Although he never complained, I could tell he was exhausted and in pain.

When William entered the room, Simon began speaking calmly but quickly. "We don't know how many revenants they have with them. Max plays games. We will have to be very careful and pay attention to every detail around us." He leveled his gaze at William. "And William, *do not act brashly.*

There is a child down there and this could end disastrously. You fired far too quickly last night when we were attacked."

"I had three revenants' snapping jaws coming at my neck. I'm sorry I don't have your cool—"

Suddenly my vision blurred, my ears rang. My stomach lurched. I fell forward onto my knees.

"Abbie?" Simon caught me quickly. I saw his face above mine before everything went dark.

I awoke on the parlor floor, William sponging my face. Perspiration poured out of every crevice of my body.

What happened?

Was I ill?

As my vision sharped, Simon's face also came into view above me. "Abbie...your eyes..." he muttered. A thousand questions lingered in his voice.

I blinked. The room became clearer. *Remarkably* clearer. I sat up suddenly, startled. My vision was so sharp I could see the film of dust on the curtains in the dining room.

"What's happened to me?" I muttered. I glanced at the clock on the wall. I had only been unconscious for fifteen minutes.

William smiled widely.

Why did he seem happy that I was ill?

But I wasn't ill. Strangely, I felt stronger. When I held my hands before me, my skin glowed with more color than it ever had before.

"What's happened?" I murmured again.

"'Impossible things'..." William muttered. "Now we will have nothing to fear."

I stood slowly, feeling slightly disoriented. My senses

seemed heightened somehow; my body felt light yet engaged with all around me. I could feel the carpet fibers through my boot soles. I felt strangely *more* alive and connected to the material world around me.

I hurried to a nearby mirror and stared at my reflection. Perspiration blurred my vision and began streaming down my face, as if I had been in a rainstorm. Wiping it away from my eyes, I stared, my heartbeat quickening.

My eyes.

The brown of my eyes shone with unnatural brightness—bright as Max's leopard-green eyes.

"Dear God..." I said, touching my damp face.

Then suddenly I understood.

The elixir.

William had been alone in the laboratory, setting it on fire as Simon and I ran upstairs.

This perspiration was my body cleansing itself from within. Although I felt stronger by the second, the rapid process as the elixir raced through my bloodstream was disorienting. I understood now why the Conclave rested each time they consumed it.

Both Simon and William watched me in the mirror.

"William..." Simon said, his eyes still on me. His voice trembled in fury. "What did you do to her?"

William beamed proudly at me, his face flushed. "I gave her what we need to survive tonight."

"The wine..." I said, still staring in the mirror at my unnervingly bright eyes. They seemed almost gold, like liquid amber.

Before I could say another word, Simon turned and punched William in the face, knocking him to the floor.

———————— �֍ ————————

When we arrived at St. Pancras Old Church, the whole property was as quiet and still as it had been on the night we exhumed Polidori's grave. Simon had suggested that I stay back at the house, but I insisted on going with them. Still, he was keeping a careful eye upon me, worried about the effects of the elixir.

We were both furious at William. Although I'd helped him off the floor and attended to his blackened eye, Simon and I had said very little to him as time pressed upon us to meet with Max's new Conclave.

While Simon knelt at the front gates of the churchyard picking the lock, I hissed at William, "I cannot *believe* that you poured that into my drink."

Although a bruise was blooming around his right eye, William remained unapologetic. "Abbie, don't you see that this is the best way? We must have someone on our side who's as strong as Max."

Finished with the lock, Simon silently opened the gate. His pale marble face was so severe, he might have been a beautiful Angel of Death. "What you did, William, was *reckless*. We cannot be certain how the elixir will affect her body. Furthermore, I'm not sure why you trusted that it was in fact the elixir of life in that bottle; it could have been any number of formulas, or even poison. I would *never* trust Max's word for a second."

"And it was a betrayal, William," I said quickly. "Even Max would not force the elixir down my throat."

"No," William growled as we walked toward the church. "He was just going to kill you when you *freely* refused to take it." He paused. Flushed with anger, he held my arm and pressed his face close to mine in the darkness. "What I did will help us *survive*. That is all I care about at this point."

Simon started to speak, but William interrupted him. "If there is any time to be reckless, it would be now."

Simon narrowed his eyes but said nothing.

The door of the church stood unlocked, opening easily as we entered. Both William and Simon held their revolvers fully cocked. I clutched my bowie knife and made certain that the knives at my belt were secure.

The narthex of the church was dark and silent.

We walked through the sanctuary, trying to watch everywhere at once. Three votive candles eerily illuminated the statue of Mary. Part of me wished I could believe that a prayer, a candle, could bring down something as sweet as a miracle. But I couldn't, so I gripped the knife handle tighter.

We walked behind the altar and into the sacristy, where Simon pulled out our torches and lit them. Then he slid his long pale fingers along the door crack and pushed gently. Almost immediately, it opened, revealing the stone steps twisting downward into darkness.

"Why do I feel like we're about to enter Dante's Inferno?" William whispered.

"Because, in a sense, we are," I replied.

William and Simon tried to go ahead of me.

"No," I murmured, chuckling. "Now that I'm on the

elixir, *I* go first." Although I'd stopped perspiring so much, the strange changes continued within my body, and I still felt stronger by the minute. But my mood was also changing. Like a rolling sea wave building momentum, my confidence was increasing and my fear was abating.

William stepped aside, smiling.

"Abbie," Simon whispered, "we don't know what is down there."

"All the more reason for me to go first." Keeping hold of my torch and knife, I began the descent.

We descended several levels. At times the spiraling turns of the stairs were so sharp that we were in danger of plunging forward. The stone was cut unevenly.

"We must be at least five stories below the church," William murmured from behind me.

"At least," I replied.

A rat ran away from the stream of my torchlight. The atmosphere gradually became damper and cooler.

The stairs finally ended in an enormous, oblong hall with a domed ceiling. Roman-era archways flanked both sides, and in our torchlight we saw faded mosaics of gods and battle scenes. Patches of lichen spilt across the walls and ceiling like ink spots. Cobwebs draped through some of the archways. The air felt moist—it was like stepping through cool vapor. I distantly heard the sound of rushing water.

"Careful," Simon said, and we paused.

Even with my sharpened vision, I was unable to see into the darkness beyond the arches.

Movement caught my eyes and I spun around, keeping hold of the torch and the bowie knife. Simon instinctively stepped in front of me, his revolver out. His torchlight caught the folds of a tattered skirt just beyond the arches. I swung my own light about and saw a pair of milky eyes.

"We're surrounded," William whispered.

As I stared into the darkness, listening to the rustling of bodies, something like a sharp coil wound within me. That building wave of fearlessness. Amid all of these beings stalking us, *I* began to feel more like the predator.

I tried to see ahead of us, but it was far too dark to see the end of the hall.

William whispered softly into my ear. "They made us the offer of the elixir—they have to be near. I don't think they would slaughter us without at least a word first. And these revenants appear to be restrained."

Suddenly, three large torches bolted against the wall at the far side of the room blazed up, all at once.

Max, Byron, Polidori, and Laura stood in front of the torches. Both Polidori and Byron were dressed in trousers and white shirts; Lord Byron had a red sash around his waist and a sword in his belt. The two men had revolvers aimed straight at us. I saw the flash of a knife blade in Max's hand, just behind Laura's head. She was quivering in fear, tears running down her cheeks. The raspy breaths in the shadows around us increased.

"Set your revolvers down or the child dies," Max said flatly as we approached.

Laura's face was pale. She whimpered and her knees buckled, but Max jerked her upright again.

"Set them down," I whispered to Simon and William.

Keeping his revolver aimed at us, Polidori narrowed his eyes in my direction. He smiled.

"I don't *believe* it," he said, stepping forward and staring at me. "She's taken the elixir."

Although he was still several feet away, I tensed, my mind racing for a way to get Laura away from them. My rising confidence shifted, and suddenly I felt reckless and even a little ruthless.

Polidori continued walking toward me, and as the space between us closed, I saw the extent of his astonishment. My transformation was irresistible to his physician's mind.

I restrained myself as he stopped close to me, his revolver aimed at my heart. "It's marvelous!" he said. "Bartlett, you were right! Her eyes are like yours. Her skin *glows* under its influence."

Then his eyes glinted at William, beside me. "Did you take it?"

"No and I never will, you bloody bastard."

"*Daddy* to you."

"I only took it to kill you," I said quickly.

Polidori sighed dramatically, a small pout forming on his lips. "I assumed that."

"Bad form, Miss Sharp," Lord Byron exclaimed, clucking his tongue. "Taking the elixir and yet refusing to become a member of the Conclave was not part of the plan."

Max arched an eyebrow. "Neither was burning our Highgate home to the ground. On this night, it seems that the ever-virtuous Abbie Sharp has not only taken the elixir while refusing to join us, but she has committed arson."

The arson part was true, and I certainly wasn't going to

tell him that I was tricked into taking the elixir. So I shrugged. "I've played a little dirty. It's not like your hands are clean, Max Bartlett."

He didn't retort, just watched me, a greedy look in his gaze. In this form, I was as he'd always wanted me.

Polidori glanced at Max, then turned his attention back to me.

No, they wouldn't kill me quite yet.

Staring at me as if I was an exotic specimen, Polidori muttered, "I wonder, Max, if she shares *all* of your powers."

Max smiled, still watching me.

"Abbie," Polidori said, pointing to the nearest archway. "Climb that wall."

I chuckled. "No."

"I think she needs a bit more motivation," Byron murmured.

"Mostly certainly." Max pulled Laura closer to him. He pressed the knife blade to her throat. She screamed, and I heard the murmurs of the revenants as they crowded together in the shadows.

"Stop!" I yelled. Both Simon and William stepped forward, but I pushed them back.

"Watch me *carefully*," I whispered to them through clenched teeth.

I walked over to the nearest archway. As I placed the bowie knife in my boot, I finally saw the revenants. My mind ticked away, trying to calculate how badly we were outnumbered. There weren't as many as I'd previously thought. I saw only five in the shadows near me. One woman, in a housekeeper's bloodstained uniform, snarled at me.

I placed my fingers on the stone. Focused.

Although the stone appeared smooth, I felt grooves, ridges that I could not see. I remembered feeling the carpet fibers through my boots before we left the house tonight. Simon once theorized that for Max, his psychic energy was so intensified by the elixir that he could propel his body into doing the seemingly impossible. Simon's theory seemed to apply now, for me. As I reached my hands up and clutched the stone, my fingers clung tightly to its surface.

I hoisted myself up, lifted a boot, and climbed three feet up the wall.

My body felt weightless, and I paused. Even amid the danger, I marveled at what had happened to me.

Polidori clapped his hands together and exclaimed, "Amazing! Truly amazing!"

I climbed, quickening my pace. I was like an insect scaling a wall. My fingers grasped the stone as if it were thick ivy, and my body propelled itself along as lightly or as heavily as I wished. Gravity itself seemed fluid, flexible, and at my beck and call.

I was almost to the ceiling.

"*Beautiful.* She is like a shooting star!" Byron exclaimed. Then he added sullenly, "Unfortunately, one that must fall tonight."

"Yes," said Polidori. "Such a pity. Such a waste."

I glanced down just as I reached a thick ledge that bordered the base of the domed ceiling. I clung to it, my hands striking out against sticky cobwebs. Dried rat feces fell upon my head like crumbling plaster.

I was almost directly above Polidori, Byron, and Max.

"You could have been such a remarkable physician, Abbie," Max said languidly, staring up at me. His knife was still pressed into Laura's throat as she watched me with fearful, curious eyes.

"That's been the plan," I grunted, propelling myself upward for a stronger grip on the ledge. "But you and your fucking Conclaves keep getting in the way."

"I like her," Polidori chuckled. "She's a fiery bitch."

"You have no idea!" I shouted, catching Simon's eye. Quick as lightning, he grabbed his revolver from the floor and shot at Max's head.

Max released Laura and spun away, and I lost sight of him. Pulling one of the knives from my waist, I aimed at Byron's right arm and threw the knife hard.

Byron cursed, shouting as he pulled the knife out.

I scrambled down the wall easily. Suddenly, ten revenants came running from the archways on either side of us. William grabbed his revolver and aimed at Polidori, who stood just in front of him. But his hand trembled—he was unable to shoot his father at point-blank range.

Laura screamed in terror, cowering against the wall under the torches. As I had in the cemetery, I pushed her behind me, against the wall.

"They are 'orrible!" she screamed, tears running down her face. "Thaur's more in cages beyond! They ur worse than these!"

"*Where?*" I yelled, slashing the throat of a revenant woman in a tattered dress. "Where are they?"

"Near where ye and the doctors entered! Thaur's another big room 'olding 'em!"

In my peripheral vision, I heard cries and curses, William yelling out in pain. At least five gunshots rang out, and then I heard what sounded like a revolver sliding fast along the stone floor.

I threw a knife into the neck of an oncoming revenant. Placing my bowie knife in my mouth, I snatched a short-bladed knife in each hand and stabbed the necks of two more revenants, simultaneously. Vaguely, as I pulled my knives from the bodies of all three, I thought of my friend Roddy. I'd never dreamed, back in Dublin, that I would someday use my knife-throwing skills to slay revenants.

With the pile of four bodies in front of Laura and me, I paused, scanning the great hall. Four more revenant corpses lay near where William and Polidori struggled, and one more lay beyond, a bleeding gunshot wound in its head. William and his father were locked together as they fought; William held him off well as he struggled for Polidori's revolver, which Polidori was gripping tightly. Another revenant man kept lunging at William with snapping jaws.

Byron was slashing at Simon with his sword. But the arm I had wounded was useless, so he fought clumsily using his left arm. Simon skillfully blocked the sword with his extinguished torch while swiping at Byron with his knife.

I scanned the enormous room and ceiling for Max, but I couldn't see him anywhere.

"Stay here!" I shouted to Laura as I ran toward the revenant near William. He lunged at me, stronger than the others, and I fell with him in a tangle of limbs upon the floor, my bowie knife rolling out of my hand.

I tried to grab the knife, barely keeping the man's gnashing teeth away from my throat. With his great weight on top of me, I couldn't reach the knives at my belt.

I could see Polidori, off to the side, pummeling William to the floor. He hit William in the head with the revolver handle; William yelled in pain but didn't lose consciousness. Beyond us, closer to the middle of the hall, Simon was still fighting Byron.

Finally, when my fingertips reached the bowie knife handle, I blindly stabbed upward into the revenant's chest. Oily blood burst out upon my shirt.

Pushing the body off me, I leaped to my feet.

I heard a sharp grind of metal in the darkness, behind the arches at the far side of the hall. Near the entrance.

Laura screamed hysterically as she backed against the wall, her fists balled in her mouth. We all paused in our fighting and stared in the direction of the noise.

"Why the bloody hell is he releasing them?" Polidori yelled to Byron. He punched William in the face.

"Damned if I know!" Byron shouted, slashing clumsily yet again at Simon. "Let's finish this and get the hell out of here!"

But Simon, quick as lightning, took advantage of the pause and stabbed Byron hard in the side of the chest.

Byron cried out in pain and stumbled away, blood gushing from his wound. Simon leaped forward to stab him again, but then turned and ran toward us, leaving Byron on the floor as at least fifty feral revenants came snarling at us from across the hall.

Seeing a door just behind one of the nearest archways, I grabbed Laura and ran to help William. Simon had almost reached us. The mass of feral revenants fell upon Byron savagely, and I heard the wet tear of organs amid his increasing screams.

"Sorry, dear boy, such a pity," Polidori said suddenly. He pointed his revolver at William, who was struggling to his feet.

"*No!*" I screamed, grabbing a knife from my waist. But I stumbled over a revenant's body and fell to the floor, the knife clattering away.

Within the next second, Simon threw his body against William—and took Polidori's bullet in his heart.

"*No!*" I screamed again, horrified. I heard gunshots ringing out far beyond us.

William stood up and knocked Polidori to the ground. Snatching the revolver, he shot his father in the head.

Twenty-five

I experienced a moment where time seemed frozen. Cold fear swept through my blood. Laura cried frantically, pulling at me, screaming for me to get up. But my eyes were locked on Simon's pale, lifeless face. Far too much blood was gushing from his chest wound.

The revenants would fall upon us at any moment, yet I couldn't move.

"No...no, no, no, no...Simon..." I muttered, stumbling to my feet.

Vaguely, I heard shouts around me. Vaguely, I heard more gunshots and the screams of the revenants. It would only be a few seconds now, and then we would be lost in a sea of gnashing teeth, sour breath, and oily blood.

William ran to me as I stood unsteadily on my feet, my eyes still on Simon.

"Take Laura, William," I whispered. "Get out of here."

Scooping Laura into his arms, William tried to take my hand, make me flee with them. Perspiration streamed down his face; he had a bleeding cut on his chin. His chest heaved so sharply he could hardly speak.

"*Leave me!*" I shouted, pushing him away and running to Simon's body.

I smelled something like burning charcoal. Heard the gunshots. But it was all background noise now.

"Simon."

I held his head in my lap, his lifeless blue eyes staring up at me. I touched the bleeding wound on his chest, and my hand accidently smeared blood upon his cheek—so red against his white skin. Then my tears fell onto his face, streaking through the blood.

Why couldn't time be unwoven, just a bit, like yarn off of a spindle? If I could undo this past minute, Simon would still be alive.

"Abbie!" William yelled, crouching beside me. In his arms, Laura hid her face against his chest. William glanced toward the far end of the hall, beyond me. "Help is here, but we *must* leave! Now!"

"*Abbie…*" In my mind, Max called my name.

"He's still alive. Max is. He needs to die," I said, my tears falling onto Simon's face. I kissed his forehead, shut his eyes, kissed his pale blue-veined eyelids, and laid his head gently back down upon the ground.

Then, quickly, I stood and wiped the tears from my face. They would do me no good now. Collecting my knifes from the ground, I stuck the bowie knife inside my boot. "I'm going to kill Max."

"You can't," William said. "I won't let you go!"

"As if you could stop me. Goodbye, William."

"No, Abbie!" A tear streaked down his face, and Laura screamed for me.

Glancing at the back wall, I saw a small door near the torches and ran through it with great speed. I felt the elixir's warmth pulsing through my veins. William could never keep up with me.

"Abbie…"

Max's voice beckoned me, and soon I found myself in another long tunnel.

My eyes adjusted a bit in the darkness. The sound of rushing water grew stronger, and soon I realized that I was running parallel to the River Fleet. Its waters churned and flowed beside me.

"Simon." I said his name as I ran, and my tears began again. My grief was fury now.

I still had my bowie knife and four remaining short-bladed knives.

In the darkness, I almost smashed into a worn, tiled wall. I turned sharply and ran left, then saw an image pulse through my mind—of a large hole at the end of another tunnel.

He was leading me to him.

I veered left again, this tunnel more narrow than any I had been in. Cat-sized rats ran along the edges.

Simon.

He had given his life so that William could live. So that I could still have William. His sacrifice split my heart in two, and I didn't know how I would live with it.

I ran until I neared the end of another hall. The architecture suddenly became more Gothic, with a slightly vaulted ceiling and rotting wooden buttresses. A large gargoyle's face covered with moss projected from the wall directly in front of me. Fissures cracked throughout the stone walls around it.

"Where now?" I growled.

But then, as I stepped forward, I screamed, falling into a large round hole. Quickly flinging my arms about, I grasped a stone side of the hole, held on, and looked below me. The drop was very far. Wryly, I thought of Alice's fall down the rabbit hole just as I saw a grayish flickering light far below me.

Water.

Letting go of the wall, I surrendered to the fall.

I crashed hard into foul water, accidently swallowing some. Coughing and choking up water as I broke the surface, I saw that there was more light in this area than in the tunnels above. I was in some sort of round pool with walls of stone, like the tunnel directly above me.

A healing pool. This must be one of the old Roman pools that Simon had mentioned.

I heard, from somewhere nearby, a faint, crackling melody. I swam to the side and hoisted myself onto the floor. Coughing up more water, I remembered Roddy again, and that day when I almost drowned.

I was tired of losing people.

I wrung my hair out and squeezed what water I could from my clothes, checking the bite on my upper arm. It would need bandages, but it wasn't terribly deep.

Stepping away from the pool, I surveyed the room, trying to look everywhere at once. The place was large, circular like the pool in its center, and lined with several closed doors.

I walked toward the door nearest me, where the music played. A weak stream of light spilt out from under it. I paused, my ear to the cold surface. Beethoven's "Moonlight Sonata" wafted like a scent toward me.

Made only of warped wood, the door opened easily.

The rooms by the pool seemed to be some sort of monk cells, perhaps an underground retreat for meditation and healing. But someone had brought modern furnishings into this room. A bed with yellowing lace coverlets took up most of the room, pillows propped upon it. The phonograph played on a nearby desk, next to a small gas lamp. Quickly, I stopped the phonograph and stared around me, listening to the silence.

He was near. He must be near. Yet I heard nothing.

A trunk rested at the bottom of the bed. Carefully, I opened it. Inside was a green ruffled gown, bloodstained about the chest. A red gown, also stained. Several nightgowns.

Mariah. They had kept her down here.

I stepped back out into the main room and looked around again. The water in the pool glimmered in the dim light.

Light poured from the bottom of another door. When I opened it, the smell of an oriental cigar overwhelmed me. A lamp glowed in this room also, and my heart pounded with mingled fear and anticipation.

As in Mariah's room, tapestries hung on the ceiling and walls, and a bed took up most of the space. Then I saw them— several dried, yellow letters spread about the bed like butterflies. Carefully, I picked one up. As I examined it, my heartbeat quickened.

"Dear Max, I have told you that our love would be impossible…"

Before I could read the middle section, I stopped, scanned to the end of the letter to read, *"Caroline Westfield."*

Dear God. These were letters from Mother to Max.

A rope looped around my neck and pulled me violently backward. I dropped my knife and clutched at my throat, struggling to breathe. Max whipped my arms to my sides and held them there in a vise-grip as he threw me down on a nearby chair, the rope still tight around my neck.

"Didn't anyone ever tell you not to pry?" he asked, loosening the rope as he tied me to the chair. With my throat released, I choked, sucking in air and cursing myself for letting down my guard. Even with the elixir in my system, I must be smarter in the way I pursued him.

Now I was immobilized in the chair, facing the bed.

Max picked up my bowie knife and sat upon the bed, amid the letters. He watched me in the semi-darkness.

"Quite a scene up there," he said, smiling.

"I'm going to kill you."

"Ahhh…" His voice dropped. His mouth curved into a smile. "Yes, I expected that. Your friend is dead. He was a loyal one, wasn't he? Always fighting battles that weren't his own."

A tear trickled down my face. Max reached a large finger out and wiped it away. He examined my eyes, my different appearance. "There, there. Don't cry. You'll be dead too by morning."

"Get your hands off me!" I glared at him, furious. "What the hell happened up there? Why did you release those revenants? You must have known that they would kill Byron and Polidori, unlike the other revenants."

He smiled and leaned back, playing carefully with his curved-blade knife, his elixir-green eyes on me. "Truth be told, I was weary of those two. And now, with our laboratory burned down, we have no more elixir."

Yet there was no defeat in his hard gaze, and I wasn't certain if I believed him about the elixir.

"Tell me about my mother."

He leaned back upon the bed and lit a cigar, then scooped all the letters into a small bundle and placed them inside his shirt. He kept his eyes on me.

"I'll tell you what I want to tell you in a bit. But you tell me why you decided to take the elixir."

I pulled on the restraints, at the knot at my wrists, but it was too tightly woven. "I took it only to defeat you."

He inhaled from the cigar, chuckling. "I don't believe that for a second. In spite of what I said to you up there, you're far too morally tortured to do even that." He paused, cocked his head. "Did William put it in your drink?"

I said nothing.

Max laughed and blew smoke into the air. "I *knew* it! The only smart thing that boy's ever done. Of course, I'll still murder him at dawn."

"You won't!" I yelled, pulling against the restraints.

He placed his back against the headboard and stared at the nearest tapestry, inhaling deeply from the cigar. "It was quite brilliant, actually. Killing you *will* be more difficult now that you're as I've always wanted you."

I glared at him, my mind spinning for a way out of this.

He patted the letters at his chest. "I'm certain that you have questions, Abbie. And I might answer a *few*."

I stopped struggling to watch him. My bowie knife lay on

the bed near him. If I could just have a knife, I could cut these ropes, then his throat.

He tapped ash onto the floor and smiled languidly in my direction. "You know that my family's name is not Bartlett. It's Aguillon. I was an assassin for the French monarchy for almost ten years before the Conclave approached me."

"Of course you were an assassin," I spit out. "That seems to be about all you're good at."

He glared. "Still the spitting cobra." Then his voice slipped briefly into a French accent. "Ah Abbie, you have no idea how many people I killed, infants, children. If I was given an order, I followed through."

"You're soulless."

He chuckled. "Perhaps. But when you're the bastard son of a duke, a lucrative career is always a shadowy one. I was discreet. I traveled, learned many languages, to do what I did skillfully. But, well... there was the French Revolution. Power shifted rapidly, even by the day. I was being led out to the guillotine when two hooded figures approached me."

"Julian Bartlett..." I murmured.

"And Robert Buck. They were powerful, able to halt the execution order. And, of course, I soon learned that what they offered me was marvelous."

"I want to know about my mother. What is in those letters? Were you and Mother lovers?"

His expression darkened, drifting into a well of memories that I was not privy to. "She loved something she saw in me."

Desperately, I wondered if Mother knew he was a murderer when she fell in love. In the glimpse of the letter that I'd seen, she said that their love "would be impossible." Was she drawn to something in Max that I couldn't see? Now, one year after her death, I couldn't decide if she was wiser or more foolish than I was, and once again I felt hopeless in the face of her mystery. She was like a set of nesting dolls, a different little painted face on each body.

"But were you lovers?"

He shifted now, his expression darkening with a wave of grief. Suddenly I was perplexed by *him*. How could he still *feel* for her after poisoning her?

"Enough. I won't talk about her anymore!" He threw the glowing ember of the cigar in a nearby ashtray. "We will finish this *tonight*, love, but not here," he added. "*Above* ground."

He walked behind my chair and put his hand upon my scalp, twisting his fingers in my damp hair gently. I felt his hand quake and I shifted uncomfortably, suddenly wanting to sob at our reluctant connection. Like the dodo birds, we were the only two of our kind in the world now. A horrible, mismatched pair.

This truth lingered between us like a paused breath.

A tear slid down my cheek.

Then, after a few quiet moments, he regained control and placed the bowie knife in my bound hands. "I'm leaving, but I assure you we'll find each other shortly. You'll find an exit at the back of this room, through a narrow archway and a rising tunnel of stairs. *Au revoir.*"

After cutting myself free, I ascended the many wet and mud-stained stairs. I kept the bowie knife out, alert at every corner, constantly looking behind me for any straggling revenants. I wondered where William and Laura were. I remembered the gunfire, how William had said that help had arrived. They must be safe. Simon. I struggled to believe that he was dead. That the world around me could survive without his cool reason.

Finally, I reached a small vent partially covered by mud. I pushed it out easily and crawled onto the banks of the Thames. It had to be the very early hours of the morning, perhaps one o'clock. The sky was dreadfully dark and silent, and storm clouds were rolling in from the east.

I stood on a long earthen ledge overlooking the mudlarks—orphans and old women in rags who were sifting through the muddy Thames banks for rings and other valuables.

The clouds moved aside like a blanket, the moon slicing light over the shifting waters.

"Your friends—all but one survived," a man's voice said from behind me. He spoke with a thick Irish accent.

I whipped around, my knife ready. A man I had never seen before stood before me, dressed in an unassuming suit. He had a thick moustache upon his face, and his hair was slicked back. He looked a bit younger than Wyatt, perhaps late thirties.

"Pardon me, Miss Sharp, but I'm here about Case X. Her Majesty has requested your presence immediately."

"Who are you?"

"William Melville." His mouth twitched. "Few people know my name, but then again, Miss Sharp, you now know a great deal that most others don't."

"Where is Wyatt? I thought only one advisor knew about Case X."

"He's been removed from the Secret Service Bureau."

"He's not alive anymore, is he?"

Melville said nothing, and suddenly I understood. Wyatt knew too much, and with his drug addiction and his attempt to get the elixir for himself... I was certain now that he was the one who'd searched my room. For the monarchy, he'd become a liability, and now he was dead.

Melville watched my face coolly. "You've taken the elixir."

"How do you know?" I kept my hand clenched at the knife's handle.

"Your eyes gleam like... *his*. And your skin. Well... the change is obvious." His eyes scanned my torn trousers, my clothing. "Of course, you will be dressed more presentably when you appear in Her Majesty's presence."

I started to speak but Melville interrupted, gesturing for me to follow him. As we walked up the muddy ledge toward the carriage, he said, "Your friend who perished—"

"Simon St. John," I said, my voice cracking.

"Yes. Please, come with me. Your other friend, the little girl, they are quite safe."

"I have other business..."

"It can wait," he said as we reached the carriage.

With great speed, I was bathed and dressed by four ladies-in-waiting at Buckingham Palace. They put me into a ridiculous ornate gown that I would never have bought for myself—the dress was made of heavy layers of black lace and crinoline, with a ring of fresh orange peonies sewn around the neckline. They placed fingerless black lace gloves upon my scratched and still-bleeding hands. Discreetly, I smuggled my four remaining knives and the bowie knife into a small clutch attached to the dress.

One of the women led me to a small room, offering me a glass of absinthe before she left. A small clock on the mantel chimed the two o'clock hour.

My hand trembled as I held the absinthe glass.

Here I sat in Buckingham Palace, waiting to meet Queen Victoria. I knew I should be more in awe of the moment, but it didn't matter to me now. It seemed merely like a pompous obstacle preventing me from finding and killing Max. My body still pulsed with the elixir, but a gnawing pain was growing in my heart over Simon.

Oh God, don't cry again.

I took out a handkerchief, wiped the tear away, and put it back in my small purse.

Then the Queen entered, with one of the ladies-in-waiting.

I rose and curtseyed.

Queen Victoria was much less impressive than I had imagined. She was short and very stout, wearing a plain black dress with a plaid shawl draped over her shoulders. The skin dimpled in deep jowls upon her face, sagging with the consistency of pudding.

"That will be all, Cecilia," she said lightly. The lady behind her bowed and quickly left the room.

"Please sit," she said, gesturing toward a chair. She seated her round body upon a nearby ottoman and sighed. "So, this is the young miss who has taken out my Conclave."

"Yes." I tried not to stare at her, tried to keep my head bowed. "With the help of two others. One of whom died tonight."

She placed her fat, heavily ringed fingers upon her lap and cleared her throat sharply. "Miss Sharp, I assume you have a great many questions for me."

I should have been tongue-tied. But I wasn't. Time was precious to me now. "Your Majesty—did you know what the Conclave *did*?"

"I knew of their existence. But I left them alone."

That didn't answer my question.

She was quiet for too long, then said, "You've been crying, Miss Sharp."

"I am grieving the loss of my friend, Your Majesty."

She cleared her throat again, uncomfortable with my emotion. "My men executed all of those ... creatures. They burned the bodies of John Polidori and Lord Byron. They retrieved the body of your friend."

"Thank you."

She played with one of the rings on her finger. "Let's speak not as queen and subject now, Miss Sharp, but as woman to woman."

I looked at her quizzically.

"What I truly think, or feel, doesn't matter. I am born into a position to play a role. We must all play a role within our lives. You will have many roles within your life. You might be a physician, a wife, a mother. My particular role here is queen. I inherited the Conclave. It's not my place to question its existence, and I'm only involved now to protect my nation from disaster given that the group has gone awry."

She paused. "Melville tells me that you've taken the elixir."

"It was slipped into my drink. The effects will wear off in a year."

She pushed a small lamp toward me and leaned forward. "Yes ... remarkable. I see it now. Your eyes shine like I've heard his do." She stared at my hand. "Might I?"

I held my hand out and she gently touched the skin above my gloves, then looked up at my face. "Your skin is so vibrant." She released my hand. "Am I to understand that you are made in the same mold as the remaining Conclave member, and that the elixir has the same strengthening effects?"

"Yes."

"We are almost finished with this Conclave business. Melville told me that they just learned of another residence the group used, in Highgate. That it was burned to the ground. Are you behind that?"

I glanced at the clock. Half past two.

"John Polidori kept a laboratory there," I stated. "I believe the last of the elixir was there. Many of their most important notes. We had to destroy it."

"You have done well," Queen Victoria said. "I arranged this meeting to see if I might impose a final request upon you." Her tone was light, as if she were asking me to return for tea. "You are presumably the equal now of the surviving Conclave member. I have lost too many men. Might *you* ... rid us of him?"

"I will rid the world of him."

PART IV

"'I can't stand this any longer!' she cried as she jumped up and seized the tablecloth with both hands: one good pull, and plates, dishes, guests, and candles came crashing down together in a heap on the floor."

—Through the Looking-Glass, and
What Alice Found There

Twenty-six

Billowing clouds pulsed through the sky, amid thunder and a light rain, as I walked away from Buckingham Palace. Within seconds the rain picked up, soaking my dress. I pulled off the orange peonies and tossed them onto the dirty pavement of Trafalgar Square.

My conversation with the Queen needled at me—the way she'd evaded my questions, the light manner in which she'd made her request. My anger rose, and that strong pulse in my veins from the elixir began again. My heart beat rapidly against the steady sound of Big Ben chiming the three o'clock hour.

I needed a plan.

William and Laura were safe only temporarily. Grandmother and Richard were unprotected at Kennilworth. Christina was unprotected here in London. I was tired of living this way, scrambling to protect those I loved.

This had to end tonight.

The rain picked up, pouring in sheets about me. Few carriages rode the streets; the square was practically empty as

I neared the base of Nelson's Column. Hair plastered to my head and eyes, I clenched my fists so tightly in fury that my fingernails broke through the black lace over my palms, drawing blood.

I had to find Max, but all my silly undergarments and layers of fabric were weighed down with rainwater. Fighting Max in petticoats and crinoline wouldn't do.

Taking a deep breath, I ran through the rain. To any onlooker, I would have appeared insane, running with long wet hair, a soaked gown, and no shawl over my bare shoulders. And as my damned skirts tripped me in the wet grass of Kensington Park, I chuckled, feeling every bit the madwoman.

I would go to Simon's house to change, and then I would somehow find Max.

"Where are you, you bastard?" I muttered through the rain.

As if in answer, a vision of Grandmother's house pulsed through my head. Rain fell down its darkened windows.

I reached Simon's house in Kensington, breathless, but not tired even after the long run. I tugged hard on the door, twice. The house was empty and locked.

Lightning cracked through the sky above me, illuminating the empty street.

I grabbed a large rock from the St. Johns' flowerbed, and with the next thunderclap, I smashed it through the glass of the front door, reached inside, and flung open the two door bolts.

I soaked the carpets while running up the stairs three at a time to Simon's bedroom. Once there, I flung open the doors to his wardrobe and grabbed a pair of riding breeches and a long white shirt, but not before pulling out the shirt closest to me and inhaling his scent of soap, tea, and old books. I stripped off my dress so quickly that buttons popped off, scattering about the floor.

After buckling my boots and securing them over the trousers, I ran to my bedroom across the hall. I took another short-bladed knife from my case so that I had five throwing knives again.

Another vision of Grandmother's house appeared, rising up slow and grainy before dwindling away again, sand kicked up from a pond's floor.

He was getting impatient.

"I'm coming," I growled, grabbing the bowie knife. Once again, I secured the throwing knives in my belt and put the bowie knife in my boot. I pulled my hair back in a comb and ran out the front door.

Lightning illuminated the empty streets of Kensington, and the rain continued unrelenting as I ran the short distance to Sheffield Terrace. When I reached Grandmother's house, I paused and looked up through the rain.

The windows were all dark. The house, like Simon's, appeared empty.

I laughed lightly as I pulled out the bowie knife and stepped up toward the front door.

This was absurd—meeting Jack the Ripper in Grandmother's home, which she had spent years decorating and furnishing to proudly display to her friends.

I tried the doorknob with my free hand.

Unlocked.

Cautiously, I stepped into the dark entranceway, tightening my grip on my knife.

Lightning, sharp as a photography bulb's flash, illuminated the large foyer.

Posters and newspaper prints from the Ripper murders lay strewn all over the large oriental rug of the entranceway. An illustration of Annie Chapman's pudgy face. A photograph from Scotland Yard of the dead Polly Nichols, her nose severed from her face. An enlarged photograph of the letter Max sent the authorities, taunting them about the murders and signed only "*From Hell.*" Also strewn about the floor was a page from *The Times* reporting the murder of Lionel Millbrough and another page reporting the murder of a priest in Covent Gardens. I bent over and picked up a long lock of hazelnut hair. It smelled of seawater, and could only have been from Seraphina's head.

The room went dark again as I dropped the lock. Then, just as my eyes adjusted, in another blinding white flash of light from the storm outside I saw the last line of the Ripper letter:

"Catch me when you can!"

Images of the first time I'd seen that letter came to my mind. Abberline had shown it to me, along with the jar containing Annie Chapman's severed kidney.

My wet boots dripped rainwater across the strewn papers as I crossed the floor, trying to see everywhere at once. I glanced upward, as Max very well might be on the high ceiling, or on Grandmother's large chandelier dangling far above me.

But the ceiling was empty.

He wasn't on the staircase or landing.

I peeked into the dining room.

Nothing.

I stepped into the nearby parlor.

Empty.

I walked across the foyer floor, water from my boots smearing the faces of the murder victims, the dramatic illustrations of the crime scenes.

Cautiously, I began ascending the stairs.

When I reached the landing I saw, nine steps above me, that the carpet near my bedroom remained peeled away from where Richard had scrubbed Ellen's blood from the floor. As I continued to ascend, I looked carefully through the bannister spindles at the darkened second floor hallway, but saw nothing.

Just as I reached the top, a newspaper rustled on the foyer floor below me and I whipped about.

Max.

The rain pounded, pelting against the windows all around us.

I saw first his wet spiraling hair as he slowly ascended the stairs toward me. His eyes gleamed green with wild fury in the darkness.

I wondered, curiously, whether his anger could match the tempest inside me, fueled by love and loss.

"Abbie Sharp, you received my invitation."

"I'm here, aren't I?" I kept a hard grip on the bowie knife, unafraid as I faced him now.

Max stopped a third of the way up the stairs, cocking his head sideways; his mouth curved into a small smile as he scanned my trousers, Simon's shirt. As he lingered upon that sixth step, his smile slipped from amused to slightly crazed. He knew he would never have me. I wondered if he also knew that whoever my mother had been, I was *not* her.

"I'm going to kill you," I muttered through clenched teeth.

"Cute, because that's what I'm going to do to you. But first, I thought we might have a bit of fun before I cut your pretty throat."

"I'm not interested in *fun*."

Max only smiled and continued his ascent.

I had to stay in control of this game.

Still holding the bowie knife, I whipped my hand to my belt, pulled out one of the small knives, and threw it hard at him.

But he ducked swiftly and the knife flew past the chandelier, sticking into the wall high above the front door.

Max looked at the knife, then back toward me. He clucked his tongue. "Not very ladylike, love."

"Whoever said I was a lady?"

He reached toward a sheath, which I hadn't noticed, near the belt of his trousers. He pulled out a knife with a thin six-inch blade. The Ripper knife. The blade glinted in the continuing flashes of lightning.

Max chuckled and took three more steps toward me. "I stand corrected. But don't you tremble in fear at what's about to happen to you? You've *seen* what I can do."

"I don't give a damn about anything now except killing you."

I glared at him, then past him as I estimated the floor-to-ceiling distance of Grandmother's entranceway. It was at least eighteen feet to the lowest dangling crystal of the chandelier. I almost smiled. Grandmother had ordered that chandelier from Prague.

Sorry, Grandmother, I thought, just as Max lunged up the remaining stairs toward me. *Here we go.*

I clenched the blade between my teeth and leaped upon the wall, crawling across the ceiling over the staircase. My fingertips clung to the rose-patterned wallpaper; I felt every ridge, every raised petal shape.

My energy coursed through me like an electric bolt.

He stood below me, staring upward, amused.

I watched him, waiting for his next move, planning mine.

Thunder rumbled outside.

Then Max threw his head back and laughed maniacally, his white teeth gleaming in the flashes of lightning. "You could have been like this with me for centuries. Even medical school—you could have attended it and had years and years to perfect your knowledge and your practice."

Hard mirth overtook me. With one hand, I snatched the knife from my mouth and stuck it into my belt. It was my turn to laugh.

"Yes, yes, Max, but at what price? Would you butcher my patients every fifty years?"

His green eyes glowed with that unnatural elixir brightness. I'm certain my eyes were glowing too, and I felt as if I might burst with my own energy. With our eyes locked, I felt our energy billowing and connecting as if it were one living being. The air vibrated with our shared fury, crescendoing until breaking glass sounded all around us.

The glass of the front door had shattered, and wind and rain swept into the foyer.

"You killed my mother. Simon. Mariah. I think I've got a right to be a little mad." Snatching one of the knives from my belt, I threw it at him.

With lightning speed, he put his hand out and caught it. Then, sticking it hard into the wall, he stuck the Ripper knife in his belt and leaped onto the wall, crawling upward toward me.

I eased quickly out along the ceiling to the bolted top of the chandelier and waited. Holding on to the plastered ceiling, I pulled out the bowie knife. As he crawled quickly toward me, I eased down the heavy chandelier chain. The bolt at the top shifted a bit with my weight.

I had never liked the chandelier; it was a monstrosity in design. Large gas bulbs tipped the ends of the giant, dusty ormolu arms that swooped out from the center.

Still clinging to the chain, I stepped onto one of the arms.

Max crawled like a terrible insect down the five-foot chain toward me. If I could just stab him once and stun him into falling, I could finish killing him on the floor below.

When he reached me, his head at eye level, I stabbed fast at his back with the bowie knife, but he grabbed my hand and jerked me to him.

The chandelier rocked dangerously as I struggled against him. Keeping one hand on the chain, the other squeezing my wrist painfully, he swung downward, his knife still in his mouth. He leaped onto another arm, and I heard the bolts of the chandelier coming undone. Ceiling plaster powdered down upon us.

Pulling my third short-bladed knife out of my belt, I swung it heedlessly at him, nicking his cheek. He yelled in pain and released my wrist in the struggle, but my bowie knife dropped to the floor.

Blood oozing from his cheek, he whipped out his knife. Perspiration dripped down his face; dark stubble lined his jaw. "Aw...Abbie, my love, you shouldn't have done that."

I could tell by the glint in his eyes that he was going to make this fight last, play with me like a cat with a mouse.

But *I* was the cat in this game.

Another bolt came loose and we tipped dangerously to one side.

Another rain of plaster.

This was not a good place to fight, so while Max stepped toward me, I threw myself against the center of the chandelier, rocking us hard in one direction. Then, just as it swung back toward the wall above the front door, I propelled myself off of it, grabbing onto the wall just inches from the ceiling.

I wasn't a second too soon.

Just as I found my grip, the entire chandelier crashed to the floor. I heard the sound of glass spraying everywhere, and another cloud of dust and plaster rained around me.

I shot my glance downward through the dust, but I did not see Max.

Movement caught my eye. He had leaped the other way and now hung from the wall just under the stairway balcony.

He smiled widely, clearly enjoying this game.

As I scrambled to the floor, Max leaped down, and we faced each other from opposite sides of the mangled chandelier.

"Let's take this elsewhere," he said quickly.

"*Anywhere*. So long as you're a corpse by morning."

He ran toward me. I grabbed my bowie knife from the floor and swung it at him, but he caught my wrist, pushed me hard against the wall, and kissed me. He tasted like rainwater, like the blood running down his cheek.

"Catch me *if* you can!" he shouted, before running out the front door.

Twenty-seven

I chased him, my three short-bladed knives and my bowie knife in my belt. The torrents of rain continued as I ran through Kensington. I saw him in the distance. I picked up speed, but he cut through two manicured yards and leaped over the gate to Kensington Park. Between the rain and the trees, I lost sight of him.

Still, I followed, running fast.

Thunder roared in the sky. Instead of passing, the storm seemed to be increasing. There was more wind now, and rain blasted into my face, my eyes. Lightning bolts cracked through the sky and raindrops pounded the surface of the Long Water. I saw the outline of the Serpentine Bridge.

I paused in the rain, staring about me.

Where was he?

As if in answer, the Wellington Arch near Hyde Park appeared in my mind, breaking shakily through the rain, and suddenly I understood. He was taking me back to where this all began—Whitechapel Hospital.

I ran east, heading toward the main streets edging the park. My boots slapped heavily upon the ground; my hair fell around my face in heavy wet locks. Although few pedestrians or carriages were out, I kept my knives hidden. Running through the streets wearing men's clothes and armed with knives was improper, to say the least. If caught, I would be sent to Bethlehem Royal Hospital as a lunatic.

But I was at the mall now, closing in upon the Whitechapel district.

I would be less conspicuous there.

Still running hard, I realized that this was the same route I had taken in my long dress last autumn, chasing the pickpocket who'd stolen Mother's brooch. I remembered, clear as a photograph, Grandmother's thin-lipped chagrin at my behavior. She had wanted me to act ladylike; she had wanted me to follow rules.

I chuckled now, picking up my sprint.

Ladylike had never brought me very far.

As I ran along the mall, the storm increased even more. I tasted salty perspiration as it mixed with the rainwater coursing down my face.

Through the torrents, I saw the sparse outlines of buildings, heard the groan of carriage wheels and the light lash of whips on horses' backs. I heard the bells tolling at Christ Church. Then just as I reached the empty Spitalfields Market, I tripped over something like a very large bundle. I fell forward, scraping my left knee upon the ground.

I leaped up, warm blood seeping through the fabric of my trousers.

I had fallen over a man's body. He looked to be about

fifty. His bowler lay where it had fallen nearby, and his eyes stared, lifeless, up at me. Blood flowed from a wound in his neck and ran on the street under my feet.

Another one of Max's casualties. Another reason why he had to die tonight.

Quickly, I closed the dead man's lids and resumed my run, ignoring the throbbing pain in my knee.

The body was a sign for me that I was heading in the right direction.

"I prefer *visions*," I hissed breathlessly in the stormy darkness.

The Ripper's chuckle reverberated in my ears.

New fears rose inside of me. If he was heading in the direction of the hospital, was he planning a killing spree? He didn't have the Conclave's "rules" to constrain him now.

I ran even harder.

As I made my way eastward along Commercial Street, I squinted through the storm ahead of me. A vision of the hospital's dull brick side pulsed into my mind. The plaque—*Whitechapel Hospital for Women. Est. 1883*—flashed before me.

He was indeed running to the hospital.

Why?

I thought of the nursery, the children's ward, all the expectant women there.

"*Hurry, Abbie…*" I murmured to myself.

I had taken the elixir, and I was his equal now. I reminded myself that there was no reason Max should outrun me in this race. I bit my lip so hard that I tasted blood as I sprinted those last few blocks. Once I crashed, hard, into an inebriated pedestrian who swore a streak as he lurched away from me, and then at the corner of Dutfield's Yard I stumbled into a large muddy puddle of water smelling vaguely of urine.

Soaked and breathless, I didn't care about any of this.

"No, no, no…" I muttered to myself, just as I saw the dark hospital looming ahead of me. If Max murdered anyone there because I wasn't fast enough…

Finally, I reached Whitechapel Hospital's front steps.

I bolted up them but stopped, startled at his hideous whisper in my head: *Look up, Abbie.*

I flung my face upward, rain pelting against my eyelashes. In the shadows near the flat roof of the hospital, I saw a dark figure against the already-dark bricks.

I ran into the alley.

Carefully but quickly, I began crawling up the wet bricks, digging my fingertips, palms, and boots into the gritty surface. My left leg, still stunned by my fall, trembled violently as I scaled the side.

Five feet from the flat ledge of the roof, I paused, listening for sounds above me. I heard nothing but rain.

At the top, I curved my fingers around a muddy, leaf-strewn gutter and pulled, heaving myself onto the hard, flat roof of the hospital. I pulled the bowie knife from my belt and gripped it hard in my right hand.

"Abbie Sharp."

I whipped around to face him.

He stood several feet behind me in the middle of the roof, his knife gripped in his hand. He bowed, a maniacal smile on his face.

Furious, I grabbed one of my short-bladed knives and

flung it at him. But Max merely stepped aside, and I heard it clatter on the stone surface behind him.

Stupid, Abbie. I couldn't react like that and waste knives.

"Our last dance ends here," Max said fondly. His shirt was plastered wet against his skin, his hair slicked back with rain.

My mind scrambled.

A flash of lightning, a thunderclap, and my mind flashed back to a sunny afternoon in Dublin, Roddy teaching me some common fighting techniques.

"*Distraction can sometimes be the best weapon,*" he had said.

Distraction.

My mother had always moved Max.

She would be my lure now.

"Yes, here we are, Max. Indeed, our last dance."

I let a rumble of thunder play out. Then I walked toward him.

"You have about as much respect for me as you did Mother. You killed her, and now you think you'll kill me"—I swept my gaze toward his knife—"like a butchered animal."

Even in the heavy rain, I saw his jaw clench.

"*Poison,* Abbie. I didn't butcher her."

I laughed as I neared him. "It's all the same in the end. Killing is all that you're good for. You kill and kill and kill like clockwork. But you've lost your flourish, and now, with the elixir gone, you have only a handful of decades left. In fact, in another year you'll be just like the rest of us."

I stepped closer to him, so that our chests touched. His knife was lowered, ready, at his side.

I stayed alert, my knife in hand, ready to whip out one of my small blades if needed. But Max didn't move; he stood statue-like, his eyes boring down hard into mine.

A cat and mouse game. That was all it was. As long as I remained the cat, I would be fine.

I reached up to twirl one of his wet locks of hair in my fingers, pulling his face toward mine. A spectator might have thought I meant to kiss him.

My eyes locked onto his. The rain blurred his face like a smeared painting. As I blinked away raindrops, reading his expression carefully, I saw fury—but also something else—rippling on a pond surface. I continued funneling into his world; the storm faded into the background.

"*You*, not me, have squandered life," I murmured. "You killed Mother, the only person who might have mourned your death."

The mystery of her relationship with him needled me even now, but I pushed it aside.

We were both soaked, drenched in rain. And for some reason, the slippery water made me even more reckless. I pressed closer against him and felt his heaving chest pause, only once.

I had caught him, hooked him in his weak spot.

Mother.

My distraction.

With my free hand, I plunged the bowie knife into his side, withdrawing it before he could whip away. Max screamed in pain, and I leaped away from the sweep of his knife.

Blood seeped rapidly through the side of his clinging wet shirt.

Yelling, I ran at him.

This time he was ready, and, lunging hard at me, he pushed me to the ground. My bowie knife clattered away, leaving me with only two short-bladed knives.

As Max fell on top of me, his knife aimed for my throat, I threw my feet up to his chest and propelled him hard away from me, onto his back. I leaped onto him, straddling him. I grabbed a short-bladed knife and without thinking stabbed it into his rib cage, close to the other wound.

Although he yelled in pain, his wet curls breaking out about his head, the wound wasn't very deep and he was able to swing his free arm upward, catching my wrist. My knife fell to the ground.

Sitting up, his black curls falling over his face, he squeezed hard about my throat.

Pain, blindingly sharp like a hot poker, shot through my left rib cage as I felt his knife make contact with bone, then slide out. He released my throat and a thunderclap drowned my screams.

Max smiled, his eyes gleaming green just inches from my face.

I dizzied. Reflexively, I shot my hand to the wound in my side and felt blood, muscle, the hard surface of bone.

He kissed me savagely in the rainstorm, biting my lip, and then threw his head back in a hysterical laugh.

Another flash of lighting illuminated both of us.

We were both wounded, but he must die.

I knew I would lose consciousness soon. Blood spread out

around us in the rain. We were about nine feet from the roof's edge. Amid my vertigo, trying to cling to consciousness, I looked around me. There was no barrier on this edge; the guttering had fallen away.

Max stopped laughing and grabbed my throat again, squeezing harder, his face close to mine.

I saw stars in my peripheral vision.

"How does it feel to be about to die, when you could have had *everything*?" He laughed again, but I heard a raspy edge in the sound. He was in pain.

"Know this, Abbie Sharp. After I kill you tonight, I will kill *everyone* you love—Lady Westfield, that little girl, Richard. But I'm going to start with William."

No.

I was losing blood. I clung to consciousness. It was like staying above water when drowning.

I needed another distraction. I grabbed his shirt, pulled him to me, and returned his kiss, biting his lips until I tasted blood.

It worked. As he kissed me back, I eased my hand toward my belt and grabbed my last knife.

This one had to count.

My dizzying mind twirled strangely through my textbooks. *Wounds to the liver cause rapid exsanguination. Death can occur in minutes.*

I had missed it before, but not now. I stabbed deep into his upper abdomen, plunging the knife upward.

As he screamed in pain, I pulled away from him. Blood and rainwater streamed down both of our chins. I twisted the knife and pulled it out.

This one was fatal. Blood gushed from the wound. He had minutes to live.

He grabbed my neck again, furious.

Max—who had gutted those women last autumn, and killed so many others as well—knew this was the end.

But he wasn't about to go alone.

He squeezed my throat harder. I gagged, choking on burning vomit as he crushed my windpipe and cut off my air.

Then suddenly he let go. I dropped my knife, gasping hard and coughing up vomit. My lungs burned painfully. He pushed me onto my back and rolled on top of me, and I screamed at the pain resurging from my stab wound. He fell upon my sore wrist.

Slowly, leaving a trail of blood, Max rolled our bodies toward the precipice.

I was too weak to fight him now. My wrist was certainly broken. I was losing blood. He murmured nonsense into my ear as we rolled toward the end, his accent French again. "We'll be together after all, Caroline. You will be forever mine."

Oh God, he thought I was Caroline. I might die up here on this roof, but I was certainly not going to fall with him; I wasn't about to meet my death with this lunatic in that alley below.

No. I'd die by myself up here, thank you very much.

My mind raced for a way to escape his embrace.

As he rolled me hard onto my back, again, I felt the bowie knife under me.

With my unbroken hand, I grabbed the handle. Max was too delirious to notice. His energy was so drained that he'd stopped rolling with me; now he crawled along on his belly like a snake, his arm about my waist, over my painful wound, pulling me along with him toward that edge. We left a trail of blood behind us across the roof.

We were two feet from the edge. Amid the rain and my wavering consciousness, I tried to keep my wits. This would be all about timing.

Summoning my last ounce of strength, I buckled up my knees and thrust him to the edge, hard. He sailed over it, but grabbed onto my injured wrist.

I screamed, jerking myself back to full consciousness as I slid close to the precipice. His eyes gleamed crazily at me, his face unearthly white from the loss of blood. He was slipping, and I was sliding toward him.

He would pull me over.

"No!" I screamed. I swung the knife around. I would cut my own hand off before I would let this happen.

But instead, I stabbed his hand with a furious yell. His eyes locked with mine, and then he fell out of sight.

I crawled to the edge and looked down. Through the storm, I couldn't hear anything. Then, in a flash of lighting, I saw Max lying dead in the littered alley, upon his back. His eyes stared upward, lifeless. His leg twisted backward at a strange angle.

A fitting end—dead in this nasty little alley, bleeding, alone, just as he had left his victims.

This now done, I rolled away from the edge, onto my back. The sky lit up around me and I smiled up at it.

But I was fading.

"*Abbie!*" I heard my name called out, distantly. The next flash of lighting was too bright, so I shut my eyes.

"*Abbie…*" Mother called.

"*Abbie!*" Her voice was clearer this time. I opened my eyes and found myself in the sunny small barn behind our house in Edinburgh. I lay at the bottom of the crude wooden stairs, a glass pot I'd been carrying shattered about me. I felt a shard, the one that would scar my thigh, under my leg.

"Abbie! There you are," Mother said as she came into my view above me.

Stunned, the wind knocked out of me, I couldn't speak. I just watched her.

"You." She smiled affectionately and bent over to help me up, her long red hair loose, as she wore it when not giving lessons to children. "My girl. Always so clumsy."

Who are you? I wanted to ask her.

But she lifted me up, brushing the glass off. Sun glinted through the windows around us.

Who are you? I tried to ask.

"*Who are you?*" the caterpillar asked Alice.

Then the vision faded into darkness.

Twenty-eight

I opened my eyes but could not see clearly. My vision was filmy, as if I peered through water.

I tried to move, but pain shot through every part of my body.

As the pain increased, I tried to move again. One of my hands felt weighed down and I couldn't move it. But with my other hand's fingertips, I felt bedsheets and the coarse fabric of a hospital nightgown about me. Although I couldn't yet move my head, my vision slowly focused.

The room was darkened, except for the soft glow of a lamp outside of my vision. I realized I was lying on a bed in the small room where we performed surgeries. A trolley of medical instruments sat beside me, with bloody cloths, bandages, a jar of carbolic acid, and two bottles of dextrin.

The pain bloomed increasingly at my left side, and that part of my chest began to throb with every breath.

I groaned.

"*Abbie!*"

Then I saw William's face above mine.

I touched his face, ran my thumb upon his unshaven jawline. He took my hand and kissed my fingertips. I noticed the dark brown blood staining my cuticles. My blood. Max's blood.

I looked away as my memories flooded back.

"Max..."

"I know—he's dead," William said gently, sitting down on my bed. Then he lay down carefully beside me and stroked my hair out of my face.

I cast an anxious glance toward the door.

He caught his smirk as I turned my face toward him. "I stitched up your side, so there's no point in hiding."

My face burned with embarrassment.

"Don't worry. Nurse Josephine was in here, so it was all very proper. Yet your virtue is ruined. You certainly have to marry me now."

I chuckled before promptly moaning in pain. It felt like a knife was caught in my lung.

"Careful..." William lightly touched the stitched wound. "I'm afraid you might have pneumothorax."

"He punctured my lung?"

"It could be worse, but you'll be in pain for several weeks. And your hand..."

I looked down and saw the splint and the bandages. Dried now.

"It will heal, but it's broken." He reached his hand across me and touched the bandages. "A distal radius fracture."

My mind wearily tried to put together the pieces. "Max, his body... how long has it been..."

William relaxed beside me; the gaslight glowed from

across the room. He put his temple against my ear, his brown curls tickling my cheek, and I inhaled his smell of perspiration and rainwater.

He traced, at the base of my throat, the top of my scar from Seraphina. "With Laura safe, I wanted to find you again. I'll admit, finding you here was pure luck. I must have been just behind you. I ran to Simon's home, then to your grandmother's ... "

He shifted his head so that he met my eyes, amused. "All I found was the newspaper mess, one of your knives in the wall, and that mangled chandelier ... it must have been one bloody hell of a fight."

"It was," I muttered.

"I decided to take my chances that you might return to the hospital. I ran part of the way before I found a carriage. When I saw the crowd gathering around a man's body in Spitalfields Market, I leaped from the carriage and ran here. I panicked when I couldn't find you anywhere—in the laboratory, in the offices. Then I heard you scream. I saw him fall past the window ... "

William paused. I knew he wanted to ask more questions about the details of the fight, but I stiffened and closed my eyes. I'd felt like a different person up there—so savage and cruel. I remembered the blood, the biting. I didn't like to think of myself in that way.

"Go on ... " I finally said.

"I ran up there ... God ... " William clutched the fabric of my nightgown and buried his face in the curve of my neck. "There was so much blood. Your face ... I thought you were bleeding to death. I brought you down here immediately. I was afraid we would have to do a blood transfusion, but as I cleaned and stitched the wound, I thought it an unnecessary risk. I gave you a heavy dose of laudanum once your heartbeat steadied. You've been unconscious now almost ten hours."

"And Max … is his body … "

William's gaze darkened. "Yes, he's dead." Then he turned to me and smiled. "*Very* dead. You did well, love."

"Don't call me that," I said flatly.

William considered me quizzically but didn't pursue the matter. "As soon as you stabilized, at about five o'clock in the morning, I ran outside to make certain his body still lay where it fell. Fortunately, he had fallen into that small alleyway, not the street. Only a few dogs had found him. I covered the body with a canvas until I could decide what to do with him. Calling Scotland Yard would—"

"Raise too many questions." I smiled, a cut from under my lip cracking a bit at the effort. I tasted blood.

William leaned over me and wiped it away with his thumb. "You have these rough little cuts about your lip … "

"So what happened to him?"

"Before I could decide what to do with the body, Agent Melville's carriage arrived. He talked to me briefly before taking the body away to be 'discreetly disposed of.'" William's gaze darkened. "Although he didn't inquire, I told him that you were under my care, but very injured."

"They were just using us—using *me,* under the effects of the elixir—to defeat Max," I muttered darkly. "It was brilliant, actually."

"It was awful. But Abbie … " William turned on his elbow

in the little bed to face me. "Max will never be in our lives, in anyone's life, ever again."

I said nothing, because William's words were only a half-truth. Max's memory would always linger with me. I could not think of Mother now without thinking of him. Mariah. Simon. Max had taken so many from me, and yet Simon's death was perhaps the most painful. His death fell slowly, crustily, upon me now like an autumn leaf.

Other questions. You have other questions, I reminded myself. I wiped a tear away from my eye. "Laura—she's safe?"

William nodded. "She's with Christina now. But did you *hear* me, Abbie?"

Gingerly, he pulled me to him and kissed me lightly. "He's dead. He cannot hurt you, or me, or Lady Westfield, my aunt, the child... *anyone*. This should be an enormous weight off of you. I am relieved."

I kissed William and stared back across the room at the light. "Yes. Yet nothing will bring back Simon."

"*Ashes to Ashes, dust to dust...*"

For a funeral, the day was cruelly beautiful.

"Ashes to Ashes..."

This ashes part was the only part of the service that I could entirely embrace. At least *that* part was true. We were all dust eventually, in spite of any twists and turns we might take to hold off impending mortality.

It was Simon's funeral, and we stood in a small circle

around the St. John mausoleum. Lady St. John would have insisted upon an elaborate affair, full of gloomy pomp and ceremony, but Rosamund had pleaded with her to keep the service intimate and simple, as Simon would have liked it. Simon had cultivated few friendships within his class, and only a dozen or so attended out of respect for his mother.

The priest's words droned on in the background as I stood in the mottled light just outside the tomb, exactly where its cold shadows met the bright outdoors. Grasping my red-rose nosegay with my free hand as I stood flanked by Grand-mother and William, I watched Simon's two sisters.

I had met them and his mother only a few times. I wondered if they even knew that Simon had loved me.

Probably not.

I couldn't imagine him telling them. Now, as I stared at them, I was grateful for the awkward, hot, black crepe veil and bonnet that hid my tears.

I couldn't stop staring at Rosamund and Annabelle; they looked so much like Simon, splinters from the same wood. Tall, thin, blond, and pale in their dark dresses, the sisters even had his stoic expression. Neither shed tears, but rather flicked a fingertip upon their eyes sporadically, their move-ments efficient and graceful, as if whisking away an eyelash.

I wondered what lie they'd been told about his death. I wished they could know the truth.

Rosamund, the slightly taller sister, would particularly miss him, and I saw her fingering a large brooch upon her neck. My chest tightened, as I knew she would have a lock of Simon's hair within it. As for me, I had nothing but my memories.

Unlike at Lionel Millbrough's service, Grandmother was

shedding real tears. She had loved Simon. Laura stood soberly near Grandmother's skirts. Christina stood behind them, a small figure almost swallowed by her own heavy black dress.

I cast a sidelong glance at William, who had been silent and sober since his arrival with his aunt. He had said little about Simon since his death, but his jaw was set tight, his dark eyes hard upon the priest. William's emotions as always shone transparent, and now his grief was real but uncomfortable. William was here, alive, only because of Simon; Simon had saved his life as a gift to me.

This truth tightened at my chest with more pain than the still-aching wound in my side, and for the remainder of the service, the liturgy and Grandmother's soft weeping faded into the background.

I stepped into the cool mausoleum with the other mourners and placed the nosegay on the floor's small pile of flowers. Simon's resting place was near the bottom, so I crouched and ran my fingers along the edge of the small glass window to see the satin-covered oak head of his casket, and then, as others moved forward to pay their last respects, I quietly stepped away. William touched my hand lightly, but I pulled away and walked out of the mausoleum. I kept walking.

I left the main roads of the cemetery, choosing meandering paths because I wanted to be alone and lost. The summer heat sweltered around me, and perspiration soaked my wrist splint. After a bit, when I felt far enough away from the other mourners, I pulled off the bonnet and the suffocating veil.

The warm summer air blew into my face like hot breath.

I walked past a few more mausoleums and then small clusters of graves. Thorny brambles clung to my skirts. When

I reached a large marble tomb shaped like an angel, I stopped, pressed my forehead hard against the stone, and sobbed.

I recalled my dream about Mariah and our conversation about heaven. I tried to picture Simon's heaven, but my mind went blank. Simon lived to care for others, and who suffered or needed anything in heaven?

I slumped down at the base of the tomb, my skirts crushing the dried twigs and dirt as pain shot through my knife wound. I played with the bonnet's lace and rested my splinted hand upon my lap. I felt weary of surmising about heaven's existence when all I wanted was for Simon to be here with me now.

My eyes sore and dry from crying, I looked up through the patterns of leaves above me, sharp and dark against the sky. I saw an empty bird's nest, tilted dangerously upon a low limb.

I heard the snap of a twig.

I didn't even turn around. I knew it was William.

"Everyone's gone," he said quietly. "Even his sisters."

Yet I was reluctant to leave. Leaving meant Simon was truly gone, that I would have to find a way to move beyond this grief. Doing so was hard to imagine.

"I'm coming," I said, holding my bonnet in my hands.

William led me back to one of the main roads, and we walked in silence through the pressing heat. My breathing was labored from my still-healing punctured lung.

The path curved as we walked around a tomb shaped like an empty urn. A young fox peered at us through the foliage.

As we neared Egyptian Avenue, William finally broke the silence. He chuckled darkly. "This is probably an awful time to say this, but Simon makes me feel guilty even after he's dead."

I didn't reply. My body felt weak, and I was lightheaded.

The whalebones about my corset squeezed hard across my chest and my knife wound throbbed. Vaguely, I recognized symptoms of dehydration, possible heat exhaustion. Then I almost laughed—my expiration would be much less noble than Simon's had been. Death by mourning dress.

The sunny world about me spun for an instant before I felt William's hand upon my arm.

"You're ill." Then, before I could protest, he led me to the shade of the entrance to Egyptian Avenue.

"Put your head down," he said, gently.

I did, lowering my head to my knees. I leaned against the creeping ivy of the nearby column. The vertigo lessened in my bent state, but my tears started all over again.

Still facing the ground, I muttered, "William, I don't know how to do this."

After a brief pause, he said quietly, "You've done it before. With your mother, Mariah..."

"I know," I said, wiping my eyes. "But now..." It wasn't right to speak of my feelings for Simon in front of William, but my grief overwhelmed me. "I can't live with him as a memory. I'm sorry." I stood up, turning my face from William.

We said nothing for a few minutes. There was no noise except for the lark's calls around us, the buzzing of bees in a nearby cluster of wildflowers.

"Abbie," William muttered. "Look at this."

I turned and faced him through my tears. He touched lightly one of the large lotuses carved upon one of the columns flanking Egyptian Avenue.

"Do you know what the lotus symbolized to the Egyptians?"

I shook my head, remembering when I stood in this place with Simon.

"Rebirth. That's why it's here. The Egyptians believed this flower mimicked the sun, sinking under the water at night and then rising, freshly bloomed, in the morning." He traced the curves of the lotus blossom with his fingertips. "The petals arose cleaned and unstained, even after pushing through the mud."

"Yes, very clever Christian symbolism … like resurrection, returning … "

"No, Abbie," he responded with uncharacteristic patience. "Yes, the intention was obviously to point to a religious notion that … but let's break away from that. Think of the message of what is lasting, resurgent, and good. Ashes to ashes, yes, but there are some things, some *people*—" William chuckled and shifted uncomfortably. "Bloody hell, I can't believe I'm saying this about him, but"—his voice cracked—"there are some whose goodness lasts beyond death."

We stood silently. It was a fragile moment.

"He gave me a gift, Abbie. I'm here with you only because of him." William chuckled again, and this time a small tear lingered at the corner of his eye.

Holding my bonnet in my good hand, I stared at the lotus blossom.

Resurgam.

Resurrection.

Christian orthodoxy, or mad science—but *this* was resurrection in its best form.

"Simon's act was a gift for both of us. But now, what are we to do with such a gift?"

William didn't answer.

Twenty-nine

William's silence weighed more than words in my mind. He was giving me time, but I knew the pressing issue: *marriage*. It weighed upon me in the coming weeks as I rested, healed, returned to my studies.

"They'll wither and die now," William said of the dodos one evening, as we sat on the bamboo swing in the menagerie.

"We all will," I replied, watching Laura play with the birds in the middle of the floor.

We had donated all of the other animals to the London Zoological Society. But the dodos, for obvious reasons, we kept.

"When, Abbie? After medical school?"

I bit my lip, watching the seeping twilight crack through the now-empty cages and across the floor. I loved William, so I was unsure why marriage seemed so difficult for me. There was just something so arbitrary, so disturbingly sanctioned, about it.

I couldn't imagine Mother ever marrying.

But then again, I was having trouble imagining her at all anymore. I couldn't peel back even one layer of her mysteries.

"When I marry, it will be to you, but William... there is too much ahead of me, too much behind me now to solidify our plans."

"Life is brief, Abbie. Why waste—"

"I can't, William." I wasn't entirely certain about my reasons. I couldn't imagine being married while still in medical school. And Simon. The only reason I had William with me was because Simon was dead.

It was a muddled mess. Muddied waters.

Laura squealed happily as a dodo nipped at her skirt. She was playing with them, leaving a circle of bread crumbs behind her.

"It's him, isn't it?" William asked, grumpily. "He lingers like a ghost between us."

I couldn't answer. There was too much truth in the statement.

He stood and left the menagerie abruptly.

I walked over to where Laura played with the dodos. The last stream of sunlight from the day poured through the windows, and I picked up a small handful of bread crumbs. I sighed, tried to blink away the film of tears in my eyes.

"Ye and Dr. Siddal said they will die now. Are they ill?" Laura asked quietly. We had not, of course, told her the truth behind it all. There were no lies; she simply knew nothing of the elixir.

"No..." I kept my eyes on the birds. Beautiful. Their existence unbelievable.

I wondered why I couldn't reaffirm the promise I'd made to William that night in the mausoleum. Why did marriage feel like a misplaced stitch to me now?

Then I felt Laura's warm fingers on my cheek. I turned and pressed my face into her palm, then smiled widely and met her gaze.

"They're certainly not ill." I stood up and brushed bread crumbs from my skirts. "But they have a limited number of days, like we all do. They should make the best of those days, don't you think?"

She nodded, watching me carefully.

"Come," I said, leading the dodos into their enclosure and then taking her hand. "We are to have a bit of pudding with Lady Westfield, and then you and I must finish reading our book."

She took my hand, a smile playing at the corners of her mouth. "Does *Alice in Wonderlain* end 'appily?"

"Hmmm..." I tried to remember how it ended. "Oh, yes, she woke up from the dream, and she had so many paths before her at the end. So yes, Laura. Wondrously happily."

Although William and I often took tea in the library upstairs, he went to bed early that evening. I cringed, thinking of the slump in his shoulders as he'd left the menagerie. I felt certain about my love for him, but everything else... I couldn't.

After tucking Laura into bed, I met Grandmother in the parlor. She was seated, studying one of Laura's paintings. She set it aside as I entered.

Bridget had already drawn all of the curtains. The house was unbearably quiet now that we had sent away the animals.

I was used to the occasional roar of Petey, to the distant shrieks of the birds and monkeys. Now there was nothing.

Richard had already cleared away our bowls of bread pudding, and now he brought us brandy.

"Thank you, Richard," I said quietly.

He caught my eye and smiled.

Grandmother sighed as he left the room. "There are so many questions now about what to do."

"Indeed..." I muttered into my glass.

"I don't think that I will be returning to London."

I stared at her, surprised.

"I've decided that I like it here. Catherine... Violet... they can visit me, but..." Her glassy eyes stared ahead. The thin folds in her skin were like cracked porcelain in the parlor's dim light. "I'm not certain that they've always been good for me. I've had more time to read here, and I rather like the quiet ease of this place."

"Certainly," I said. I'd never imagined that Grandmother would *not* wish to return to London.

"London holds too many memories now. Since you told me about your mother, about this history that I did not know of... that life feels so insincere. I would rather live here."

She was quiet, and her hand trembled. "I cannot tell you enough how sorry I am that I *sent* you to them. That I was so blind to their natures."

I sat silently, hoping that she would keep talking. We had talked very little about this since I'd returned to Kenilworth. I think it had been too difficult.

I felt her eyes upon me, and then I saw her looking at my splinted hand. "He is gone... those men..."

"They are all gone, Grandmother, and they will never trouble us further."

We remained silent for several minutes. We hadn't discussed the matter of Laura's education yet, but I knew it was a lingering topic. I feared that Grandmother and I would disagree upon the matter. She would want Laura to attend a girls' boarding school.

But Grandmother's voice broke into my thoughts. "I was thinking that perhaps the child might remain here with me. Perhaps bring a governess here for a year. Then you can find a suitable school."

I smiled, happy that for once Grandmother was thinking along the same lines as me. Laura needed a year with us. She didn't need to leave so soon for a school where she would be chided by sharp-mouthed headmistresses and have her accent mocked. Of course, she would meet all of that soon enough. But for now, she needed Grandmother daily.

"Yes, I completely agree."

"Good," Grandmother said, sipping her tea. "I'll start advertising for a governess tomorrow."

My brandy glass was almost empty.

"But I suppose I cannot dissuade you from marrying William Siddal. I had always hoped that you could do better..."

"Grandmother..." I stopped, caught between tears and a laugh. Simon lingered between Grandmother and me also.

She sighed. "I supposed that you'll marry him."

Even now, she couldn't bring herself to like him. She was still Lady Westfield.

"Yes, probably so, Grandmother." I stood and kissed

her forehead. "But it will not be for a good while. There is medical school first."

She sniffed loudly but said nothing else.

William came and went from Kennilworth for the rest of the summer, working at Whitechapel Hospital but still spending most nights with us. Christina dined with us frequently. I was to return to London soon, to settle matters with Grandmother's house and to find a place of my own to live before taking my exams and beginning medical school.

The night before I went back to London, William asked to inspect my stitches in the library. I felt guilty for not caring more about propriety, but that concern felt so inane now.

Unlike in the rest of the house, the large square windows of the library had no curtains. With only the desk lamp on, we had very little light; only a watery, periwinkle twilight moving through the windows.

Grandmother thought we were in bed.

William turned away while I unbuttoned my dress and then my corset, which was difficult with the still-binding splint.

"You have been applying the salve nightly?" he asked, an awkward rasp in his voice.

"Yes." I was almost to the last stay.

"And your breathing?" He tapped his knuckles awkwardly as he stood near the lamp.

"Better each day."

In the semi-darkness, I finished with the stays and tried to hold my dress up around the loosened corset as I walked toward him. His face remained turned away, near the lamp.

When I was just next to him, I unbuckled the fastener. At the click, he paused. "Are you ready?"

"Yes." I couldn't meet his eyes as I turned.

He cleared his throat. "You'll have to take off the corset for me to see it properly."

"Turn around again, please," I whispered.

Holding my dress up awkwardly, I slipped out from under the corset. Goose bumps broke out on my exposed arms and across my exposed breasts. I held the dress as far up to my chin as possible and stepped closer to the lamp. "I'm ready."

He stepped closer. I turned away, feeling his breath upon my neck. I slid my dress down on that side, making certain to keep ahold of it around the waist.

I felt his warm fingers on me, gently feeling the stitches about the wound. The skin prickled softly under his touch.

"There is still some inflammation, but the salve has helped and there is no infection. The stitches are not ready to come out, though. They should remain in place for at least another week."

His fingers remained, pressing gently against my skin.

Then, he kissed my neck. My breathing became irregular. And all of the pain at my side stopped. I felt only pleasure. He slid his hand forward, from the stitches to my belly. Bare under his touch.

"Stop, William. Please, turn and let me get dressed again."

He paused, then stroked my stomach a bit more. I almost turned to kiss him before catching myself.

"William, if you do not stop now, I will have no will-power to stop you."

He paused again and sighed against the back of my neck. Removing his hands, he placed them on my shoulders. With a deep sigh, he kissed my cheek and turned away.

While his back was turned, I quickly dressed.

"When?" he asked, pouring himself a small glass of water.

"At *some point* after medical school."

He turned around and smiled. "I was going to wait to give you this until after you passed your medical exams, but..."

My heart pounded.

"Christina gave me this ring. It belonged to Elizabeth Siddal."

"Was it..." I stared at the thin rose-gold band, an amethyst stone set upon it.

"Yes. It was upon her finger when she was buried. When Gabriel exhumed her body to retrieve his poems, he quietly requested that it be brought back to him. See, even married, you'll never be traditional."

I laughed.

William put the ring on my finger, and I kissed him.

Thirty

After selling Grandmother's house, I used the money to move into a small flat in Bloomsbury near New Hospital. Living alone and unchaperoned was not ideal, but I enjoyed the autonomy. In my small front parlor, I hung Gabriel's painting of my mother as a lamia, and my desk nearby was littered with notes and open textbooks. My entrance exam for the London Medical School for Women was in two weeks.

A few days after I moved in, Christina stopped by with a bouquet of roses in her hand.

"If I didn't know better," she said, glancing slyly at my ring, "I would think that you've chosen to live as an eccentric spinster."

I laughed. We sat down to tea, and talked mostly about William and the three new "friends" Christina had living with her. I noticed that the circles under Christina's eyes had deepened since I'd last seen her. And she seemed even thinner, if that was at all possible.

"Abbie, why wait? Unless you're unsure if you love him," she was saying.

"No, it's not that at all." I looked down at the worn Oriental rug under my feet. I shuffled uncomfortably.

Christina looked away. "I didn't wish to pry ... "

"This is all a terrible mess," I muttered quietly. "I'm still grieving Simon. There's medical school. I know that I love William, but love always muddled everything for Mother. I don't feel like I understand her ... or like I understand myself enough to marry." I chuckled awkwardly. "And marriage itself makes me uncomfortable. It has so many entailments. Mother did it only so that I might be born legitimate. My last name, Sharp, shouldn't be—"

"Ahhh ... " Christina cut me off and took another sip of tea. "I think I understand. By all means, take your time with the matter." Her eyes shot to the scandalous portrait of Mother. "Abbie, I didn't know Caroline. Truthfully, what she had with Gabriel was ... " Christina's lips tightened. "Short-lived."

"Of course it was," I said bitterly. *Short-lived, like her relationship with Max?*

I looked away but felt Christina's eyes upon me. After a few minutes of silence, she said quietly, with just a hint of mirth, "Abbie, I have experience, obviously, with ... *complicated* family members."

I met her eyes and laughed a little. "That's rather an understatement."

"Of course it is. I'm merely saying that you will drive yourself insane, set yourself on a very unpleasant and never-ending carousel ride, if you try to make sense of everyone who has loved you."

"But she was my mother."

"She was *human*, Abbie." Christina leaned forward. I could smell the faint scent of the roses she'd held against her blouse. Laying her hand on my knee, she whispered, "You cannot expect more."

I took in her words. But the acceptance of this truth—that I would never fully know who Mother was—might take a lifetime.

Carefully setting down her tea, she wiped away a tear from my face that I hadn't even felt fall. "Come…William is coming home early tonight. Why don't you dine with us?"

At the end of that week, I was to visit Kennilworth. Whenever William didn't need me at Whitechapel Hospital on the weekends, I went to see Grandmother and Laura.

But before catching the train, I had one more stop. This final task had to be completed.

In Westminster, I walked into looming Scotland Yard and made my way directly to Inspector Abberline's office.

He sat behind his desk. Three empty teacups rested before him. I saw the same map on the wall behind him that had been there during the Ripper murders, but now he had pins placed upon new spots, different crime scenes. I wondered if the case on Cleveland Street had been wrapped up. His head was bent as he wrote furiously in a large notebook.

I cleared my throat.

"Miss Sharp," he said, startled at my presence. His eyes

were red-rimmed as always; I suspected that he hadn't slowed down much over the past weeks. "Miss Sharp, please sit down."

As I sat in one of the uncomfortable wooden chairs across from his desk, I remembered being here last autumn with William and our assistant, Mary Kelly. The police, thinking they were pursuing the Ripper, had only managed to arrest us.

"I can only stay for a moment, Inspector." I leaned forward, lace from my wrist brushing the corner of his desk. In spite of his red-rimmed eyes and pasty skin, there was something softened about Abberline. Strangely, I didn't feel angry at him now. For anything.

"For some reason," Abberline said in a low voice, "I feel as if I know what you are about to tell me."

"Why?"

He shrugged his fleshly shoulders. "A mere premonition."

"The Ripper is gone."

He stared at me. "Was that how your friend, Dr. St. John …?"

A lump formed in my throat. Abberline wasn't *completely* unaware of the happenings in my circle. "Yes. It was not without a great cost."

"I'm sorry to hear that," he muttered uncomfortably.

I paused; I couldn't weep in front of this man.

"Thank you." I took a deep breath. "I came here because I know that you cared about the Ripper case. I know that it truly troubled you that the murders had remained unresolved. You need to know that it's over, and the cemetery attacks should be over now also."

His old bloodhound expression resurged for an instant. "I suppose—"

"No," I said quickly. "I cannot tell you any of the details. I merely thought that you deserved closure. You deserve to know that the Ripper is gone."

He stared hard, then more gently. His eyes flicked briefly to the photograph of his wife. Then he looked up and caught my hand in a warm grip.

"Thank you, Miss Sharp. My gratitude is sincere, and I'm very happy that you are here safely to tell me this news." He paused, grunted, and stood at the same moment that I stood to leave.

"Goodbye," I said awkwardly as I moved to step out of the room.

He cleared his throat. "And now, what is there for you after this? What do you seek now, Miss Sharp?"

I paused only for a second. "Possibilities."

When I arrived at Kennilworth that evening, I read to Laura for an extra hour even though I was weary. Then Grandmother and I sipped brandy in the parlor.

The first governess to be interviewed would arrive the next afternoon. We were in no hurry to fill the position. We wanted someone qualified, but also someone who would suit Laura's sensitive personality.

After Grandmother retired to bed, Richard came in to remove the glasses.

"Richard, I'd like another brandy, please. And"—I smiled and caught his eye—"I would like you to take one with me."

He returned with the drinks, and it felt very odd to be sitting with Richard as an equal. William and I had told him all that had occurred, but Richard had said very little. He had attended Simon's funeral, and I knew that he mourned him quietly.

I took a sip of brandy. Richard sipped his too, with a sigh, and then crossed his legs and relaxed. Today was washing day, and he'd helped Miranda and Bridget with the task. He smelled faintly of lye.

"How do you do it, Richard?" With my free hand, I played with the leaf of a nearby potted plant.

"Do what, Miss Sharp?"

"Move on..." I wiped a tear. "From Simon, from all of *this*..."

I felt his eyes upon me in the darkness. He set down his brandy and fumbled for a handkerchief, placing it gently into my hand.

My shoulders heaved. Richard shared my grief in a way that William could not. William still didn't know Simon's painful family history, and I wasn't certain when or if I would tell him of it.

Gently, Richard pulled me to him and stroked my hair. "Hush, dear..."

I clutched the folds of his neatly pressed jacket.

"I have had many losses in life. I have seen terrible things. Losing Simon was..." His voice caught. "*Particularly* difficult. But with every loss, with every interlude, one must wait for what is to come. There is always something else to come.

When I arrived first at your Grandmother's house, I was so lonely, and now I have my niece, her child...*you*."

He pulled away from me, his blue eyes watery.

"But it all seems so difficult. I wouldn't have believed that Simon's death could do this to me."

"I know, darling," Richard said, stroking my hair. "I know."

Epilogue

FIVE YEARS LATER

Sunlight streamed into the first floor of the New Hospital for Women, spreading across the room, catching the glint of my engagement ring. I'd tried not to look at it for the past few weeks; Dr. Anderson had made a suggestion that I could not stop thinking about. It needled at me, making the whole question of my impending marriage that much more complicated.

"Just a sting, a small bee sting," I said as I stuck a syringe into the blue-veined arm of an old woman. Her appendix had been removed yesterday and she was still in great pain. She barely winced at the needle.

Now, as I tried to make a decision, the past five years of my life played out clearly in my mind. I'd finished medical school and was working full-time as a physician at New Hospital. William still worked at Whitechapel Hospital, and I saw him almost daily. Although Whitechapel had other physicians, most soon moved on to more prestigious locations. William's dedication to the hospital surprised me.

Over the past few years, I'd helped him reorder many aspects of Whitechapel. Although William didn't pursue any of Simon's experimental practices, such as hypnotism, he agreed with Dr. Anderson about attempting to use only minimally invasive methods for delivering babies, as well as the importance of having wards filled with sunlight, flowers, and widely spaced beds. I couldn't do much about the lack of sunlight in our wards, but I often brought fresh flowers in to brighten the environment. Still, Whitechapel Hospital had many needs, particularly an additional ward, and its third floor operating room needed to be changed into an operating theater to accommodate the increasing number of medical students working under William.

I had finished my clinical rotations at New Hospital the previous year, and now, along with my own work, I also had the responsibility of teaching rising medical students. After making the elderly woman comfortable, I went to the hospital's operating theater to demonstrate an appendectomy to a small crowd of female students.

"The cut is made here, at this point, between the iliac crest and the umbilicus," I muttered softly as I made the incision. Although appendectomies were a fairly common procedure, I bit my lip nervously and steadied my hand. The sedated patient was only twelve years old.

"Sepsis is the main danger … " I muttered automatically as I focused upon cutting through the layers of fat. The child was about the same age as Laura.

Laura was doing well. We had educated her with a governess for the first three years, but now, at age thirteen, she was thriving in a reputable boarding school near Kent. The school had rigorous classes and a caring headmistress. Grandmother and I had visited no less than eight schools before deciding upon that one.

Many weekends, Laura returned to Kennilworth to stay with Grandmother and me. She still painted and sketched often, but she rarely talked about her past in Orkney. None of her surviving relatives had made any attempt to contact her. After the deaths of Max and his cohorts, she never spoke of any more visions. I never asked. My own visions had stopped with Max's death.

Grandmother had grown used to her life at Kennilworth. Richard continued to work as her butler, and for the most part she accepted William. She still had the occasional flare-up with William, of course, but it was no greater than a passing summer storm.

As I worked, I spoke to the medical students about the importance of properly disinfecting the area. I removed the inflamed organ and then demonstrated how to stitch the wound so that the patient would have minimal scarring.

While watching one of my students bandage the stitched wound, my thoughts turned once again to my conversation with Dr. Anderson. I couldn't seem to banish her suggestion from my mind. I hadn't spoken of it to anyone, yet the idea had taken root, and it batted its wings against my heart like a butterfly.

I knew my decision, and it would hurt.

I washed my hands and then splashed my face with cold water in the supply room that adjoined the operating theater.

"Dr. Sharp." One of the young nurses stepped into the room. "Dr. Siddal is waiting downstairs for you."

"Thank you. I'll be down in a moment."

I stared at my reflection in the scarred mirror. Thankfully, my eyes had turned back to their normal brown color. The elixir had stayed in my system for an entire year, pulsing and pulling in my bloodstream, and I was relieved when it dwindled away—there was something comforting and very right about casting my lot with the rest of the human race. I reached my fingers to my throat, touching the curve of the scar that poked out from the collar of my dress. I had half-moon circles under my eyes. I was overworked and exhausted, but wondrously happy.

Then I frowned into the mirror. It was Tuesday, mid-morning. William never came to the hospital at this time.

What could he want?

My mind raced a bit. Over the past five years, my love for William had not changed. He had remained constant to me. His touch still thrilled me, and I thought of how many heated moments we'd shared. I blushed even thinking of it, but one time we became far too passionate after an autopsy, late at night at Whitechapel. I definitely wanted to be with William... but marriage would likely be an obstacle to the new adventure I had decided to embark upon.

Still, a nagging part of me feared that I was squandering my chance to live a life of love with William. I cursed the gods for strewing so many appealing paths at my feet.

I dried my face and hands and swung open the door, almost colliding with William.

"*William*...I thought you were waiting downstairs."

He had come straight from work, and seemed overworked and very anxious. A line of dark stubble marked his clenched jaw, and he had that faint odor of carbolic acid and lime chloride that we all carried upon our clothes.

"What—"

But he stopped my words with a kiss.

"There's something different about you, Abbie. Something is heavy on your mind, and I must know." He glanced down at my ring. "Are you reconsidering...?"

I played with the ring, slowly rotating it around my finger. I wanted to suggest that we go on a walk. I wanted to lie, tell him anything except what I knew I had to tell him now.

"William..." I swallowed hard. "I still love you, as much as always. I planned to marry you, but..." I paused. His eyes searched mine.

"A two-year position for a female physician has opened in Dubai. Dr. Anderson recommended the position to me, and I have decided to take it."

Tears pricked my eyes. I had second-floor rotations in twenty minutes.

"I'm sorry, I must," I added weakly.

"*Why*, Abbie?"

"There are so many needs there. Because of their culture, men are not allowed to attend to female patients, so there is a desperate need for female physicians. It will only be for two years..."

William slammed his hand onto a nearby trolley of medical supplies. They rattled, and three scalpels fell to the floor.

I wiped my eyes.

"I have waited five years," he snapped. "I have been constant. Abbie, I will turn twenty-nine this year."

In the soft light of the operating theater, his face betrayed the five years that had passed. Yet he was still breathtakingly handsome.

"I must do this, William."

"Marrying me is no betrayal of *him*."

I looked away. Simon was with us even now. His dedication to his work had infected me.

"You know that if we marry, you can continue to work. But there is no reason for you to leave, to do this, other than . . . " His voice drained away. "Do you love me?"

"Yes." I chuckled through my tears. "I cannot *not* love you. How many times have I told you that? You know that I would *die* for you, William. But . . . " I struggled with the way to put my feelings into sincere words. "I want to marry you, but I must do this. I cannot betray myself."

"I cannot go with you," he muttered. "My aunt. The hospital."

My heart clenched a bit. With each passing year, Christina's health weakened. She continued to lose weight, and she'd stopped taking in "friends."

I shook my head. "William, the hospital in Dubai is terribly understaffed." I swallowed as the lump in my throat grew. I hated the aching look on his face. "A typhoid infection swept through that part of the city last spring . . . "

Alarmed, William raised his voice. "Abbie . . . you *can't*—"

I waved my hand. "It has passed. But the few female physicians they had were evacuated. The midwives who stayed on, died. Women are dying in childbirth, and this hospital is particularly reliant upon our graduates. I have no children. No husband … it would be irresponsible for me not to go."

William sighed loudly, ran his fingers through his hair, and shook his head.

I started to take off the ring. Tears pricked my eyes, as I knew what this would do to him.

"I do not have any right to preserve this engagement," I said. "I want it more than you could know. But to make you wait for two more years, after these past five … I can't do that to you."

He took my hand. He was angry; his eyes narrowed. He pushed the ring back into place and growled, "I'll wait. There will be no other way."

Without looking at me, he kissed me, turned, and left, slamming the door to the operating room behind him.

I leaned over the edge of the stern, the land no longer in view. Although I'd purchased a relatively nice second-class room, I wasn't used to living in such close quarters with strangers, so I'd come up to the deck as soon as it was possible. While boarding, I'd noticed that many of my fellow passengers seemed to have come straight from Kensington—expensive white sunhats, parasols—and brought along an inordinate number of children as well as several spaniels in satin collars, who ran about the wide spaces of the deck.

Never having been on a steamship before, I found it remarkably loud. Despite the propellers churning noisily below me, I liked being up here, alone with my thoughts as I watched the sun sink, coppery, into the distant horizon.

I had said my goodbyes to Grandmother, Richard, and Laura at the dock, promising to write to them often. Grandmother had taken the news surprisingly well, particularly since the hospital in Dubai was operated by the British. William had been with me when I'd told her my plans; she'd narrowed her eyes and glanced at him before saying to me, with far too much hope, "Some distance might cool certain feelings..."

I would miss Grandmother.

Laura. In my bag, below deck, I had a miniature watercolor that she'd painted for me as a parting gift. It was of the dodos—their beaks together, their bodies forming a heart shape. They were gone now. As was Hugo, William's dog. The week before I left, William, Laura, and I had buried Hugo's body in the front garden, next to the dodos' little graves.

William.

We hadn't talked very much about my departure. I hoped he knew how much I still loved him. Playing with the ring upon my hand, I knew that I couldn't fault him if during this time he met someone else, fell in love again.

Was I making the right decision?

I hoped so. I thought of Alice and all her paths in Wonderland. There were so many. Each represented possibilities, but also closed doors. I remembered my last kiss with William, after I'd said my goodbyes to Christina. His expression had seemed to be marked by almost physical pain. He'd told me that he couldn't be at the docks today.

I watched the waves below me fold upon one another. The sun had set, and the sky was dark. Vaguely, I thought that I should return to my room, but I couldn't yet. I stared past the hull, knowing that the distance between myself and William was increasing with every minute.

A light rain began, just as I wiped away a tear.

"Miss me already?"

I jumped, startled, and whipped around.

"*William!*" I blinked, unbelieving. William stood behind me, looking quite handsome in trousers, a neatly pressed shirt, and a tweed jacket, his cravat knotted just under his chin.

I clutched the rail behind me, still unbelieving.

"William, oh dear God, how, *why?*"

He kissed me hard, stopping all of my questions. "After you left, Christina forbade me from staying for her. She said she would die early just from thinking of you and me so far apart."

Christina and her unyielding selflessness.

"And the hospital?" I stuttered, pulling away.

He shrugged. "I spoke to Josephine this morning. She wasn't happy about my departure, of course, but we've recently hired two newly minted physicians. I promised her I would return—when I return with you."

I blinked, hoping yet again that this wasn't a dream. William, here, giving up everything to be with me.

"Besides, I would be absolutely no good for the hospital without you."

The rain continued falling lightly around us, but I didn't care. The evening shadows spread across the deck as we kissed. A warm sea breeze picked up, whipping softly at us. Most passengers were below deck now, and we were outside alone.

I pulled away again, troubled by the details. "William, I'm not certain how this will work... do you have a position there?"

"No," he muttered softly against my hair. "But I doubt, with the hospital in such dire circumstances, that they will send me back to London. I have a perfectly decent medical degree."

I couldn't deny that.

"William, this hospital is terribly traditional. You will only be allowed to attend to the male patients and possibly children. And... us being together, unmarried, might be concerning. Dr. Anderson sent me with excellent recommendations, and—"

"We're on a ship now, aren't we? With a captain?" William looked down and gently brushed drops of rain from my hair.

Suddenly, understanding washed over me like a tidal wave.

"We could at least do something about the unmarried part," he said softly.

"Cad... " I muttered, yet I couldn't stop smiling.

Photography by Roger Hutchison

About the Author

Amy Carol Reeves has a PhD in nineteenth-century British literature. She lives in Columbia, South Carolina, where she works as an Assistant Professor of English at Columbia College and writes young adult books. When not teaching, writing, or spending time with her family, she likes jogging with her Labrador retriever, Annie, and daydreaming about Brontë novel hunks. *Resurrection* is her third novel.